Am Bratach Sith of Dunvegan

Duncan Hamilton

authorHOUSE®

AuthorHouse™ UK Ltd.
500 Avebury Boulevard
Central Milton Keynes, MK9 2BE
www.authorhouse.co.uk
Phone: 08001974150

This book is a work of fiction. People, places, events, and situations are the product of the author's imagination. Any resemblance to actual persons, living or dead, or historical events, is purely coincidental.

© 2008 Duncan Hamilton. All rights reserved.

No part of this book may be reproduced, stored in a retrieval system, or transmitted by any means without the written permission of the author.

First published by AuthorHouse 3/11/2008

ISBN: 978-1-4343-5729-8 (sc)

Printed in the United States of America
Bloomington, Indiana

This book is printed on acid-free paper.

Dedication

This book is dedicated to my lovely wife Sandra, who I love deeply and without her by my side, life would be a lot less mystical and intriguing.

May your God walk with you always Sandra.

Acknowledgements

Chief John MacLeod of MacLeod the 29th Clan Chief of Clan Macleod who sadly died March 2007.

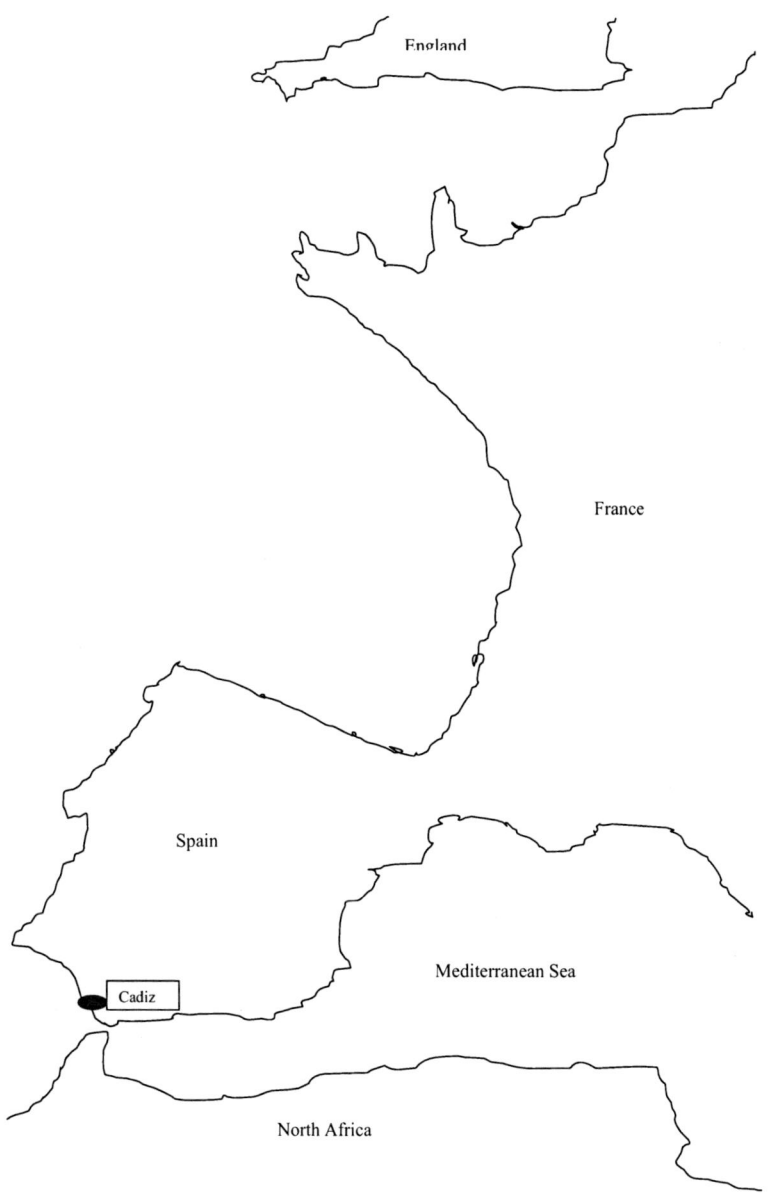

Table of Contents

Prologue — xv

CHAPTER ONE
The MacLeod's — 1

CHAPTER TWO
Olaf's Quest — 13

CHAPTER THREE
Witch wood — 25

CHAPTER FOUR
The Fairy Queen — 37

CHAPTER FIVE
Lady of the loch — 47

CHAPTER SIX
Return to Mann — 57

CHAPTER SEVEN
A new beginning — 67

CHAPTER EIGHT
A Clan is born — 77

CHAPTER NINE
   Clan MacLeod   87

CHAPTER TEN
   Rory's Quest   97

CHAPTER ELEVEN
   Gregor's shame   107

CHAPTER TWELVE
   Farewell to Gregor   117

CHAPTER THIRTEEN
   The voyage home   127

CHAPTER FOURTEEN
   Jack's destiny   137

CHAPTER FIFTEEN
   Return to Dunvegan   147

CHAPTER SIXTEEN
   The Witches curse   157

CHAPTER SEVENTEEN
   David's secret   167

CHAPTER EIGHTEEN
   Megan's search   177

CHAPTER NINETEEN
   A Fairy lullaby   187

CHAPTER TWENTY
   Angus plots revenge   197

CHAPTER TWENTY-ONE
   Revenge of the MacDonald's   207

CHAPTER TWENTY-TWO
   Fairy flag unfurled   217

CHAPTER TWENTY-THREE
   Christmas in November   227

CHAPTER TWENTY-FOUR
   Dark days of Dunvegan   237

CHAPTER TWENTY-FIVE
   Fight for freedom   247

CHAPTER TWENTY-SIX
   Iain's farewell   257

CHAPTER TWENTY-SEVEN
   The lost picture   267

CHAPTER TWENTY-EIGHT
   Iain comes home   277

CHAPTER TWENTY-NINE
   Home to Skye   289

Prologue

'Ay bonnie boat speed like a bird on the wing, carry the lad who was born to be king over the sea to Skye,' these words taken from the 'Skye boat song' for me conjure up all sorts of thoughts, mystery, bravery and romance.

The first time my wife and I visited Skye in June 2003, we found an Island full of natural beauty charm and history, the one thing that stood out was the romantic mystery of Skye.

As you may have guessed already we fell in love with this windswept, unforgiving and rugged Island that is often cloaked in a shroud of mist.

While on a short break we wanted to see as many of the sights as we could fit in.

On the first morning we decided to drive round the middle and top half of the Island in a clockwise direction, the scenery was breathtaking.

Having made an early start we passed few other cars and soon we reached Dunvegan castle, home of the Clan MacLeod, only to find the grounds to the castle did not open for another forty-five minutes, not being people to stand around waiting we decided if the castle didn't want to see us we didn't want to see the castle.

We continued on our adventure of discovery taking in various points of interest including the monuments to giant Angus MacAskill and Flora MacDonald, the museum of Island life, Kilt rock falls and the Old man of Storr.

Having past through Portree heading back to the hotel at Broadford we came to the road junction at Sligachan, where we had earlier that day turned towards Dunvegan castle.

At this point we stopped, looked at each other, there was no doubt we both knew what had to be done, drive back to Dunvegan, it was as if something was pulling us towards the castle.

As a rule we would never consider going the nineteen miles back to anywhere but whatever or whoever changed our minds we will always be grateful.

The castle grounds were beautiful, on their own worth the entrance fee, the garden were so peaceful only the birds and the splashing of the various waterfalls could be heard, with the afternoon sun cascading through the trees and Dunvegan castle looming above in all its majesty, this was truly a place of romance and fairy tales.

The entrance to the castle was as gothic and intimidating as you could imagine, although the castle is now laid out for the tourists it does retain the essences of a great fortified stronghold, the sort of castle a clan would have needed during the numerous battles and feuds between rival clans and the English over the last 800 years or so.

The history of the Clan MacLeod is laid out for everyone to see, from the impressive portrait's of previous

Chieftains and artefacts of the Jacobite rebellion, to the dungeon where many captured enemies would have perished, starved to death if nothing else.

One artefact captured my imagination, Am Bratach Sith (Fairy flag) it appears to be a very old piece of delicate silken cloth, yellow in colour with a faded red pattern not unlike berries.

The Fairy flag is now so delicate it is kept behind glass in a frame, what stories could be told if only it could speak, I stood looking at the Fairy flag too long other tourists began to wonder what I was looking at, I could feel their stares burning into the back of my neck, it made no difference the Fairy flag had captured my mind.

The Clan MacLeod is clearly able to acknowledge its chequered past and how the clan Chief's have managed to "HOLD FAST" (clan motto) in keeping the Clan MacLeod resident at Dunvegan castle for nearly a thousand years.

Following our return home I could not stop thinking about Dunvegan castle and the Fairy flag.

I decided to write a story for my wife, who is an avid reader of Barbara Erskine's novels.

The novel would be long enough to capture how the fairy flag inspired me and short enough to tell the story of the MacLeod clan and the many myths that surround the very existence of the Bratach Sith.

I do not consider myself to be an author, just someone who tells what he sees and hears.

Do you believe in fairies and the magic of the Bratach Sith? does the MacLeod clan?

I will leave you to make your own mind up to what is fact or fiction.

I do hope if nothing else reading this novel will inspire you to visit as we did and release your senses to the magic and mystery that surrounds the Isle of Skye, as well as the Islands and Highlands of Scotland.

May your clan be with you always.

CHAPTER ONE
The MacLeod's

The sound of tyres scrunching over stones on a crisp icy cold November night, Lucy's emerald green eyes sparkled like moonshine dancing over an enchanted loch, a pretty six year old with auburn hair flowing in ringlets over her tiny shoulders.

'Mummy, mummy daddies home' she ran to the door, her anticipation becoming more than she can contain, an icy shroud forced its way in as the large oak door slowly creaked open, there stood Iain MacLeod.

A well built stocky ginger haired Scotsman, he had earned the nickname of "westy" after the little Highland dogs that hold a reputation for being full of fun and fight never knowing when they are beat, this trait in his personality has landed Iain in trouble over the years but he had also gained the respect of everyone who knew him for being fair, honest and a good friend to have around when the chips were down.

'Daddy, daddy,' Lucy screamed, she flung herself into the air towards him, knowing she would be held in the loving embrace she had been eagerly waiting for, she was not disappointed, Iain held her as if he hadn't expected to feel the love and magic of Lucy's hugs ever again.

Iain twirled Lucy round and round until she squealed with delight, they both became so dizzy they fell into an old chair that was kept in the hall, breathless Lucy began to talk without stopping, her excitement over whelmed her.

'Lucy let your father get in the house, he's had a long journey,' Anne leaned over them both and welcomed Iain with a long loving kiss, without ending their embrace she slowly drifted round the side of the chair as if she was floating and sank lovingly onto his lap.

'Excuse me,' Lucy cried, Iain wrapped his arms round both of them, time was meaningless, and the future could make its own arrangements for this was their moment in an uncertain world.

Anne MacLeod, a slim twenty-something, curly raven haired beauty with deep blue eyes twinkling with a playful wickedness, Anne was Iain's bonnie lass, that was clear for every one to see.

They had known each other since childhood, from the first day at school Iain would tease Anne, pulling her hair, she would call him carrot top, she knew he hated that, he would chase her, she was a quick runner, he only caught her when she wanted him too, that was the last term of high school, they remained lovers and were married in June 1934.

Lucy was born a year after, their family was complete, Iain and Anne were advised by their doctor, she should not have any further children due to the bad time she had when carrying and giving birth to Lucy, this disappointment was discussed, buried and never mentioned again.

Am Bratach Sith of Dunvegan

Iain was a squadron leader in the Royal Air Force, he flew Spitfires.

Lucy said her dad was an angel because he could fly and went close to heaven.

Iain didn't talk about the RAF, Anne never asked, she knew it bothered him but he would do what the RAF asked of him, in his mind it was helping to keep her and Lucy safe.

Iain had been granted a five day pass, it had already taken him fifteen hours to get home, he caught the train from London to Edinburgh and left his car with Sean MacLean, who agreed to meet him at Edinburgh station.

Sean had been a friend since Sean's family moved from Skye to the mainland looking for work, they started their first job together working for Andrew Askew a local landowner.

The job was not much, it was hard work but he did not mind that because it meant he did not have to go to work in the Glasgow ship yards or join the fishing fleet, Iain was not keen on water, he never learned how to swim, something he liked to keep quiet.

Andrew Askew an Englishman, who had moved to Scotland towards the end of the First World War, he was one of the 'twenty minuter's,' he told Iain, anyone who flew planes during the first world war was only expected to live twenty minutes before being shot down or the plane crashing due to poor maintenance.

Andrew was no exception, he did manage four hours and nine minutes of flying in battle conditions before engine failure caused him to crash land, he was not seriously injured but it was the end to his war.

Andrew's family were very wealthy, when his father died in 1917, Andrew and his mother moved to Scotland for some peace and quiet, he brought with him his pride and joy a well maintained Tiger Moth aircraft.

On Iain's sixteenth birthday Andrew allowed him to fly with him in the Tiger Moth, Iain had sat in the cockpit before when Andrew was away, which was just magical, he would dream he was in the clouds with the wind rushing by, he was in control, he was flying.

As the plane took to the air it was everything Iain had dreamed of, it made his senses stand on end, he had never felt so alive and frightened at the same time before, he wanted to stay up in the clouds for ever.

'We're going to land now,' Andrew shouted Iain's head dropped slightly, 'before we do would you like to fly her?' Iain's head snapped up, a big grin spread across his face, Andrew realized Iain was speechless 'take the controls and don't waggle them around too much, they are quite sensitive, I'll make sure you don't make a hash of it.'

Iain held the controls, he was really flying, he was in control, it filled him with a feeling of self-belief and nothing else existed Iain was in a time warp.

'Iain,' Andrew shouted, Iain shook his head as if he had been dreaming 'this is great,' he replied trying not to appear too overwhelmed 'I'll take control now, we're going to land' these were the last words Iain wanted to hear, 'must we?' Iain pleaded, 'yes we must, low fuel, if we don't land now we will anyway,' Iain quickly guessed Andrew meant the plane would run out of fuel and crash, 'aye we had better land then' Iain shouted back.

The Tiger Moth drew to a standstill Iain sat in the cockpit his breathing was heavy, his senses still tingling unable to take in what had just happened.

Iain was forever saying it was the biggest mistake Andrew ever made, within two months Iain had convinced Andrew to teach him to fly.

Andrew knew Iain was a natural aviator, he took to flying like a duck to water, of course he never told Iain, as that would only over inflate his already enormous ego.

On the outbreak of the Second World War the RAF was already short of fighter pilots, everyone was banking on an early end to the war, when British troops invaded France.

Following the failed invasion and the heroic efforts of all concerned extracting the retreating British troops off the Normandy beaches, the armed forces were left in turmoil, how could Britain be defended against a German invasion which would now surely be inevitable.

With even less trained pilots the RAF sent out a plea for anyone who could fly to join the fight against the German onslaught.

Iain was working in the barn when a car pulled up outside Andrews house, two men wearing long dark coats, one wearing a bowler hat the other wearing a flat military type hat stepped out of the car.

They were greeted by Andrew as if he had known them all his life, Iain was curious, Andrew did not receive many visitors especially what appeared to be official visitors.

After about thirty minutes Andrew called Iain into the house, he introduced the two men as Wing Commander David Jarvis and Squadron Leader Mike Thompson.

David Jarvis was a tall slight man, he wore heavy black rimmed glasses, he looked tired and walked with a limp, this was due to having his right leg amputated a couple of years before after crashing while testing what was then a new plane the Spitfire.

Iain could tell Mike Thompson was a service man he stood bolt upright yet seemed a little loose around the edges, as if he was one step away from madness, the giant handlebar moustache did little to improve Iain's first impression of him.

Andrew explained to Iain they had come to ask him if he was fit to fly fighter aircraft.

Andrew had told them he was too crook and had lost his bottle for all that nonsense, he did however mention that a young man who worked for him was able to fly reasonably well.

Wing Commander Jarvis looked at Iain, 'I won't beat around the bush Iain, we need good pilots, and Andrew says you can fly, is that true?' 'och aye,' replied Iain, 'good, how would you like to join the RAF and fly a Spitfire laddie?' Iain was for once speechless, 'well come on man, there's a war to win, we can't stand around here all day staring at your open mouth, are you in?' 'Well err aye I suppose so,' Iain finally uttered, 'well don't be so enthusiastic, this is an opportunity of a lifetime.' Andrew had kindly invited them to stay the night,

Wing Commander Jarvis stared at Iain, 'we'll leave at 09:00 hrs tomorrow, be here at 08:45 hrs!' Iain felt as if had been given his first order.

Suddenly, reality hit Iain, what am I going to say to Anne, How did I get roped into this, 'I canny fly fighters!' he said to himself , he slowly walked home, going over and over how could he tell Anne and what about Lucy she could not possibly understand.

Iain reached the cottage, his heart both sank and was in his mouth at the same time, he had never felt so selfish, of course he wanted to fly Spitfires, who wouldn't, but how could he leave Anne and Lucy who meant everything to him.

Iain opened the cottage door as it creaked open Anne was standing in the hallway, 'what's the matter Iain?' she looked at him, she could see he was upset, 'we need ta talk,' Iain replied,

'Anne please come an sit doon,' Iain started to tell her about the two men who visited Andrew and what they wanted, Iain did not get to the part where he was asked to join the RAF, Anne was there before him, she burst into tears.

'Why yoo?' she kept saying, Iain tried to give the reasons but Anne could only see her Iain, her beloved Iain was going to war and may never return.

After some time they both gained a degree of composure, enough to talk over what was happening, they talked and cuddled most of the night, they had never felt so close, yet so far away from each other.

They decided to tell Lucy part of the truth, the bit where daddy was going to fly planes and would not come home every night, they felt Lucy was too young to know daddy was going to war.

The next morning at six o'clock Lucy bounced into her parents bedroom the same way as she always did, this time it would be different, Iain and Anne were not there, she called out for them with a hint of anxiety in her voice.

'Down here Lucy,' Iain was at the foot of the stairs, Lucy ran down the stairs almost missing the steps, 'slow doon,' Iain cried, half laughing as Lucy jumped from the seventh step into Iain's arms, she held no fear her daddy would catch her and keep her safe, Iain held her and gently kissed the top of her curly hair.

'Lucy, mummy and daddy have something ta tell yoo,' she looked up to his face 'what daddy, are we going hoot, please, please can we go ta tha loch?' 'Lucy, listen,' Iain's voice changed, she immediately shut up, her face was plain without expression, her daddy never spoke to her like that.

Iain began to try to explain he was going away for a time and he was going to learn how to fly big planes.

Lucy was puzzled, 'why do yoo need ta do that, yoo work on tha farm, Mr Askew already has a plane you can fly when yoo want ta,' this was not going well for Iain.

Anne tried to change Lucy's thinking, 'Lucy yoo will need ta help me around tha cottage an we can ask Mr Askew if he will need any help on tha farm while daddies away, would yoo like that?' Lucy half smiled, 'Does that mean a can feed tha lambs an chickens?' Anne cuddled Lucy, 'aye but we'll have ta ask Mr Askew first.'

'Daddy doon't go,' Lucy pleaded 'a have ta princess,' there was a tear in Iain's eye he had never had to make a more difficult choice in his life, he only knew this was something he had to do, if he didn't he would regret it for the rest of his life.

'Iain it's eight-thirty,' Anne's voice was low and gentle, Iain reached out and wrapped his arms round her, he looked into her tearful eyes, he could see all the love Anne held for him, she wanted him to stay more than anything but she could not stop this happening, they shared a long silent kiss which would be on their lips for ever, 'come on Iain yoo'll ba late.'

Lucy held her head down she was crying Iain tried to console her by saying he would be home before she realized he had gone, 'when?' was the last word she said, he hugged and kissed her as she hung like a rag doll in his

Am Bratach Sith of Dunvegan

arms, Anne took her from him Lucy put her head over Anne's shoulder.

Iain slowly walked from the cottage, Anne waved, Lucy did not look round as Iain disappeared down the lane out of sight.

It had been a long six months for all of them, at last Iain was back home, the only trouble was they knew he would have to return to duty in a few short days.

Iain stood by the sink drying the pots while Anne washed up, they looked at each other no words spoken, just looks exchanged, it was if they were talking without words both knowing what was being said.

With the washing up all cleared away, it was time for Lucy to have her bath, she loved her bath it was serious playtime and with her daddy home she knew she could have a really good time and get away with it.

The bath was full of hot water, Iain held Lucy over the bath and plunged her into the water, she squealed with a mixture of fear and delight, Iain picked her up out of the water and down she went again, this time she knew what was coming, her head came up out of the water she was gasping for breath, not because she was drowning, she was laughing so much she couldn't catch her breath, 'Daddy stop, stop,' she didn't really mean him to stop, she was having the time of her life.

'Look at tha mess! there's water all orr tha floor,' Anne was trying her best to look angry, Lucy sat in the bath dripping with water and soap suds, Iain was sat hanging over the bath equally wet through, they both looked at Anne and burst into laughter.

The corners of Anne's mouth started to twitch giving her away, Iain splashed water over Anne, she was not having any of that she grabbed a dish from a shelf by the bath and plunged it into the bath as she raised it Iain cringed, 'doon't yoo dare,' he shouted, 'yoo'll ba sorry!' in an instant the water was released from the dish and was flying towards Iain, Lucy shrieked as the water hit Iain in the face, 'right noo ya for it,' Iain spluttered.

Anne was already out of the bathroom door, she was always quicker than Iain unless she wanted to be caught, Iain ran after her, he caught her at the foot of the stairs, breathless, Anne thought she was safe, Iain picked her up and ran back up the stairs, it quickly dawned on her he was going to throw her in the bath, 'Noo Iain' she screamed, she struggled to break free, his hold was tight, they got to the bathroom door Anne tried to hold onto the door jam, this seemed to work for a couple of seconds, Iain managed to release her grip by turning round, 'noo,' Anne squealed, 'aye daddy,' Lucy egged Iain on, 'doo it daddy, doo it'.

The bath water went everywhere, Anne was lying in the bath completely covered in water, Lucy was standing at one end laughing uncontrollably, Iain was bending over the bath with his head under the water, Anne was holding on tight, he was struggling to break her grip, as she let go Iain's head came up out of the water, he took a life saving gasp of air.

Trying to catch his breath and talk at the same time was not easy, 'what did ya doo tha fa,' 'that'll teach yoo to drop ma in tha bath,' Anne teased, the stare between them was intense a lot of built up emotion had been released in a few short seconds.

Normality resumed when Lucy thought she would get in on the act, she splashed water over them both, Lucy looked first at Anne then Iain, had she gone too far.

Iain and Anne looked at Lucy showing no expression, then they looked at each other, all of a sudden they both

Am Bratach Sith of Dunvegan

grabbed Lucy and pulled her back into the water, this time it was too much for Lucy she started to cry, 'it's alright Lucy,' Anne whispered as she wrapped Lucy in a large soft pink bath towel, she was tired it had been a long eventful day and she was after all only six.

Towels were put on the bathroom floor to soak up gallons of water left over from bath time,

Lucy sat by the open fire, while Anne dried her hair, Lucy liked this, the fire made her feel warm and safe, she didn't like the brush being forced through her knotted hair, 'stand still Lucy it'll take less time if ya stand still,' Anne was a little impatient with Lucy because she always made a performance about having her hair brushed, Anne gave up, Lucy's hair was all but dry.

They sat by the fire, Lucy snuggled up to Anne her mother was soft, gentle and smelt nice.

Iain had changed into his dressing gown, he sat in the chair opposite Anne and Lucy, 'are yoo alright noo?' he asked Lucy, she nodded and smiled, he looked at Anne gave her a wink, she twitched her cute nose in reply, Lucy had seen Iain wink at Anne, she tried to wink but both eyes shut at the same time.

'Lucy it's time fa bed,' 'oh mummy can a stay up a bit longer?' 'noo, come on, a'll tell yoo what shall a read yoo a fairy story?' Iain interrupted, 'aye, please daddy,' Lucy's eyes began to sparkle, she loved fairy stories, she wanted to be a fairy, she had recently told her mummy if she was a fairy she would magic her daddy back home.

Iain picked Lucy up and bent down so Anne could kiss her good night, 'thank-ya mummy fa being yoo,' Anne touched Lucy on the cheek and gave a gentle knowing smile, 'good night princess, sweet dreams,' 'hold on fairy queen,' Iain stood up and they both went up the wooden hill to Bedfordshire.

Lucy jumped onto her bed from Iain's arms, she began to bounce on the bed, 'Lucy get inta bed or a wont read ta yoo,' Iain looked round for a book of fairy stories, he found one 'ho noo, not that one daddy, mummy reads that one ta me,' Lucy looked most displeased she would not get palmed off with an old story, 'have yoo got any books yoo have nee read?' Iain enquired to save him wasting time looking, 'noo daddy, I doon't think a have, we have nee been ta Edinburgh since yoo went away ta get any,' that hurt Iain, it was really the first time Lucy had commented that she was losing out.

'A'll tell yoo what, shall a make up a fairy story fa yoo,' Lucy was starting to get annoyed 'daddy a only wan ta hear true fairy stories like in tha books.'

Iain thought for a moment, 'och would yoo like ta hear tha story of tha Fairy flag of tha Clan MacLeod?' Lucy looked puzzled, 'is it true?' 'aye, it's tha fairy story of them all an it belongs ta our family,' Iain looked at Lucy her eyes widened, 'aye daddy a would like ta hear it,' she sat up in bed, Iain sat on the bed next to her, she snuggled close to him and put her thumb in her mouth and prepared herself to listen to the best fairy story ever told.

CHAPTER TWO
Olaf's Quest

His galley was all but ready to set sail, Olaf the youngest son of the King Astred of Mann stood on the quay looking at the damage his beautiful galley had taken over the last two summers since he had left home.

I hope she can get us home, I pray to the gods, grant this ship one last safe encounter with the storm demons of the seas and sky who lie in wait between Spain and the land of Mann, these demons were strong and merciless, they had taken so many of Olaf's friends in the past.

They had moored by a small fishing village on the coast of Spain to buy supplies and repair the galley, the crew deserved a well earned rest, before the last leg of their voyage home.

Olaf had left the land of Mann in the year 454 AD, he was to try and secure trading agreements with the kings of Europe, he had also hoped to make his fortune and he had been moderately successful with the trade agreements but was still without his fortune.

Olaf missed home, he had felt the north calling him back for some months, so deep had this feeling become, he knew he had to return home.

Olaf had been blessed by the Gods with twenty-three summers of life, he wasn't a big man, he stood at around five foot eight inches, his most striking feature was the deep red shoulder length hair which shone like a beacon, he believed the gods inflicted him with this hair to act as a warning for others, for what he lacked in height he made up for in courage and guile, which too many of his enemies found to their peril.

Olaf was a fine swordsman and showed no fear in battle, his crew believed in him so much they never challenged his word or judgment, they had been through a lot together over the last two summers and they did not have much to show for it.

They had a good time and won many encounters with the European tribesman but still no fortune, this really annoyed Olaf , he could see his brother's laughing at him when he got home, it was alright for them they were set to inherit his father's lands and title, he was to get nothing, it wasn't his father's fault it's how it is and has always been, title and lands passed down to the two eldest surviving children.

This has caused many a war between brother's of other families over the years, Olaf didn't hold any bad feeling towards his brother's, they had been good to him, he just knew they would not resist goading him over his lack of good fortune.

Olaf found himself dreaming of home, his day dream was rudely interrupted by a commotion, coming towards

Am Bratach Sith of Dunvegan

him were what looked like four local men carrying a block of stone on two wooden poles, two men at the front and two at the back.

Walking along side striding to keep up was a fifth man, smaller than the others with a bushy black beard dressed in long Arab style clothes, 'come on, come on, move, move,' he kept yelling at the four men.

The man stopped in front of Olaf, panting trying to catch his breath as if it would be his last, 'stop!' he finally mustered enough breath to yell, the four men lowered the stone block to the floor the man almost fell on it as he sat down wiping the sweat from his forehead, he held his hands up to Olaf gesturing to him to give him time to recover.

'Are you the master of this fine galley?' He remarked, 'yes, I am Olaf from the Land of Mann,' 'good, good, I am Ollam of Ireland, and I have business to discuss with you'.

The four men who carried the stone block were talking together, Ollam looked at them, 'Oh here,' he pulled out a few local coins from a small pouch he kept round his neck, he handed them to one of the men, 'now go,' he ushered them away with his hands, the four men moved slowly away, walking back to the village.

'Olaf my friend, you are going back home?' His words sounded more like an instruction than a question, Olaf hesitated, this man was strange, and he spoke as if he already knew what was going to happen.

'Yes,' Olaf eventually replied, 'good, good then I take it you have room to carry this stone and myself, can your men bring it on board?' Olaf nodded in agreement, then he suddenly snapped to his senses, 'we're not going to Ireland,' 'of course your not,' Ollam replied putting his arm round Olaf's shoulder as he gently eased Olaf towards the galley.

'You'll have to pay,' Olaf looked Ollam straight in the eyes, Ollam could see he was starting to lose control of the situation, he was already pleased how far he had got but if he pushed Olaf too far he may end up on the wrong end of a sword.

'Of course I didn't expect a powerful worrier like yourself to carriage for nothing,' Ollam became uneasy, 'I'll be honest with you, I have little money left, I have travelled from the holy land with this stone and if I don't get it to Ireland, I will have failed my lord and master, all I can offer is when we reach Ireland you will be paid in full,' Ollam started to sweat again, he sensed Olaf wasn't buying his promise, the silence was long and deafening.

Olaf's stare burned like the midday sun into Ollam's eyes, what was he looking for truth, lies or just a reason to kill him, did he need one, had he underestimated Olaf, was he just a barbaric killer out to make easy money.

Olaf broke the endless silence, 'I'll need something first, otherwise the crew will think I have gone soft, how much have you got?' 'Just a few coins,' Ollam stuttered, he reached for the pouch that hung round his neck he was shaking so much he could not open it.

Olaf grabbed the pouch, he tipped the contents into his powerful hand, 'is this it? This would not buy you the time I have already wasted on you,' Olaf put the coins back in the pouch and tied it onto his belt.

Am Bratach Sith of Dunvegan

'Get off my galley before I throw you to the sea demons,' Olaf half drew his sword as gesture of intent, Ollam turned and stepped off the galley, Olaf slowly eased his sword back into the scabbard and turned away as if to say end of business.

Ollam regained his composure, what had he got to lose, 'Olaf, my friend,' Ollam raised his voice 'this stone will defend you against the sea demons,' Olaf spun round, reaching for his sword he jumped off the galley towards Ollam, it was as if he was frozen to the spot, Ollam closed his eyes in anticipation of death, his lips moving in quick silent prayer, Ollam felt cold steel on his throat he could taste death but he was not afraid, why was he not dead?

Ollam slowly opened his eyes, through the bright sunlight he could see a silhouette of Olaf, 'how can this stone protect against the mighty powers of the sea demons?' Olaf's voice was uneasy, 'this stone, is the stone of destiny, the stone of kings, blessed by the king of kings, this stone will get to Ireland with or without you or me,' Ollam's words were sincere, he believed them, what if Ollam was right and the Gods would give safe passage to the stone.

Olaf slowly removed his sword from Ollam's throat, 'I will need something more than a few coins to show the crew,' it was as if Olaf was offering Ollam a final way out, 'I have nothing only my word and the power of the stone,' Ollam's voice was more a plea than a conformation of his lack of wealth.

Stepping back Olaf lowered his head, again placing his sword slowly back to it's place of rest, 'then I cannot help you,' Olaf's voice was more gentle and resigned, fate had delivered yet another lost opportunity.

Ollam suddenly stuttered, 'wait I have this, it's not much but I was given it to drape over the stone, it's said to have been worn by a true saint,' he was busy unwrapping a length of bright yellow, silky cloth with a red pattern on it from around his waist, 'I kept it hidden, it must have a value,' his words were spoken more in hope than knowledge.

Olaf held the cloth, it was delicate and weightless, cool even through it had been wrapped round Ollam, who was clearly overheating.

Olaf held the cloth to his nose it smelt of wild spring flowers, this reminded him of home, he looked at Ollam, without turning round Olaf shouted to the crew, 'get the stone on board.'

Four of the crew lifted the stone onto the galley they placed it in the middle to balance out the weight.

'We sail on the tide, be here,' Olaf looked at Ollam who nodded in agreement, 'I'm going nowhere.'

The galley slowly slipped it's moorings with all aboard, the crew rowing towards an open sea.

The sail soon bellowed in the stiff south-westerly wind, they were on their way home, with this favourable wind the gods were surely smiling.

Ollam sat next to the stone, he was not going to let it out of his sight, the last part of his long journey well under way.

Olaf sat on the stone 'we're not going to Ireland, you know that' Ollam raised his head, looking at Olaf, 'Gods will,' he smiled and turned to look back out to sea.

His words unsettled Olaf, the sky was clear, the sea unchallenging and most importantly a fair wind, the gods were indeed favouring this voyage.

Twice the sun had risen since they had left Spain, Ollam was cheered by Olaf's optimism they should see the south of Ireland within the next few hours.

Ollam started to reflect on the last few years, the near misses like when he lost the stone in Africa following an attack by local tribesman, they had dragged the stone for about a mile and suddenly left it, he believed it was Gods will, there was no other reason why they would have left the stone, even if it was without value they would have took it any way, just in case.

Olaf suddenly pointed towards the north-west, 'land,' again he pointed, 'land,' Ollam was quick to his feet 'where is it, Ireland?' he looked at Olaf with the kind of look a child gives, with the giving of a surprise, 'yes Ireland,' Olaf confirmed with a low tone to his voice, 'we'll follow the coast for a day then head east home to the Land of Mann.'

Ollam stared at Olaf, 'you said you would take me to Ireland?' Olaf glared at Ollam with a defiant grin, 'the will of the gods,' he started to laugh and looked out over the horizon as if trying to see the Land of Mann.

The wind started to freshen, it changed direction, it was now coming from the east, Olaf called for the crew to ready the oars, the wind was by now becoming a storm, rain started to fall like spears, waves swept over the galleys sides as if to push it towards Ireland, the oar beat was almost at battle speed, still the galley was losing ground.

Olaf's face was red with a mixture of anger and determination, 'keep rowing,' he yelled, 'row for your lives,' the wind caught the sail, it had not been pulled down quick enough, the sail started to rip, it was if the wind was playing with it, like a cat with a bird, knowing it could tear it to shreds in seconds, tossing it around until the sail was in tatters like ribbons blowing almost straight out from the mast.

The galley was now perilously close to the rocks, it took all of Olaf's seamanship to keep his galley from founding on the rocks, as quick as the storm started it began to fade, the sun forced its fingers through the dark clouds, they opened like curtains to welcome the day.

Ollam looked across to Olaf, who was busy counting the cost of lost oars and the bits of sailcloth which only a short time ago bellowed with pride in a south-westerly breeze.

With both hands lost in his soaking red hair Olaf looked at Ireland, he turned sharply; 'this was your doing and that stone,' he caught Ollam round the neck, 'why should I not kill you now,' he squeezed tighter and tighter.

Ollam could feel his life force draining away, he became limp, he was ready for death but this was cruel, would he not feel Ireland beneath his feet, was it to be the place of death when he believed he was bringing life to his beloved Ireland.

A shout went up, 'harbour, harbour,' one of the crew shouted he pointed to a small inlet, Olaf threw Ollam to one side, he was almost with his god, he gave one gasp for air, his god granted his wish, choking Ollam regained consciousness, he stumbled as he tried to get to his feet.

By now the galley was making it's way into the inlet, as it moved further in Olaf could see the inlet opened up into a sheltered harbour, there was a small fishing village on the left, he could make out the villagers running around, he smiled to himself, they believed they were being attacked.

Olaf waved as if to show they were friendly.

By the time the galley came to rest by a flat rock that jutted out into the sea, there was no sign of the villagers.

Olaf knew what was going through the crews minds, pillage, Olaf had other ideas, he got off the galley and waited, he kept the crew on board.

Olaf looked round no-one was there, had they ran off and left the village to be sacked or had they a surprise of their own in store, Olaf was not going to take any chances, 'we'll camp here,' 'what about the village?' one of the crew cried, 'not yet,' Olaf snapped, 'we need more from these people than a few pots and pans,' Olaf looked puzzled as if pondering over recent events.

Ollam had recovered, he stepped off the galley, still unsteady from his ordeal, he looked at Olaf, 'these people will not harm you, they are fisherman not warriors,' Olaf half turned to glance at Ollam, 'I don't take unnecessary risks,' Olaf replied in an untrusting voice.

The crew unloaded only what they needed, in case they had to make a quick get away, soon the camp fire was lit and the smell of hot food filled the cool late evening air, they all sat down to eat some kind of fish soup with chunks of near stale bread, it smelt better than it tasted, Ollam not wanting to offend anyone else that day ate most of it, saying he was too full to eat the rest.

Olaf finished his soup and went to inspect the damage to the galley, it was not as bad as he had first thought, a couple of days would see her fit to sail, his thoughts returned to home, he looked out of the narrow gap in the cliffs to the open sea, will he ever return to the Land of Mann?

Olaf positioned guards around the camp, he did not trust anyone, least of all the men of Ireland, when ever he had cause to meet these people in the past, he had always lost out, they are a most devious people, all smiles while taking your money.

The night past without incident, Ollam woke to a fine sunny morning, he smiled to himself, looking round he saw green hills and lush pastures 'home' he gently whispered under his breath, it seemed to warm him and give him the sense of safety.

Ollam looked for Olaf, he could not see him, 'where's Olaf?' he asked one of the crew, 'he's gone to the village,' Ollam quickly ran after Olaf, he caught up with him in the village, 'and what are you doing?' Olaf turned and gave a rye smile, 'nothing, just looking,' Olaf pushed open every door in the village, he shrugged his broad shoulders and held out his powerful hands palms up, 'where have they all gone?'

'They probably thought you were going to kill them,' Ollam was stating the obvious anyone in their right mind would run if they saw a fighting ship heading towards them but then again Olaf did ask the question.

Olaf took a few bits and pieces he thought would help to repair the ship and they headed back to the camp.

'Can you ask the crew to unload the stone?' Olaf stopped and looked at the ground as if he was tired of saying what was happening, 'I told you the stone is going to the Land of Mann,' Ollam checked himself from saying anything else.

The galley was almost ready to sail when Ollam decided he was going to stay there, Olaf looked at him, 'as you will,' and carried on with what he was doing, 'you won't leave here with the stone, you know that don't you,' Ollam started to slowly step backwards, he did not wish to encounter Olaf's sword again, 'you know that storm was sent to force you to land here?' Ollam was hesitant, Olaf shook his head, his long red hair catching the suns rays as it danced round his head, 'we're ready to sail,' he looked to the cloudless sky, 'what is going to stop us? you stay if you want, me I'm going home.'

Ollam stood on the flat rock as the galley slipped from it's moorings, he looked up to the heavens for a miracle, nothing happened, the galley headed towards the opening of the inlet, he breathed out in a sigh of disbelief, all hope was lost, he had brought the stone of destiny to Ireland only to lose it, after all this time and effort.

Ollam looked at the galley, it had started to list to the right, there must have been more damage to the underside than Olaf had thought, the galley turned round, within minutes, the galley was once again moored against the flat rock.

Olaf jumped from the galley, he approached Ollam with great strides, Ollam turned to run, ' stand,' bellowed

Olaf, 'you can have your stone, it's nothing but trouble,' Ollam could hardly believe his luck, the crew appeared only too pleased to unload the stone, it was soon laid on the flat rock, Olaf looked at Ollam, but it was as if he was looking through him, Ollam turned round, Olaf could see the villagers returning, Olaf looked in disbelief, 'why now,' he murmured.

Soon Olaf could see a few of the villagers were walking towards them, not enough to cause them any trouble, they watched the small group approach without making any comment.

At the front of the group was a tall heavy set man, wearing a long creamy white gown like a holy man, 'greetings, greetings to you all, I am Tomack follower of St Columba, as you see we wish you no harm, please join our village,' Ollam introduced himself and Olaf.

Tomack looked at the stone, 'where did you find this?' Ollam began to explain why he had brought the stone to Ireland, 'this is the stone of destiny!' Tomack walked slowly round the stone with one hand dragging on top as if he could not believe what he was seeing.

CHAPTER THREE
Witch wood

The cool evening air started to form a mischievous mist in the valleys between the small hills, demons of the twilight played tricks on unsuspecting eyes, this was a time to know who your friends are.

Ollam had earlier gone to the village with Tomack, they seemed to have a lot to talk about, they had taken the stone with them, the crew cheered when it had taken six of the villagers to lift and carry the stone, when four of them could lift it easily.

Olaf looked to the darkening sky, he could feel a growing discontent with his gods, after all what had they done for him during this voyage, nothing, they even let this new god take this stone from him.

He shrugged his shoulders and rallied his crew to make their way to the village.

The village was deep in some sort of celebration, Olaf walked between the small fishermans cottages, all made of heavy stone with small windows and doors that a big man would need to squeeze through to get in, the damp thatching on the roofs glistened in the glow of the fire, he looked round, the mist was closing in like a shroud around the village.

He could see a red glow from what must be a large fire, he made his way toward the glow, he walked round the last cottage into an open area, most of the villagers were sitting close to the fire eating a kind of broth 'Olaf, over here,' he looked to where the shout came from, through the smoke and flames of the fire he could make out Ollam gesturing him to go over 'come and join the gathering, sit here,' Ollam patted a wooden stool, Olaf sat down, he was handed a wooden bowl containing a fish broth and a chunk of bread, Olaf was not keen on fish but he was hungry and the broth tasted pretty good.

Most of the crew joined the villagers, some were left with the galley, and Olaf did not trust this situation enough to completely let his guard down.

Olaf looked around the fire everyone looked relaxed and appeared to be enjoying this eerie evening as if it was normal, he turned to Ollam, 'what's the celebration for?' Ollam looked at Olaf the happy grin disappeared from his face, 'the stone of course, remember, the stone you were trying to steal from me,' Olaf felt something was wrong, had they been lured into a trap, he looked at Ollam, suddenly Ollam's face cracked into laughter 'want a drink, be careful it may be too strong for you' Olaf snatched the bowl from Ollam's hands, he knew he had been made to look a fool, he drank the liquid and began to cough, 'I told you it was strong,' Ollam laughed again.

'What is this, it's like honey with the bit of a sea demon?' Olaf wiped his mouth, 'want some more or is it too strong, there is some milk if you would like that?' Ollam obviously felt secure enough to goad Olaf in this way, Olaf grabbed the large jug containing the demon drink and started to drink straight from the jug, after about six gulps Olaf could feel his legs start to buckle, he stopped drinking, the jug dropped into Ollam's hands, Olaf felt very strange, everything started to slip round, he fell to his knees, then onto his face, he was out cold.

Olaf woke with a jolt, he felt icy water being splashed over him, 'come on, you can't lie there all day' he could hear Ollam's voice but his eyes could not focus, 'what have you done to me?' Olaf began to panic, Ollam could not help but laugh, 'don't blame me, you did this on your own, I tried to stop you,' Ollam chucked another bowl of water over Olaf, he spluttered and started to shake with cold, 'enough,' Olaf held out his arm for Ollam to help him to his feet, his eyes were beginning to clear, the bright sunlight burned like hot coals.

Olaf turned away and looked at the ground, his vision slowly returned, he looked at Ollam who was holding a small bowl, 'drink this,' he held the bowl out for Olaf to take, 'what is it?' 'drink it , it will do you good, it will get rid of the demons pounding in your head,' Ollam still held the bowl out towards Olaf, he took it and held it to his mouth, he caught a smell of the liquid, it made him wrench, 'I can't drink that!' he held the bowl out away from his face, 'don't be a child, drink it,' Ollam was beginning to lose patience with Olaf, he again held the bowl to his mouth, this time he held his breath, he drank as quick as he could and threw the bowl to the floor, 'that was horrible, what was it?' 'Best you don't know, as long as you feel better,' Ollam put his arm round Olaf's shoulder as they started to walk back towards the galley.

Sure enough Olaf started to feel better, his thoughts began to turn towards repairing the galley, how could he get the galley out of the water to repair the damage.

They talked like old friends, gone was the mistrust, Olaf reckoned if Ollam or the villagers were going to kill them it would have been last night.

As they approached the galley Olaf looked at the shoreline, there were two flattish rocks which had been under water at high tide, he thought if they could manoeuvre the galley over the rocks at high tide and anchor it there, the next time the tide went out the galley would almost be high and dry.

The question was would the galley sail over the rocks without causing more damage, he looked at the high tide mark on the rocks at the opening to the inlet, he felt deflated, judging by the tide marks the water would not be deep enough.

Ollam looked puzzled, 'what are you thinking?' Olaf told him his idea but he did not think it would work because at high tide the water would still be too low.

Ollam looked at the two rocks Olaf was talking about, 'how deep does the water have to be?' 'at least as high as a man,' Olaf mumbled, 'there was a fat moon last night, if the moon remains fat tonight the water could rise higher than normal, this sometimes happens when the moon is fat, I'll go and talk with Tomack, he may know more of this and when it happens.'

Tomack was busy cleaning the stone, it had suffered some damage during it's travels that was clear to see, it

Am Bratach Sith of Dunvegan

had got to look at its best before he could present it to St Columba.

Ollam asked Tomack about the high tides, 'yes this happens, sometimes the cottages too close to the shoreline become flooded, I would say it happens about four or five times a year,' he started to clean the stone again, when was the last time of high water, Ollam hoped for a positive answer, 'about three moons ago, yes I remember the Moon was large and bright against a black night sky, it was so bright you could walk without fire, which was good too because the cottages were flooded and we had to move their belongings out to dry land, it would have took longer if we had to light the way as well,' Tomack started to ramble about other high waters, 'thank-you that's what I wanted to know I'll leave you to get on,' Ollam eased his-self away thanking Tomack again.

Ollam hurried to the galley, 'Olaf, Olaf!' he waved his hands in the air to try and attract Olaf's attention, Olaf looked at Tord one of the crew, 'the man's possessed by demons,' Olaf shook his head and started to walk towards Ollam, 'calm down what's wrong?' Ollam was so out of breath he could hardly speak, 'the water!' he gasped, 'the water will be high tonight,' 'are you sure?' Ollam gave another gasp for air 'yes.'

Olaf placed his hands on Ollam's shoulders, 'if your right we have a lot to do, come on,' Olaf let go of Ollam's shoulders, Ollam fell forward still out of breath, he stumbled to regain his balance, 'come on don't stand there all day,' Ollam held his hand up to acknowledge Olaf who had suddenly been filled with hope.

The water in the inlet started to rise, the crew were in position, everything that could be taken ashore was now off the galley, the crew started to pull the galley towards the two flat rocks, they needed to position the galley before the rocks were covered by water other wise they could cause more damage or if the position was wrong the galley could tilt too far to one side and wedge between the rocks when the tide went out, then they may not be able to refloat her.

The water began to rise, the galley was pulled bow first towards the two rocks, it became difficult to hold the galley in place because of the narrow opening to the inlet the water was being forced through the gap causing a current against one side of the galley.

Olaf moved more of the crew to hold the galley against the current, it wasn't working the current was too strong, the galley was starting to drift, the crew held on, they were starting to lose footholds and grip on the ropes.

Sweat poured out of Olaf, he was holding on as if his very life depended on it, his long red hair was soaked and hung across his face, sweat trickled down his hair and stung his eyes until they watered so much he could not see clearly, he shook his head to clear the sweat from his eyes and hair from his face, it did not work, he needed to wipe his face with something, hanging out of his tunic was the corner of the silky cloth Ollam had given as part payment for his passage, he tugged it out with his teeth, he secured the rope round his waist as best he could and grabbed the cloth and rubbed his face, he felt the ropes become easier to hold, the galley was not fighting against the ropes, the galley was brought back into position, all they had to do is hold on for a bit longer, Olaf heard the splashing of people behind him the villagers had come to help, with their help the ship was easy to hold in place over the rocks, Olaf gave the signal to move the galley over the rocks, as it slowly started to slip over the rocks Olaf could feel the galley scraping against the rocks, he became nervous the water would not be deep enough, the back of the galley moved to one side, the front suddenly lunged forwards taking every one by surprise, the galley slowly eased over the rocks, when it was in position Olaf gave another signal and the crew moored the galley in position.

It was a relief to everyone, they all sat where they could catching their breath, resting tired legs and arms, it was quiet for a while, all that could be heard was the breathing of tired souls and the gentle lapping of the water against the galley.

After what seemed like an age, the crew and the villagers got to their feet each helping the other, Olaf looked around the moonlight was indeed nearly as bright as day, he could see the people from the village walking back, his crew sitting on the large flat rock where the galley had first moored, lights from small fires made the village looked like the fairy villages his mother used to tell stories about when he was a child, one word came to his mind, magical, this was indeed a magical place, as he stood up he felt something drop onto the ground, looking down it was the silky cloth, he crouched down to pick it up, he remembered what happened when he had pulled it out to wipe the sweat from his face, no it couldn't hold magical powers, it was just another piece of cloth, he pushed it back under his tunic.

At first light Olaf could clearly see the damage to the galley, he needed to work quickly, on inspection of the damage it was not too bad but it would take a few hours to repair, he woke the crew gave them instructions and set about repairing the damage to the galley.

While stripping off a piece of wood to fit one of the holes Olaf spotted Ollam walking towards the galley, 'hello my friend,' Ollam shouted, 'where were you when we needed you?' Olaf joked, 'from what I hear you did alright on your own,' Ollam's reply caused Olaf to drop his head and smile.

'Olaf my friend I am leaving, the stone needs to be presented to St Columba, what happens then I don't know, my life for the last few summers has been that stone,' Olaf looked up, 'don't worry I'm sure your god will have plenty in store for you,' Olaf held out his hand, Ollam grabbed it with both hands, 'the cloth will protect you, it has been blessed, Olaf don't lose it promise me,' Olaf looked at Ollam for the last time, he could see true friendship in his eyes, they embraced each other knowing their paths would now be in different directions, 'go now before I slit your throat,' Olaf tried to take the feelings out of the situation Ollam laughed, then nodded he knew what was happening, Ollam slowly at first walked away towards the village without looking back, Olaf looked across at Ollam striding away, shook his head, smiled and carried on working.

All had gone well the galley was sea worthy again, which was all to the good because the sea was rising again.

Olaf hoped refloating the ship would be easier than last night, the rise of the water seemed too far below what they needed to refloat the galley, Olaf looked towards the gods, he pointed in a threatening way, 'just once, just once,' his voice tapered off, he didn't want to anger the gods but all that had gone wrong for him, a little piece of good fortune would be useful.

With the galley stranded until the next high water all they could do is relax.

The crew helped the fisherman to land their daily harvest of prime fish Olaf smiled and thought to himself this village will never starve.

During the days that followed Olaf became more anxious to leave, waiting around wasn't his style, he started to walk into the hills and woods, villagers had warned him not to get lost or the leprechauns, goblins or even worse the witches would take him, he did not show any fear of these creatures to the villagers but he was careful to mark his path and return before nightfall.

It was on one such walk Olaf encountered a beautiful young woman, like him she was in the middle of nowhere, she walked towards him, she smiled as she passed him and carried on, he stopped and looked round, she had disappeared, he ran back down the path, she was nowhere to be seen.

In front of him there was a narrow path into the woods, she must have gone in there he thought, against all his instincts he went into the woods, he would be alright, he could always double back, there was only one path, he went deeper and deeper into the woods, it started to become dark, the leaves on the trees were blocking out the sun, it was more like twilight, he kept on going, after a short time he came to a small clearing, a sun beam shone through a small gap in the trees, after his eyes became adjusted to the sudden bright light he saw the young woman again, he looked at her she was most beautiful, hair as black as the darkest night cascaded in ringlets over her milky white skin, bright green eyes shining like emeralds in the sun.

'Who are you?' Olaf finally asked, 'I'm Sandaira,' her voice was as sweet and clear as spring water.

'What brings you here Olaf?' Olaf was caught off guard, 'you know my name, how, are you a witch?' Olaf became frightened, what if she turned into a wretched old hag, he could be turned into a toad or worse, eaten, he had heard of this before, he slowly moved his hand to his sword, having managed to secure a firm grip on the sword he asked again, 'how do you know me?' Sandaira smiled, 'from the village of course, we know you and your crew,' this puzzled Olaf more, 'who's we? I haven't seen you in the village,' Sandaira stopped walking, 'the we is myself and my mother, we don't live in the village,' she turned to walk off again, 'wait,' Olaf raised his voice, 'where do you live then?' he was almost too frightened to ask, 'in the woods!' came the reply Olaf's heart sunk, why did he follow her, surely he could not have fallen into this trap so easily, what a fool.

She started to walk off into the woods, 'wait!' Olaf shouted, again she looked round, 'are you coming or not?' her words suddenly had a steel edge to them but he could not help himself he had to follow her, the walk was short and silent, they came out into a larger clearing, the back was a sheer rock cliff with a waterfall down to a crystal clear pool, there were wild flowers growing all around, sun light danced on the pool causing a rainbow in the fine

Am Bratach Sith of Dunvegan

mist from the waterfall, Olaf believed this was truly an enchanted place.

Sandaira had walked on as if this was nothing, Olaf ran through the wild flowers, the scent was intoxicating, his head began to spin, 'this is my home,' she pointed to a small cottage almost hidden at the base of the cliff, Olaf became even more frightened, he still believed Sandaira was a witch, his curiosity overcame his fear, Sandaira slowly opened the door, 'mother I'm back, I've got someone with me,' Sandaira stepped out of the doorway, Olaf slowly moved into the cottage, his eyes were wide open, what was he walking into, at first he looked up, there were all manner of instruments hung from the roof joists, he looked across to the fire, there was a cauldron on the fire bubbling away, was this it, was he going to be a witches feast, he could run, how would he find his way back.

'Welcome Olaf,' he looked to the back of the cottage in the fire light he could see a woman, older than Sandaira but still pretty, she moved forward towards him, she stood proud with a blue dress and apron that covered the front of the dress, her hair was red the same as his own, this seemed to comfort Olaf, 'I am Sadie, please sit,' she gestured to a chair by the table, her hands were long and slender, not the hands of a working woman, more of a woman of wealth, she wasn't a hag, Olaf was still worried would they both turn into wretched beast woman and eat him.

'Olaf would you like something to eat?' Sadie was holding a bowl, 'it's good broth I made it this morning,' Olaf looked at the bowl, 'I'm not that hungry,' Olaf tried not to show fear, 'he thinks we're witches mother,' Sandaira picked up a bowl and ladled in a portion of broth, 'I'm starving,' she sat down and started eating.

'I am a witch,' Sadie looked at Olaf, 'but not how you think, I am a pure witch, and I only do good not harm, please trust me and try the broth,', she again offered Olaf a bowl, 'if I was a bad witch I could have killed you the first night you became stranded here,' Olaf looked at her, what did she mean, 'remember the liquid you drank?' Sadie remarked, how could he forget, 'and the potion Ollam gave you in the morning, I made them both, now will you trust me when I say I will not harm you?'

'While you eat the broth I will tell you how I came to live here?' Olaf picked up a wooden spoon and tasted the broth, and much to his surprise it tasted good, 'what is it?' he enquired, 'Venison, not the eye of toad and bats wings you were expecting,' Sadie replied.

By this time Anne was standing in the doorway to Lucy's bedroom, 'did yoo know she's asleep?' Iain slowly moved off the bed, they both kissed Lucy then tucked her up, she was sound asleep.

CHAPTER FOUR
The Fairy Queen

'Shall we go ta bed noo Iain?' Anne looked at Iain with a glint in her eye, the sort of glint that Iain could not mistake, they had not been together for six months, Anne was not going to let Iain being tired get in the way, she had her own itch that needed scratching.

They both felt a little strange as they undressed for bed they had been apart for so long 'do you still fancy me?' Anne looked sheepishly at Iain, 'come here,' he grabbed her and held her close to him, 'a had forgotten just how beautiful yoo are,' he could feel her naked body under her nightdress, he slowly moved his strong hands over her back and down to her bottom, he eased the slender straps of her nightdress off her shoulders, the nightdress dropped to the floor, he kissed her neck, then they shared a long kiss Anne's lips were full and ripe, Iain needed a shave but Anne found this strangely erotic, she had never kissed Iain with so much stubble before.

Iain picked her up and carried her the short distance to their bed, he laid Anne on the bed, he moved his hands over her naked body following all her contours, Anne raised her arms and gently pulled Iain into her, she guided his swollen manhood into her waiting body, it was like their first night, intense, exciting and playful.

As they lay exhausted in each others arms, Anne looked thoughtful, 'what's the matter?' Iain asked 'Ho nothing, a was just thinking what happened next in tha story?' Iain raised his head and looked at her, 'what story?' Anne smiled, 'tha one yoo were telling Lucy!' he slumped back on the pillow 'that can wait till tomorrow night,' Iain replied, 'noo tell ma noo,' Anne raised herself onto her elbows, 'a'll make it worth ya while!' she smiled at Iain, Iain sighed, 'alright, but noo fa long a'm tired'.

Iain teased Anne, 'noo let ma see where did a get ta?' Anne jabbed Iain in the ribs, 'ahh tha witch'.

The witch started to tell her story, 'fifteen summers ago, I was walking through the hills along side the woods when I heard a baby crying, I looked round but it was clearly coming from the woods, I was frightened to go into the woods because of all the stories of witches, wolves and leprechauns I had been told as a child, my mother would have scolded me if she found out I had been in the woods alone.'

Sadie sighed, 'the baby was still squealing, I could not ignore a baby, what if it was with it's family and something had happened to them, I took a deep breath and followed the babies crying it was deeper in the woods than I had first thought, I kept going, then in a small clearing a beam of sunlight was shining on the baby as if to keep it warm.'

Sadie looked at Olaf, 'I picked the baby up and it stopped crying, it was wrapped in a silky yellow cloth with

Am Bratach Sith of Dunvegan

red strange markings, I quickly found my way out of the woods, it didn't seem to take me long, I ran home to the village as quick as I could.'

'What happened then?', Olaf became more interested, 'when I showed the baby to my mother and told her where I had found it, she didn't believe me and threw me out of the cottage calling me a witch and a whore, it started to rain, no one would give me or the baby shelter.'

'What did you do then?' Sadie stared at Olaf, as if to say stop interrupting, 'I walked back to the woods, at least there was shelter in the trees, I seemed to walk for hours, still the baby did not cry, I sat down in a clearing and drifted to sleep, I had a dream, fairies came out of the woods and built a cottage next to a waterfall, there were wild flowers all around, it was warm and plenty of things to eat.'

Olaf began to fidget, 'I woke up in the very place I had been dreaming about, my dress was drenched in milk, I could even feed the baby, I soon became used to my new life, it had everything I wanted apart from other people, I did miss my mother and the other people from the village, the summers past, Sandaira grew from baby to child, she was the only company I needed.

When she was old enough to come with me we set out to find the village, it took time but found it we did, the women beat me with sticks, calling me a witch, they took Sandaira from me and left me for dead on the path from the village.'

Sadie continued, 'I didn't know what they would do to Sandaira or even if she was still alive.

I made my way back to the cottage, I was battered and bruised, and it took me days to get back, when I opened the cottage door who was sitting there? Sandaira, how she got away I don't know.

'You visit the village now?' Olaf looked puzzled, 'that's another story, some five summers ago we were at the edge of the woods, a man from the village was staggering along the path, he fell as we got to him, he had got a sickness we dragged him to the cottage, I gave him a potion, I had used on myself a number of times when I was unwell, after a couple of nights he seemed to come out of the sickness, he told me all the village had the sickness and the children were dying, the villagers believed I had put a curse on the them.'

'When he was well enough to travel we went to the village, as you can imagine I didn't receive a warm welcome, the man convinced some of the villagers that I had cured his sickness, they took the potion, what could they lose if I had cursed the village they would die and if the potion killed them what's the difference, thankfully the villagers who had the potion all recovered, so the others who were still alive wanted it.'

'I am still a witch and they remain frightened of me but they would accept my help if they needed it, which includes the liquid you, drank on your first night.'

'You made that, what was it?' Olaf referred to the mixture with both curiosity and admiration, 'that's a secret you will never know,' Sadie turned to Sandaira, 'more broth?' 'No I've had enough,' 'Olaf, more broth?' 'I don't mind if I do,' Olaf felt himself starting to relax.

Am Bratach Sith of Dunvegan

With the meal over Olaf sat looking at Sandaira, who was she, where did she come from the more he sort answers the more questions were raised.

'You will stay the night?' Sadie looked at Olaf somehow he knew that was a question with only one answer 'aye it's too late to be making my way back' Olaf sat back on the chair, he had eaten too much broth.

The open fire was hot and crackled, flames leapt into the air in a hypnotic dance, Olaf could not take his eyes from the fire, he could feel tiredness and sleep overcoming him, and nothing would prevent his eyes closing.

Olaf woke his body felt as if it was being caressed, his senses tingled, the hairs on his arms stood up as if he was cold but he wasn't, he looked round there was no sign of Sadie or Sandaira, he moved slowly to a small window, he could see a shape in the pool below the waterfall, it was a woman, the moonlight danced on her shimmering body as the waterfall cascaded around her, he could not tell who it was, he sat watching for a while as if mesmerized, he had never witnessed anything more pure and beautiful, suddenly he heard a voice, a sweet clear delicate voice calling his name, he looked round there was no-one in the cottage, he looked back through the window, startled he stepped back from the window.

The woman was beckoning him out of the cottage, who is she, he could hear the voice calling him again, what should he do, he opened the cottage door, slowly he stepped out, he walked towards the pool, his eyes were fixed on the woman, could this be a trap, he felt for his sword, not there, the woman slowly enticed him into the pool, he could not resist, he was firmly in her spell, he felt his legs moving, was it his will or hers?

The woman moved towards him, she hardly made a ripple in the clear water, her face white as milk, with bright dark green eyes, her deep red wet hair hung over her shoulders, they were close, so close he could smell the heavy scent of wild flowers which surrounded her.

She slowly removed his tunic and leggings revealing his naked body, she kissed his large shoulders, her touch felt like butterflies dancing over his rough skin, he felt a calming sensation tingling through his body, he wrapped his strong arms around her slender body, her breasts pressed against his chest, her lips red and swollen touched his, their kiss was long and deep, he held her waist as he slowly entered her body, she gasped as she gently gyrated against his powerful manhood, he was unable to control the overwhelming power rising in his loins they both withered with delight as their bodies reached their destiny.

They collapsed among the wild flowers which covered the banks of the pool, exhausted by their moment of passion, the woman turned to Olaf, 'give me a token of your love for me,' he looked at her, 'I have nothing to give,' she looked at his wet tunic lying close by, 'what's that?' she pointed to the cloth Ollam had given him, 'that will do,' 'take it if you want it,' 'No, you need to give it to me otherwise it will mean nothing,' Olaf reached out, he could just reach the cloth with his finger tips, he pulled it towards them, 'I give you this cloth as token of my love for you,' the woman held the cloth to her breast and lay back among the wild flowers.

Olaf finally woke, he looked round, he was alone, his tunic and leggings lay at his side he picked them up, it was dry, how long had he been asleep, did he dream about the woman, had he been bewitched, he turned towards the cottage, was any one in there as he walked back a voice called him, his head turned towards the sound, there walking into the meadow was Sadie, she waved as if glad to see him, as she became closer she looked at him with a puzzled expression on her face 'what's wrong, you look worried' she touched his face, he jolted back 'how long have you been here, where's Sandaira?' 'In answer to both your questions, I have only just returned from the village and I have no idea where Sandaira is, I thought she was here with you?'

'No, no she's not here unless she's back in the cottage,' the cottage the door was still open as Olaf had left it, they went inside, Sandaira was not there, Sadie scanned the dimly lit cottage, 'where could that child be?' she muttered under her breath.

'You are acting strange Olaf, tell me what's wrong?' Sadie sat down at the table and started to peel some root vegetables, she looked at him, 'come on you look troubled,' he sat down 'you went to the village last night?' still continuing to peel the vegetables, 'yes that's right not long after you went to sleep,' she smiled at him, 'why did you not wake me?' Sadie looked up, 'I tried, you were like the dead you must have needed the rest.'

'I had a dream, well I think it was a dream, I'm not sure' Olaf's voice was hesitant, 'spit it out,' Olaf sensed Sadie was becoming irritated with his lack of response.

Olaf began to tell her the whole story, still unsure if he had been dreaming.

Sadie stopped peeling the vegetables and listened, Olaf told her how the woman in the pool enticed him to join her and they had made love, then she disappeared, Olaf felt for the cloth, it was gone, it must have happened, he stood up, 'where are you going?' Sadie snapped, 'to see if the cloth had slipped out of my tunic by the pool,' he walked slowly towards the door, 'don't bother you had no dream, she was real,' Olaf looked at Sadie, 'how do you know?' Sadie stood up and walked slowly towards him, 'it was Sandaira,' Olaf looked at her in disbelief, 'No it wasn't she was a woman not a young girl, she had red hair,' Sadie gestured to the stool, 'Sit down we need to talk, I need to explain.'

'You will find this hard to believe but it is the truth, you will need to believe, otherwise this would all be for nothing,' Sadie sat next to Olaf, 'when I found Sandaira she was like a gift from the gods, even through I was not welcome at the village, I knew I had got to raise Sandaira as my own.'

'I too had a dream, in fact many dreams as the years, each telling me what I was to do, at first I paid little heed to them, then I began to realize they were showing me the future path Sandaira was to take.'

Sadie glanced into the air, 'I believed Sandaira had seen fifteen summers, but the last dream I had, showed her as a woman heavy with child, she was not here, she was in a mysterious, peaceful place full of light with fireflies dancing around her, during the dream she told me she had to go, her destiny had been fulfilled and I would always be watched over by the guardians of the forest, that was the last dream I had and that was a number of moons ago, I thought it meant she would be here until she was older, now I don't know.'

'I still can't believe the woman was Sandaira, but she knew me!' Olaf was more puzzled than ever.

'I'm going out to the pool, I won't sleep this night' Olaf picked up his sword and went out of the door.

He stood by the pool looking into the clear water, it seemed like for ever, his reflection changed, he could see Sandaira, she was rising up out of the water, she was smiling at him, Olaf was speechless, she stood next to him, it was as if she was there but in a kind of mist.

'Olaf I want you to listen carefully to me, I was the woman you made love to, I needed your seed to protect the line of my people, in return you and your family will receive protection at times of extreme peril, I asked you for a token of your love for me, you gave me this cloth, I now give it back as a token of the joining together of our two families, when your family is in peril you can call on my family to help, I cannot tell you in what form help will be given, all I know is your family can ask for help only three times, on the third time of asking, help will be given but the cloth and the person asking for the help will disappear from your world to mine, this cloth will hold it's own magical powers again only the power in the cloth will know when it is needed, use the cloth wisely.'

Olaf reached out trying to touch Sandaira, his hands just went through her shape as if she was not there, Sandaira continued, 'Every so often a girl will be born into your family, this child may not be born to the head of your family but to a direct descendent of you, this child will have a destiny either to protect members of your family or to lead when hope appears to have abandoned your family, be careful not to scorn this child as she may appear different, to help you identify such a child she will have long deep red hair and emerald green eyes, she will always have a connection to my world, be wise Olaf, don't use the cloth in haste remember the cloth is to protect, never harm.'

Sandaira's image started to disappear, 'who are you, who are your people?' Olaf was even more puzzled, Sandaira whispered, 'don't you believe in the fairy people Olaf?' He stood in disbelief.

'A'm glad yoo didn't tell Lucy that part of tha story,' Anne said amusingly, 'a would have never told Lucy tha story in that way,' Iain then saw the funny side of Anne's comments.

Anne was tired, she looked at Iain, his eyes closed, he was seconds from sleep, she snuggled up to Iain and drifted into a security she had not felt for months.

CHAPTER FIVE
Lady of the loch

Sunlight streamed through a small gap in the blackout curtains onto Anne's face she was still asleep, Iain looked at his bonnie lass he was truly a lucky man.

Ian heard tiny footsteps, the bedroom door slowly opened every time it gave a creak it stopped only to open a bit further until a small face with bright eyes and a mass of unbrushed red hair appeared round the door.

'Daddy are yoo awake,' Lucy enquired knowing the answer, 'Yes but mummy is still asleep, I'll get up an we can make mummy breakfast in bed,' Lucy bounced with joy at that idea, she was always a bundle of energy, which could be overpowering at times and often got her into trouble.

They both quietly made there way downstairs, this was difficult as Lucy was like a coiled spring and the stairs were old and gave loud creaks when anyone stood on them.

'Right what will mummy like fa breakfast, eh Lucy?' Iain looked at Lucy, she shrugged her shoulders, 'eggs an bacon would ba nice,' Iain smiled to Lucy, 'aye that's what we'll have then.'

Iain could not believe how clumsy he had become in the kitchen, he could not find anything much to Lucy's delight, she thought it was funny watching daddy look silly.

They finally managed to cook breakfast, Lucy carefully carried Anne's breakfast, she knew she had to take her time or it might slip out of her hands and spoil the surprise, Iain carried the cups of tea, Lucy's and his own breakfast, they gingerly made their way up the stairs to Anne's bedroom.

Anne was pretending to be asleep, she had woken up a couple of minutes earlier, hearing the commotion that was going on downstairs she thought it best to stay out of the way.

Lucy put Anne's breakfast quietly onto the bedside table and jumped onto the bed, 'wake up mummy, wake up,' Anne opened her eyes, instead of being half asleep as Lucy believed she was, Anne grabbed Lucy and started to tickle her, laughing Lucy cried, 'stop it mummy we've done yoo breakfast.'

'This looks nice what have I done ta deserve a surprise like this?' Anne looked at Iain, he gave her a knowing wink.

After the breakfast dishes had been washed up it was decided to go for a drive to Loch Lomond, the loch was about twenty miles away and the roads were narrow and only tracks in places so it would take some time to get there.

The drive was pleasant in the crisp November air, the heather had turned like brown velvet as it clung to the hills, only a couple of months earlier the hills had been clothed in a majestic purple cloak as the heather had been in full bloom, the tops of the hills were capped in the first snows

Am Bratach Sith of Dunvegan

of the coming winter, they passed shepherds working the sheep, well the dogs working as the shepherds whistled and shouted commands to the ever eager to please sheep-dogs, the pace of life was slow and sure, not an easy place to live and work but a very easy place to belong.

They reached Loch Lomond shores in good time, the autumnal sun hung like an orange in the cloudless sky barely warming the icy shroud left during the night by Jack Frost, each breath of cold air was replaced by smoke as Lucy would say as the warm air rushed out of her mouth.

Loch Lomond stretched out before them, it looked like a mirror, no wind to ripple the water only the odd fish topping to catch flies or water birds gliding across to one of the many islands that inhabited the loch, there was a mist lying over the loch like a blanket on a bed, you could hardly see it close up but it appeared quite thick in the distance, 'is this tha sea?' Lucy looked at Iain for an answer, 'noo but it is part of tha story I'm telling yoo, it is associated with tha MacFarland Clan who once owned this area,' Lucy danced around Iain, 'daddy will yoo carry on with tha story when we get home?' Lucy again looked at Iain for conformation, 'aye I'll carry on with it, but don't keep on.'

They walked arm in arm for a couple of hours, Lucy throwing stones into the loch and running all over the place, it was so peaceful, tranquillity took on a new meaning, Iain loved this beautiful, rugged, hard and sometimes uncompromising country, this could only be Scotland.

Lucy had found a rock that hung over the water she was lying on it looking into the clear water, as Iain and Anne came closer to Lucy they could hear her talking as if there was someone in the water, 'Lucy who yoo talking to?' she looked round, 'tha lady in tha loch,' Lucy turned back and looked at Iain, 'she's gone noo, yoo frightened her away,' Iain and Anne both looked into the water they could clearly see the bottom of the loch even through it was about six feet deep, 'were yoo talking too a fish?' Lucy gave Iain a cruel look, 'noo I told yoo, I was talking too tha lady in tha loch.'

Lucy started to become annoyed, it was clear Iain and Anne did not believe her, she started to run off in front again.

The afternoon was drawing to a close when they got back to the car, 'we had better make a move, a want too get back afore it gets dark an too icy,' Iain's comments meant they had been too long already.

The drive back home was not too bad, it was dark when they reached home, the frost was starting to bite any exposed flesh, and Lucy had a scarf wrapped round her face so you could only just see her eyes.

Anne opened the door the heat from the fire was welcome, Lucy stripped off her coat, scarf, gloves and wellington boots and sat right in front of the fire, 'sit back from tha fire Lucy,' Anne was quiet abrupt, Lucy hotched her way back about two feet, Lucy could feel the warmth tingling through her body, she was soon warm, 'I'm hungry,' Lucy moaned, Anne had earlier made a broth which she had left on the range to cook through, it was served in a matter of minutes.

They all sat round the fire talking about the lovely day they have had, Lucy was sitting on Iain's lap staring into the fire, 'what did tha lady say ta yoo?' Iain was hoping to catch Lucy out, 'what lady?' Lucy was unimpressed, Iain's voice had broke her trance, 'tha one in tha loch,' Lucy did

Am Bratach Sith of Dunvegan

not move, 'she told ma ta walk from tha fire,' 'fire what fire?' Anne asked as she sat up, 'a doon't noo,' Lucy was becoming agitated, 'yoo must ba tired, time for bed lassie,' Anne stood up, holding Lucy's hand she led her up to bed.

Iain came into Lucy's bedroom, 'are yoo going ta carry on with tha story daddy?' Lucy's face was more hopeful than optimistic, 'alright but only for a wee while.'

'Where did a get ta?' Iain was bating Lucy to see if she had listened, 'Daddy it was tha bit where tha man was in tha cottage with tha witch,' Lucy had indeed listened.

'Och aye, 'Olaf met a lassie by tha pool he fell in love with her an gave her tha cloth Ollam had given him as a token of his love fa her, later Olaf found out tha woman was Sandaira tha witches daughter, she gave tha cloth back ta Olaf granting his family three wishes but tha wishes could only ba used ta stop his family from coming ta any harm, she also said a girl would ba born within his family who would have special powers, they could identify tha child because she would have red hair n green eyes,' Lucy jumped up, 'like me daddy, like me?' Lucy's eyes sparkled, 'tha lassie could ba me?' Iain looked at her and shook his head, 'if yoo wan it ta ba, aye a suppose so,' Iain was too tired to argue.

Olaf told Sadie about meeting Sandaira again, he showed her the cloth he had given to Sandaira, which she had now given him back, you must leave, go back to your home, don't tell anyone about this they will not understand, you could be in danger.

Sadie took Olaf back to the edge of the forest, you know the way from here, may the gods be favourable to your journey home, Sadie patted Olaf on the back, he turned round she had disappeared back into the forest.

As Olaf walked back to the village he felt calm, somehow reassured that things were going to work out for him at last, he arrived back at the village in a short time, no-one he met was surprised to see him, they did not appear concerned that he had been gone for a couple of days.

Olaf could not work it out it was if he had never left.

He met Tord in the village, 'there you are Olaf, I've been looking for you everywhere, you seemed to disappear at high sun, we need to set sail the men are becoming anxious to get home,' Olaf just stood and looked at Tord, 'did you see me this sunrise?' Olaf's voice dwindled away Tord turned 'what did you say?' Olaf knew if he questioned any further Tord would get suspicious, 'nothing, nothing,' Olaf remembered what Sadie had told him, 'don't tell anyone they will not understand.'

Olaf went to the galley, it was ready to set sail, 'Tord you have done a good job, why don't you master the galley home?' Olaf held out his hand to Tord, he grasped it and embraced Olaf 'well come on you have to get the galley home.'

The villagers came down to see the galley safely out of the inlet, as the last part of the stern disappeared out of sight the villagers slowly made there way home.

Olaf stood on the bow of the galley, wrestling with his thoughts, did all this really happen, if it did how can he possibly explain to his father and his brothers, he had forgotten they will laugh him out of the land of Mann, with no treasure to show, yes he had arranged some trade agreements but they are often broken as quickly as they are made, he pulled the cloth out from his tunic it still smelt of wild flowers, he wanted to be back with Sandaira.

'Galley, galley coming towards us,' one of the crew had spotted a galley it appeared to be heading on a collision course, Tord steered the galley away from it's present course, as the other galley came closer they could not see any crew on board, 'try to board her,' Olaf shouted, this was not easy to do when two galleys are passing, if you time your jump wrong you could end up between the galley's and dead.

Olaf decided to jump, 'Tord you take her home we will follow,' Tord looked at Olaf, 'may the gods be with you old friend,' Olaf winked then turned and jumped towards the side of the other galley, he managed to grab the side of the galley and hauled himself onto the deck, three other members of the crew also made the jump, sadly two others did not make it, they were crushed between the galley's hulls as they passed each other.

The small crew quickly took hold of the galley and began to turn her round, once with the breeze behind them the galley was under control and they could follow Tord home, Olaf searched the galley, there did not appear to be any real damage, the deck was not nailed down very well, Olaf pulled up one of the deck planks, stored under the deck were bundles of some kind, he heaved on up onto the deck and cut the bindings, it was packed with cloth possibly silk, if they were all like this one he had a small fortune in his hands.

The rest of their journey home was uneventful, Olaf concluded, the sea demons must have been up to mischief elsewhere.

As the two galleys sailed into port on the Land of Mann a few local villagers waved to them, word quickly spread of Olaf's arrival back home, soon the quay was full of people looking to see what treasure he had brought home.

Olaf heard a voice above all the commotion, 'Olaf!' he could not mistake that voice he looked round at the back of the crowd waving was Tormid his eldest brother, Olaf pushed through the crowd as they met, each stopped and looked each other up and down, 'you have got older Olaf,' a big grin came across Olaf's face, 'and you have got fatter,' Tormid laughed they slung their arms round each other, Tormid was built of rock, a tall monster of a man, long jet black hair, beard to match, he moved for no man, he did hold a more gentle side but he did not let it show outside of his direct family, 'tell me of your adventures?' Olaf looked at Tormid, 'I don't know where to begin but I will wager you I've had an adventure you will not believe,' Tormid laughed again, 'your on, now lets see what you have brought back with you, or not,' Tormid laughed again, this was not unusual Tormid was either laughing, eating, drinking, loving or fighting he never seemed bothered which, as long as he was doing one of them.

Olaf told Tormid how the galley was adrift and all of this was stored below the decking, Tormid scratched his head, 'there is all manner of things here silks, spices, coinage, precious stones, gold and silver, I don't know of any vessel carrying this amount of goods in these waters.'

Tormid looked around, 'we had better get this lot moved to a safer place, too many interested eyes for my liking,' Olaf looked at Tormid, things suddenly appeared less jovial, 'what do you mean, what's been going on since I

Am Bratach Sith of Dunvegan

left?' Tormid let out a deep sigh, 'nothing just a few quarrels with the neighbours,' Tormid held his finger to his throat and moved it across as if to cut his throat.

The crew packed the treasure onto mules and they moved off towards their fathers castle, it was not that far but far enough to give Olaf time to tell Tormid of his adventures and brave acts, not that Olaf would embellish the truth but you have to tell a good story don't you, anyway Tormid would do the same.

It was good to be home, the mules walked slowly under the gateway of the castle into the court yard, he dismounted his horse, 'where's father?' Olaf looked round, why was he not there to greet him.

Tormid dismounted his horse, he put his powerful arm round Olaf's broad shoulders, 'come Olaf, into the castle, we need to talk.'

Olaf sensed all was not well in the Land of Mann, it was not like his father to miss something like his youngest sons homecoming, they entered one of the small rooms, Tormid poured a jug of ale for them, he turned towards Olaf handing him one of the jugs, 'drink for the gods good fortune, by the gods we're going to need it,' Olaf was becoming anxious and ill tempered, 'will you tell me what's going on, where's father and Magnus why are they not here?' Magnus was Olaf's other brother, as quick and cunning in thinking as he was brave in battle.

'Both father and Magnus are in the north of Mann, there are reports of galleys from the north, raiding villages, they have gone to reason with them or fight if need be,' Olaf could hardly believe Tormid, 'but they must be our kinfolk from the northlands, why would they want to steal form us, they only have to ask, food and shelter would be given freely?' Tormid finished his ale wiped his mouth with his long broad forearm, 'times change, we now need to fight to hold onto what we have, dark days are ahead.'

'We must go to join father,' Olaf turned and walked towards the door, 'wait, father wants me to remain here in case others invade in the south, that's why I remained here, don't you think I wanted to go with them, instead I just sit around here?' Olaf turned to Tormid, 'you were told to stay, not me?' Olaf stared at his brother for what seemed an age, waiting for some kind of reply that for once never came, he walked out of the room, no further words were spoken.

CHAPTER SIX
Return to Mann

Olaf soon found himself riding across the land he knew so well, yet his thoughts told him this was not the land he left a few short summers ago.

Villages towards the north of the land were abandoned, it had taken him the best part of the day to reach his father, the day light had all but gone, all that remained was the mischievous twilight that played tricks on your eyes, he found, what he thought was his father's camp by the coast, as he rode towards the camp he was challenged by a over zealous guard, 'stand, show yourself,' there was fear in the guards voice, 'I am Olaf son of king Astred of Mann,' Olaf moved his horse slowly into the available light, hoping the guard would recognize him, 'hold fast,' the guard was not sure, he called to the camp for help.

Olaf started to become annoyed, 'let me pass, I need to speak to my father,' the guard held his spear to the throat of Olaf's horse, this made his horse nervous, Olaf steadied his horse, he could make out men coming towards him carrying spears and swords, a sudden fear came over

Olaf, what if this wasn't his father's camp but the camp of invaders, should he stand and hope the gods are with him or should he try to escape and return in day light, he weighed up his chances of escape there was not much room to turn his horse quickly, the guard would have chance to spear his horse and him before the other men arrived, Olaf decided to wait and put his faith in the gods.

The men drew closer in the dimming light, Olaf could make out his brother, 'Magnus,' he shouted 'Magnus it's me, Olaf,' Magnus was near to Olaf by this time, 'by the gods, it is you,' Olaf started to dismount all fear of capture or death gone from his mind, the gods had surely been merciful this day.

Magnus stretched out his arms to greet Olaf, they hugged, 'it's good to see you brother, the gods could have granted us better times but at least you returned safe,' Magnus led Olaf to the camp.

'Where's father?' Olaf appeared concerned much had been left unsaid since his return, he was stealing himself for more bad news, 'right here son,' Olaf turned his head to where the voice was coming from, on a large rock in a alcove to his left side sat his father, Olaf's face beamed all his questions were answered with one look at the powerful frame of King Astred, Olaf was quick to greet his father, they embraced as only a father greeting a lost son can, after a short while when words were not needed, Astred placed his hands on Olaf's shoulders and looked straight into his eyes, 'tell me, how did your adventure go, was it fruitful?' Olaf's head dropped, 'well yes and no, I did not bring back much treasure until we were nearly home,' he continued to tell his story. Afterwards Astred held Olaf's arm, 'the gods were playing games with you, they wanted to test your resolve,' he laughed, 'come boy, no you are truly a man now, you have earned the right to be listened to, lets eat and talk some more.'

Astred told Olaf about the problems they were having with raiders from the north lands and their lack of respect for their kinfolk who have settled on Islands west of Scotland.

Astred feared they would need to move to Islands north of Mann and try to establish a home on larger islands, the Land of Mann was not easy to defend and he was becoming too old to fight.

Olaf asked his father if he could talk alone with him, 'we hold no secrets here son, speak freely.' Olaf was unsure how what he had got to say about Sandaira or the cloth would be taken, they might believe he had been bewitched or was a slave to the sea demons, believing this was not the right time to tell every one of all his adventures he passed it off and changed the subject.

Olaf wanted to know why they had camped there, his father believed the raiders would come ashore in a cove at the foot of the nearby cliffs, if they did, they would be in a position to cut them off from their galleys by going round a narrow hidden path at the base of the cliff, Astred was then hoping to talk to their leader to secure an agreement, they could land on Mann but not to carry out raids on the villages, if an agreement could not be reached they would need to repel the raiders and destroy them if necessary, this did not sit well with Astred, he longed for peace, he wanted to enjoy the last summers of his life, not having to continue fighting to survive.

The morning brought a heavy dew, the ground was wet and cold, Olaf was woken by Magnus, he had his finger pressed to his lips, telling Olaf to be quiet, when Olaf had gained his senses Magnus pointed to a rock which appeared to be on the edge of the cliff, 'follow me there's three galleys close to the shore,' they both made there way to the rock making sure they stayed low and out of sight of the galleys, Olaf peered round the side of the rock, Magnus likewise on the other side.

The galleys were coming closer to the shore, they could clearly see the oars in the water, 'we had better wake father, Olaf you stay here keep them in sight,' Magnus slowly slipped back from the edge of the cliff using the rock as cover, Olaf was soon joined by Astred, the galleys were fully crewed, no question the galleys intended to come ashore, Astred dropped his head, Olaf could see his father hoped this would not happen, 'don't worry father, they may reason.'

Olaf's words did not convince either him or Astred, 'no son, I feel this is a bad day to die, there is no honour in killing your own kinfolk, the gods will desert this day,' Astred returned to the camp Olaf stayed at the rock, he could see the men making their way down the path to the beach using the cliff as cover.

The galleys finally beached in the cove, the crew were soon on the beach and heading for what they believed to be the only way up from the beach, they appeared to be well armed with swords, axes, shields and spears, Olaf tried to count them, at best he believed them to be a hundred strong, they would need to leave at least twenty behind to protect the galleys, that left around eighty to fight.

Olaf had a good view of his father and around fifty men waiting at the top of the cliff, he would not show himself until the others had reached the beach, all Olaf could hear was the waves gently meeting the shore and a few birds twittering in the gorse behind him, the signal was given, the men had reached the beach, the raiders stopped to see where the sound had come from, they spotted the men on the beach and some of them began to run back to protect the galleys.

Astred and the other men showed themselves at the top of the cliff, this caused a few seconds of panic, the raiders did not know what to do, go back to the galleys or carry on, they soon decided to head for the galleys, Astred led his men down the cliff, the men on the beach were now near to the galleys, they were not engaged by the raiders left to guard the galleys, they appeared not to know what to do, fight or try to float the galleys out to sea, they could see they were out numbered.

One of the raiders stopped, he looked round at Astred and appeared to be assessing how strong a force they were up against, he quickly came to the conclusion they could win this fight, he called his men to fight, by this time Astred and his men were all on the beach, the raiders had formed a half moon shape to defend all sides, they did not attack, this was a good sign, Olaf decided it was time he joined his father and brother, he started half running half clambering down the cliff when he heard a shout , he looked up, the leader of the raiders had decided to attack Astred and his small band of men.

The attack was fast and somehow caught Astred by surprise, Olaf ran to be by his fathers side, many lay dead or injured, his sword drawn Olaf struck one of the raiders in the side blood gushed from the wound, his fight was over, without hesitation he thrust his sword into the stomach of another, he pulled the sword clear knowing he needed his sword to defend him-self, Olaf tried to get to his fathers side, it was difficult to know amongst the carnage who was winning, the raiders were battle hardened and desperate, they had their backs to the wall or sea in this case.

Olaf called to his father, his call only distracted Astred, a sword plunged into his side, he fell to his knees, Olaf lunged at the raider his sword cutting deep into his sword arm, again Olaf struck, this time deep into the raiders chest, he fell dead, Olaf pulled the sword from his fathers side, he was badly wounded but still alive, Olaf began to pull Astred clear of the melly, Magnus joined them for protection, 'try to stop the bleeding,' Magnus yelled, 'what with?' Olaf seemed to lose all reasoning 'anything,' Magnus yelled back as he fought off another raider, Olaf remembered the cloth he pulled it from his tunic and held it to the wound, almost at the same time the raiders began to fall back to their galleys, they were being defeated.

Astred's men appeared to find greater strength, each fighting with the strength of two men, the raiders were soon cut off from their galleys and encircled, Magnus called there leader to surrender or die, Magnus knew what they would decide, within a short time all the raiders lay dead or injured.

The battle had claimed the lives of fifty-five of Astred's men and left many injured including himself, he felt cold and believed he may not recover, Olaf and Magnus carried Astred back up the cliff, Magnus knew of a witch who lived close by, he could threaten her to cure Astred, 'no Magnus' Olaf held his arm, 'do you believe in fairies?' Magnus looked at him as if he had gone mad, 'during the battle, we were losing, don't you think?' Olaf looked up, Magnus could see he was serious, 'well, yes I suppose things did look bad,' Olaf pulled the cloth from his father's wound, he held it up to Magnus, 'when father was struck down I pulled this cloth from inside my tunic, from then on the battle turned to our favour, don't you see, I was told this cloth would protect my family,' Magnus tried to understand, 'are you saying that cloth is bewitched?' Olaf placed the cloth back on Astred's wound, he stood up, 'no Magnus, it was given to me by a fairy queen, it's a long story, I'm not mad or bewitched, let's get father back to the castle, I'll tell you all about what happened, then you can decide if you believe me'.

Olaf and Magnus left the remaining men behind with instructions to look after the injured and bring the dead back to the castle, they would be given a warriors funeral, the raiders were to be stripped of any belongings and burned on their galleys that were cast out to sea.

Olaf and Magnus did not speak much on the journey back to the castle, Magnus was deep in thought while Olaf wondering if he had already said too much.

When they finally arrived Elspeth was waiting at the gate to the castle, her long black hair streaming down her slender back mainly hidden under a white lace bonnet and shawl, her eyes brown as peat, she was a stern plain faced woman who did not suffer fools easily, She looked at her sons, they were unharmed, without a word she soon had Astred whisked away into the castle, she would tend his wound now.

Olaf could not believe she was not glad to see him after all the time he had been away, 'don't worry, she'll come round, she was distraught when you left, she did not speak to father for a month for allowing you to go in the first place, you know what she can be like, everyone was walking on egg shells for ages,' Magnus patted Olaf on the back, 'come on lets bed the horses down.'

Astred recovered from his injury in a few days, he was lucky the sword had passed through his side missing any vital organs, never the less his fighting days were over, when he was strong enough he asked to see his wife and sons together, they all gathered in his bed chamber.

'Tell me Olaf, what do you think happened during the battle?' Olaf did not know what to say, he felt he had made himself look a fool when he spoke to Magnus after the battle, he looked at Magnus, 'go on tell him what you told me,' Olaf could not believe it Magnus had told his father.

'Come on Olaf, I want to hear the whole story before I make up my mind if you are telling the truth, bewitched or just mad,' Astred gestured to Olaf with his hand to sit on the stool next to his bed.

Olaf started to tell them what had happened in Ireland, he kept saying, 'I know you wont believe me, how can I expect you to, I only know the battle changed when I pulled the cloth out of my tunic.'

When he finished telling his story, Olaf expected to be ridiculed, instead there was silence, even Elspeth did not speak, she went over to him and touched his forehead, moving his hair away from his face, 'I'm glad your home safe, you have brought back a special gift that needs to be kept within the family and secret from outsiders or it will bring more pain, if this is true we are truly graced by the fairy people, we should respect their gift and use it wisely, all we have to decide is do we believe Olaf and do we believe in fairies?' she turned walked out of the bedroom with a smile from ear to ear.

'Well not much I can add to that, do you truly believe in the fairy people Olaf?' Olaf looked at his father then to his brother's, 'yes I do, I will not renounce them,' he looked back at Astred who was still pondering, finally he announced, 'the fairy people are welcome within this family for as long as they wish or until any member of this family renounces them to outsiders,' each son in turn made the same pledge.

'That's said and done, we will pass this pledge through the generations so our children may share in our good fortune,' Astred then ushered his sons out of the bedroom, they left without a further word, each feeling a contentment they had never felt before.

CHAPTER SEVEN
A new beginning

Iain woke with a start, his eyes wide, he was sweating, he looked down at his hands, he was trembling, why could he not remember dreaming, Anne rolled over in bed without opening her eyes she asked what was the matter, she snuggled close to Iain, she felt his unease, her eyes opened, 'what's wrong?' she looked at him, 'Iain yoo staring at me, what's wrong?' Iain looked at her, 'nothing, nothing's wrong, a must have had a bad dream, only a canny remember,' Anne held onto Iain, he put his strong arm round her slender shoulders Anne felt safe all appeared well.

Iain was the first to get up which was unusual, normally Lucy would be up at the crack of dawn, Iain had looked in at her she was fast asleep, must have tired her out last evening, he went down stairs and started to make breakfast, it was good to get fresh eggs and bacon, the rationing down south was hitting everyone hard, there was always stuff on the black market to be had at a price but if he was caught with any thing he would be court marshalled so it was not worth it, any way the officers did not do too bad, every morning they were due to fly a mission they would be given two eggs with their breakfast, he stood in a day dream thinking about the squadron, wondering what they were doing, how many sorties they had flown since he left a couple of days ago, worst of all who would not be there when he returned.

'Iain,' Anne cried 'yoo burning tha toast?' Iain snapped out of his trance, 'err, a was not, leave it a can manage,' he looked at Anne, she held him, 'a canny begin ta know what it's like fa yoo ma darling,' Anne whispered, they held each other so tight it was as if they would never let go.

'Daddy, Mummy,' Lucy broke the moment as children have a habit of doing, Lucy was coming down the stairs, she had obviously been into their bedroom only to find no-one there, she was calling out to get a reaction.

'In tha kitchen lass' Anne replied, Lucy ran into the kitchen straight to Iain, she held him round his legs, 'a thought yoo had gone,' she slowly let go, 'what gave yoo that impression?' Iain asked, 'tha fairies told me yoo would leave us last night,' Iain crouched down, 'a'm going noo where until Thursday,' Lucy looked puzzled, 'how many days is that?' holding up her little fingers for Iain to count, 'four, one two, three, four,' he held four of her fingers, her head dropped, 'only four days?' Lucy held the chair as if to stop herself from falling in despair.

Anne tried to break the mood, 'what shall we do ta day Lucy?' she looked at Anne, 'can we stay in, a want daddy ta finish tha story?' Anne's face raised to look at Iain, 'what do yoo think daddy?' Iain stretched out his arms picked Lucy up, 'of course we can stay here, that's lots of tha story left still ta tell.'

Am Bratach Sith of Dunvegan

After breakfast Iain sat in his favourite chair, the large open fire burning logs they had collected, as the fire crackled it occasionally spat out a piece of wood onto the hearth.

Lucy was always bemused by the fire, she said she could see people dancing in the flames, she knew not to get to close because it might burn her.

Iain lit his pipe, a bellow of smoke rose from it, Lucy did not like Iain's pipe it made her cough and his breath smell, 'now then what about tha story, where was a?' Lucy pulled at Iain's jumper, 'yoo noo where yoo got ta, tha bit when tha king believed in tha fairies,' Iain looked down at Lucy, 'och aye, a remember.'

A long, long time ago seven galleys were being gently tossed from side to side by the sea, like a mother rocking a baby in it's crib, a whisper of breeze slowly edged them closer towards their new homeland, mist hung over the black silhouette of land like a protecting shroud, keeping the land from view, this would be a new beginning.

There was nervousness about, would they have to fight their way ashore or would these islands be less inhabited, they would soon find out.

The galleys became grounded on a small sandy beach, no hostile reception, in fact no reception at all, the men began to unload personal belongings from the galleys, there was no time to waste, the quicker they could make a camp, the more able they would be to defend themselves.

The galleys were unloaded before darkness covered the land, a main camp had been hurriedly arranged, and more like a lot of people huddled together round a large fire with sentries posted to warn of any danger.

The short spring night passed without problems, people around the dying fire began to stir, it had been a long voyage and they were tired but knew there would be time to relax when they had built a defendable stronghold.

Stevson a blood relation to Magnus of Mann stood on a headland next to the beach, his long black hair blowing over his rugged face in the freshening breeze, he looked out to sea, there was good visibility, he turned slowly taking in all the contours of the landscape, this could be defended, it was large enough for a sizable camp with only one real means of entry, as he walked back to the beach, he spotted someone looking at him from a distance, he began to walk towards the person who turned and ran away from him, he gave chase, as quickly as he had first seen the person he was gone, Stevson looked round, he drew his sword expecting to be ambushed, nothing happened, he kept looking round as he made his way to the beach, puzzled and a little nervous, someone knew they were there.

Olaus was busy doing what he believed he did best, bossing every one else around, he was under the illusion he had some kind of right to lead and others would follow, he was soon in confrontation, Connack had him by the throat, his big hand slowly squeezing the life out of him, 'Connack stop playing with Olaus, come with me,' Connack glared at Stevson, 'you want a fight I may have picked one for you?' Stevson pointed to the headland, 'I saw someone up there, they saw me, then disappeared,' Connack glared at Olaus, squeezed his throat a bit harder then threw him onto the beach like a rag doll, Olaus was left gasping for breath, Connack walked off as if nothing had happened.

Connack was indeed a mighty warrior, the sight of him would make any man tremble, he stood a full head and shoulders above any man Stevson had ever seen, he had once broke the neck of a horse that had kicked him, he was as strong as two men and showed no fear.

Stevson was not small himself but he looked like a child walking next to Connack, they reached the headland Connack looked round it was difficult to know what Connack was thinking, he was not a man of many words but if he disagreed with you he had his way of showing it as Olaus found out.

Connack nodded, 'good, we camp here,' that was that then, Stevson knew if Connack believed this could be defended no one would argue, they could try, as Stevson was sure Olaus would, but they would end up making camp on the headland with or without Olaus.

Before Stevson and Connack had got back to the beach Olaus was in more trouble, this time with one of the women, Fingula, granted she was no ordinary woman, strong as most men with a wicked temper, Olaus sure knew how to pick a fight, he could not possibly win.

Once Stevson had managed to stop Fingula killing Olaus with a stone club, he thought if he does not find something for Olaus to do or he would not see a new day.

'Olaus, you have many qualities, one of them is not ordering people about, I think you are more suited to advising people, what I would like you to do is to make sure every one knows we are going to build a stronghold on that headland and they are to move there belongings as soon as possible, do you think you can do this without getting yourself killed?' Stevson looked at Olaus for some kind of answer, 'of course I can, shall I hurry them along?' Stevson looked towards the sky, 'no Olaus just tell them, they will make their own way.'

It had taken most of that day for everyone to make their way to the headland, it was not as sheltered as the beach but it was easier to defend, some of the men were busy collecting large rocks and timber, others were constructing shelters by digging out the earth, once again darkness fell but with the nights being short they were soon busy again, by the end of the second day they had shelter and a defendable position, now they needed to find food.

Stevson decided to take Connack and a couple of other men to scout round their land and look for food, Leod was left in charge of defending the camp with the other men.

They decided to walk inland until the sun was high then turn back, Stevson was nervous of the person he had seen on the first day yet they had not see any one since, they continued to make their way inland, there were a few wooded areas and a lot of rock, not many animals, this was a concern, they had brought seeds to sow oats corn but that would take months to grow, the few hens and live stock they had brought would not sustain them for long.

Connack stopped, he put his big hand to his forehead covering his eyes from the sun, he pointed, 'look smoke,' Stevson scanned the land in front of him, in the distance was a whisper of smoke, could this be a village or just one person, the one he had seen on that first day, he had to find out.

As they approached the smoke was more visible, it must be a camp fire, they remained hidden for as long as they could hiding behind a rock outcrop, Stevson peered over the top of the outcrop, there was a fire and a shelter, he could make out five people two men two women and a child, he could also see a few chickens and a few cows,

Am Bratach Sith of Dunvegan

shaggy looking things with large horns, he had never seen cattle like these before.

Moving back out of sight he told the others what he had saw, he believed they were not warriors more like farmers, they decided to approach the shelter in a peaceful manner, if that possible with a giant like Connack with you.

They got quite close to the shelter before the alarm was raised by the child, she screamed, the two men grabbed spears as the women took the child into the shelter, the two men stood guard a short distance from the shelter, Stevson approached the men with his hands held up as if to gesture he meant them no harm, he spoke to the men, he instantly knew they did not understand him, he was close enough for them to throw there spears, they just stood holding the spears out in front making jabbing movements as if to show intent if they came any closer, they were talking to each other in a strange language unknown to Stevson.

Tordson one of the men with Stevson thought he understood some of what the men were saying, he believed they may be part of a Pictish tribe but he did not think they held lands this far west, Tordson tried to talk with them, it was difficult but they seemed less aggressive, 'what are they saying?' Stevson looked at Tordson, 'I think they are from the main land, they are like us trying to settle on the island,' Tordson asked if they had seen any one else, they said there were a few other people on the island but they were relatively peaceful.

One of the men pointed to a large iron pot on the fire, he looked at Tordson and put his fingers to his mouth, Tordson turned to Stevson, 'I think they are offering us something to eat,' Stevson looked around the camp 'they don't look as if they have enough to live on as it is' Tordson took out a large piece of bread from a sack which was hanging from his waist and offered it to one of the men, he looked at Stevson and then at the other man who nodded at him as if to say take it, the man slowly took the bread from Stevson.

By this time one of the women had come out of the shelter and was standing behind the two men, she was handed the bread, she slightly lowered her head to acknowledge his gift but never took her eyes off Stevson there was a nervous trust between them.

'Tordson tell them thank-you for their offer of a meal but we need to get back to our people if they want to join us they will be welcome,' Tordson looked at Stevson, 'I'm not sure they will understand,' Stevson looked at the two men, 'They will,' Stevson held his hand up as if to say good-bye and turned away leaving Tordson to his task.

Connack still kept looking back as they walked away from the shelter, he did not trust anyone or anything new or he did not understand, 'leave it Connack, they were more afraid of you than we were of them,' Connack stared at Stevson and a slight smile came on his face, Connack knew he had that effect on most men.

The sun was heavy in the west as they reached the stronghold, they had seen the camp fire from a distance, this was good because they knew other's who may try to attack them would be seen, Connack sniffed the cooling air he could smell food being cooked, Connack had three loves in life food, fighting and drinking not always in that order, he did not care for the love of women, he believed if he wanted a woman he could take her.

The following few weeks went by with out any real drama, the settlement was becoming established, temporary

Am Bratach Sith of Dunvegan

shelters were being replaced with stone buildings cut into the ground with turf roofs, live stock was now fenced in at night, Stevson was still concerned about the lack of any wild animals on the island they could eat, there were plenty of sea birds and a few seals but they needed to start producing their own food.

Days were becoming warm and longer, the nights less cold, when it rained it really rained Stevson had never seen rain like it and there was always the wind, even on warm days the wind could cut you in two, Stevson would smile to himself when there was such a wind, his mother would say it was a lazy wind because it would go straight through you instead of going round.

A bright golden sun rose over the sapphire blue sea, with the faint breeze coming off the sea and a cloudless sky this was sure to be a good day, Stevson filled his lungs with the clear cool air, for the first time since they landed he could see the beauty of this land.

As the camp began to stir, a smell of fire and cooking filled the morning air, it was not long before the peace was shattered by the daily workings of a settlement trying to establish position.

Connack decided he wanted to explore, he was a warrior not a farmer, Stevson agreed Connack could go for three nights, Tordson reluctantly went with him, Connack looked thick but he wasn't daft, he knew if they come across any other camps he would rather talk than fight at least first anyway, they were soon in the distance, Stevson felt strange, he could not say why, just strange.

He soon forgot his feelings, Olaus was already causing trouble, trying to order Fingula about again, will he never learn, Stevson winced as Fingula punched Olaus in the face, he fell over a pile of fire wood onto a pile of cow muck, Olaus was now more concerned in getting away from people laughing at him to worry about what ever it was that caused him to pick on Fingula in the first place.

Stevson decided to call a meeting to discuss the way forward, he asked Olaus to make sure everyone knew about the meeting, that night all the people were sat round a large camp fire, Stevson started the meeting by going over what they had achieved in a few short weeks, he then gave his concerns about the food situation, there were a number of ideas discussed how to best farm this land with it's changeable weather, most of the comments were positive a few people thought they should go back home to the Land of Mann.

This was going to be a meeting that made history.

CHAPTER EIGHT
A Clan is born

The real reason Stevson called the meeting was to pick a leader 'king of the Isle' he knew they could not carry on as they were, with the camp growing into a real community unless there was strong leadership it could cause trouble, he proposed everyone should voice the persons name they wanted to make the head of the family.

Names were shouted out, obviously there would be a lot of different opinions, did they want a warrior or a thinker or may be a farmer, Stevson stood up raised his hands until the shouting stopped, ' lets think about this over night and decide in the morning.'

With sleep being far away from his mind Stevson walked the shoreline, it did not seem two full Moons since they had first landed on this island, he wondered what the future held, would they be forced to return to their homeland through starvation or would they be part of the new beginning they all prayed to the gods for.

Stevson sat on the beach listening to the sounds of the sea, the sun began to rise, a ball of orange light pushing away the darkness of despair, filling hearts with hope, he knew this would work, it had too, they had got over the worst, all they needed to do was work together, this would be their future.

When Stevson returned to the camp people were already up and about, there was an uneasy silence, people going about their business without any real discussion or argument, this was going to be an important day, a day of decision.

The meeting was called for mid day when the sun was at it's highest, every one would be there apart from Connack and Tordson, Stevson looked out over the land where are they, he could do with them being here, if Connack was good at any thing it was keeping the peace.

People started to gather in groups round the embers of last nights fire, Stevson could see there was a lot of division between who people believed should be their leader.

After a while Olaus raised his hands in the air trying to draw the attention of the crowd, Stevson could see no one was taking any notice of him as usual, no one ever has so why should they now, Olaus was becoming annoyed, sensing this could turn ugly even before the meeting had started Stevson pulled out his sword and thrust it into the middle of the dying fire, the embers crackled, every one stopped talking, startled they looked at the sword still swaying gently from side to side, their eyes moved to Stevson, he who believes he should be ruler of this land pull the sword from the fire, a light breeze blew in from the sea relighting the embers.

Olaus could not resist the challenge, if he claimed the sword every one would have to listen to him he would be king, he stood at the edge of the fire, slowly he placed his right foot into the embers, with a crackle fire leapt over his sandal like fingers grasping, holding on, he shouted out as he moved his burning foot from the fire, this caused both amusement and unease among the gathering.

Allard shouted out, 'we agreed to pick a leader not walk through fire, I pick Cullum he's a strong man, he works hard and can be trusted,' a cry of 'No,' was heard from others in the gathering, someone else shouted out a name then another, Stevson tried to calm the gathering without much success, it was clear there were too many opinions to gain any real outcome.

Suddenly a voice was heard above the crowd, 'stop,' Stevson looked up, Connack stood there larger than life, well he always was but Stevson was never so relieved to see him, Connack moved slowly round the fire, looking always for the next threat, people believe him to be a bit slow in mind mainly because he did not say much, he had worked this puzzle out in a few seconds, 'only one man can pull this sword, this man has already been chosen by the gods,' he looked round the gathering, looking for any argument to his words, 'who?' all eyes turned to Allard, he stood firm, 'go on then tell us of this man who has the gods on his side,' Allard did not show any fear but must have felt sick to his stomach at the thought of any confrontation with Connack.

Connack glared at Allard, 'Stevson,' a ripple of discontent rang round the gathering, 'no Connack I have no divine right,' Stevson looked at Connack, 'if you did not believe someone could pull the sword why did you thrust it into the fire in the first place?' Stevson was struggling to find the reason, 'it felt the right thing to do,' Stevson was more hopeful he would be believed than he trusted his own words.

The gathering sensed this, Allard shouted, 'if you hold the right, pick up the sword, if you are not burned I will stand with you,' Stevson was shaken, he had already seen Olaus burned taking one step, Connack took hold of Stevson by the arm, 'take the sword, trust the gods it is your destiny,' again the breeze raised the embers to a glow, fingers of fire beckoning Stevson to bathe in their warmth, slowly Stevson placed his foot in the embers, fire licked round his sandal, he felt no pain, a ripple of disbelief rang round the gathering, he placed his left foot gently down, the fire appeared to leap with joy it had got another victim, still Stevson felt nothing, he took two more short steps and stood by his sword, he gingerly touched the grip of the sword fearing it to be hot, it was cold, he grasped the sword, with one pull he released it from the fire's grasp and held it up to the gods, the gathering was silent, they could not believe what they had witnessed, was it the will of the gods or witchcraft.

Stevson looked round the gathering, he pointed his sword at each and every one as he turned, first Connack stepped forward, then Allard, Stevson stepped out of the burning embers it was clear to see the fire had not touched him, no burn marks on his sandals, feet or legs, Connack dropped to one knee, 'I will hold and protect you as my king,' Allard did the same, then Tordson, soon every one was on one knee proclaiming Stevson to be their rightful King.

Stevson could not believe what had happened was he bewitched, he could not remember being bewitched, he did not know any witches, personally anyway, could he be

Am Bratach Sith of Dunvegan

chosen by the gods, he decided he wanted to be on his own to reflect what had happened, he left Connack and Allard in charge, he returned to the spot on the beach where he spent the last night, he slumped down onto his knees.

After a while he started to think of his childhood and his grandmother who used to tell stories of his ancestors and how their family became connected to the fairy people, she always told him never to renounce fairies otherwise they will desert the family when it is in the most need, Stevson began to put events together, of course this is my destiny my family will have it's own land where the fairy people will be welcome, he would need to move things along, how can he expect others to believe what his family hold as true, he would need to protect the people from the truth until it can be proven beyond any reproach.

This was strange to Stevson he did not want to be king, he was more about getting things done, it's true he did hold a vision of what he wanted but he did not want to force others to follow his dream, he decided to form a group of respected men in the village to discuss subjects of importance, so that there was an agreement based on the wishes of the whole camp, not just one man, it was agreed at the first of these meeting Stevson would hold judgment to the words said and his decision would be final.

Stevson continued to want all the inhabitants of the island to be under one rule not for his own gratification but to allow peace and security for all.

Stevson decided he would invite the other islanders to the village, not many came at first, they thought they would either be killed or held as slaves, this was a common practice in most of the known world.

The island was inhabited by a number of people from the mainland tribes mainly the Pictish people, a warlike tribe fearless in battle, they would go into battle naked having painted their bodies, however the tribesman on the island wanted no more than to be left alone, it was hard enough to keep alive let alone argue with your neighbours.

Stevson, the first proclaimed king of the isle had established a village, which was not only surviving but quite prosperous, they had found sheep suited the land better than cattle, this gave them plenty to eat, warm clothing and enough to trade with other islanders and other islands.

Stevson had also wanted all of the islands to be under one rule, this had been difficult but over the years and long since his death the other islanders had grown to rely on their protection against attacks from outsiders, there had been numerous attacks from other tribes over the years but non had succeeded gaining any more than a few sheep or killing a few islanders, the normal outcome of such attacks would be the total destruction of the invaders either by the sword or by the sea as they tried to get home in galleys that had been damaged in their attempts to escape death.

The best defence they had was the sea and the weather, it was so unpredictable any attempt to pillage the isles would end up being effected by fog or bad weather that would be the future, they still had work to do.

The following few months were relatively peaceful, this allowed the islanders to build on their trust of each other, there was no where on the island that you were not safe, on one occasion a young man from the village went missing, he was nowhere to be seen, it was feared he had

Am Bratach Sith of Dunvegan

slipped over the cliff and drowned, he turned up hours later saying he had lost the track of time, which under the circumstances was possibly true, some months after his father saw him disappearing from the village he decided to follow, the lad walked and ran most of the day cutting across the island, it was as much as his father could do to keep up with him.

The lad stopped, he looked round as if looking for someone, his father thought his son had spotted him or he was looking back to see if any one was following, the lad appeared to stare in one direction then raised his arm and waved, he then started to run so fast his father lost sight of him, his father stopped running, he continued to walk in the general direction of the last time he saw his son, he stopped he could here voices, laughter, he slowly crept round a rock outcrop only to find his son with a girl, the father confronted his son, only to be told they were friends they had met some time ago and wanted to be friends, the girl ran off, the father asked his son if he knew where the girl lived, he said he did, the father told his son to take him to where she lived.

They came across a stone building with a large turf roof, there were animals running around out side, the door began to open, a large man stood in the doorway he looked proud and strong, the man spoke, the boys father could not make out what was being said, the boy replied, his father looked at the boy what did you say 'we mean you no harm, I am a friend of Megarna' the man stood to one side as he did the girl came out of the house, she stood in front of the boy, they spoke to each other in a way neither of the father's could understand, each in turn explained to their respective fathers how they had learned each others language, after a while all was well and they sat down sharing a type of broth.

The father's allowed their offspring to continue seeing each other as long as they were at either of their respective homes, what started out as a childhood friendship ended up in a wedding the couple decided they wanted to be together, this caused it's own difficulties due to their respective culture and beliefs, there happened to be a Holy man on the island preaching about a new god, it was decided to ask him to conduct the wedding, he agreed but only if the couple agreed to be baptized as Christians, they agreed anyway they could return to their own gods once he had gone.

This was a different wedding, the bride and groom were dressed in flowers and good luck trinkets, the Holy man did not appear to approve of these references to Pagan beliefs but given this opportunity to further the teachings of Jesus Christ to a large gathering he would turn a blind eye for this once, the Holy man only referred to one god, he called Christ our lord and a wedding held in place called Cana, with no offering of sacrifice to the new god it had been an inexpensive wedding for the parents

Little did they know but the arrival of the Holy man on the island would have an important baring on the people of the island becoming closer together, more often than not religion causes more wars than it stops but in this case religion would be central to the people of the island being of one mind with one religion.

Following the wedding the Holy man was asked to speak at many gatherings, many of the people were baptized as Christians renouncing their other gods as false.

Am Bratach Sith of Dunvegan

Within a few years the whole island was considered to be Christian, that was not to say the Islanders did not keep some of their old ways, Pagan festivals used to be quiet joyful affairs with a lot of dancing and drinking, it was difficult to break the deep beliefs of people who were so close to the land, they believed the land needed care and they were all part of the land, this meant with a lot of people their Christian beliefs came and went depending on who was asking and whether there was a holy man around to keep them in line.

As the years went by a trust grew between the inhabitants of the island, it was not long before the joining of people from different parts of the island was common place, the joining of blood would begin the story of a family who would dominate the Isles for over a thousand years.

CHAPTER NINE
Clan MacLeod

In the year 1237 Leod Olafson became the last king of the Isles, from his name came the family name of this story.

His ancestry is said to date back to one of Norwegian origin and the Kings of Mann but his blood line also holds the ancestry of the Celtic Western Isles people, therefore he can be called the first real Chief of the Clan Leod or MacLeod, he had two sons Tormod and Torquil, after a period of stability there was sure to a period of change and these pair would only be too happy to provide it, the only way Leod could see of stopping them from fighting to the death would be to give them lands before his death.

Leod decided to give Tormod part of their homeland now known as Harris and Skye, then to be known as Siol Thormod (race of Tormod) Torquil's part of their homeland now known as Lewis, then to be known as Siol Thorcuil (race of Torquil) he hoped this would stop them from arguing rights between them, Leod adopted the role of Chief of the family, Tormod did not like it because Torquil had the largest part of the Isles, Leod explained the quantity of the land was not important it was the quality, there was as much good farming land on Harris as there were on Lewis, but Harris is closer to Uist and Skye which makes trading easier and Torquil will need to ask for passage over Harris to get to Uist unless he sends galleys which is time consuming and dangerous, he also reminded him he also held large areas of lands on Skye, Tormod agreed he did had got a good deal after all.

Neither of the brothers would let things remain, Tormod decided to base his authority at Dunvegan castle on the Isle of Skye, said to have been built by the Norse rovers in the ninth century, he turned this small stronghold, into a defensive sea locked castle, his prime driving force being he was not going to give up any of his lands without a fight, Skye seemed to be the Isle he would most like to defend and Dunvegan was his most defendable castle, Tormod turned Dunvegan into a formidable sight the castle rising high on the rocks, clearly visible from the western shores and the sea.

On the death of his father Leod Olafson, Tormod being the eldest son became Chief of the Clan MacLeod, he decided Dunvegan would be the castle seat for the Chief of the clan from now on, he believed Dunvegan castle sent the right message to all who would attack the lands of MacLeod.

While Tormod set about his plans for Dunvegan, his brother was making his own plans, he wanted to be the chief of his own clan, he married the heiress of the chief of the MacNicols, with this he then gained possession of Assynt and other lands in Wester Ross, having been granted a charter by David ll, he had secured independent chief status for his dependents, later to be known as the

Am Bratach Sith of Dunvegan

MacLeod of Raasa, this appeared to prevent any further arguments between the brothers but would surely stir up trouble in the future if there became any doubt of succession to either title.

Both of the brothers created their own dynasties, they fought their own battles and picked their own fights, yet later history shows the MacLeod clansmen would fight together against the English.

Lucy had started to become impatient, she wanted to hear about fairies and magic, Iain smiled at her, 'you'll have ta wait lassie, you'll only now aboot tha fairies and the magic if yoo know tha story,' Lucy shrugged her small shoulders, she looked out the window, the sun was shining on the frost that covered the hills, sparkling like glitter, this reminded Lucy, 'mummy are we going ta make Christmas cards yet, it must be soon?' Anne nodded, 'aye but I thought yoo were listening ta a story?' Lucy frowned, 'I was but there's noo fairies in it any more,' Anne took hold of Lucy's hand, 'come on lets find tha stuff we put away last year, can yoo remember where we put it?'

Lucy jumped up and down, 'aye, it's in tha cupboard under tha stairs,' she pulled Anne towards the cupboard, Lucy tried to open the door but the handle was too stiff for her, 'let me,' Anne grabbed hold of the handle, she turned it hard, it slowly turned, 'you'll have ta look at this Iain, I can hardly move it,' by now Iain was in the middle of lighting his pipe, 'hang on lass a'll ba with yoo in a wee while,' by the time Iain got there the door was open, Lucy was on her hands and knees in the cupboard, she did not get to explore this cupboard very often, 'what's this for mummy?'

Lucy was holding up an old butter pat, 'that's belonged ta ya grandmother, she used ta make her own butter, she used it with another one ta shape tha butter into a square block,' Lucy looked at the butter pat and pretended to make a block of butter, 'can we make some butter?' Anne took the butter pat's from Lucy, 'noo a thought yoo wanted ta make Christmas cards?' Anne finally found the card, glitter and crayons she had used last year, 'come on then, let's see what we can do,' Anne placed the materials on a tray, they both sat at the dinner table, Lucy was busy drawing green snowmen and red Santa's on crème card, 'they're different,' Anne remarked, 'can yoo draw ma Rudolf?' Lucy passed Anne a yellow crayon, 'a think Rudolf would ba better in brown, doon't yoo?' Lucy nodded in agreement, 'a want ta draw his red nose,' Lucy grabbed the red crayon just in case Anne forgot, Anne passed the card to Lucy, 'that's a good Rudolf,' Lucy was impressed, she then gave Rudolf the biggest red nose, 'a think he would like that' Anne smiled as Lucy held up the card, she was very impressed with her art work, she moved off her chair, 'daddy, daddy look what a've done.'

Iain was trying to free the cupboard door handle, 'och aye, it's a dog with a wee red apple in it's mouth.' Lucy was not amused, 'It's Rudolf, with his red nose, any one can see that,' Lucy looked at Iain, 'yoo can ba so silly daddy,' she gave him a gentle slap on the arm and walked back to the table, 'a'm noo showing him any more,' Anne gave Lucy another card, this one had a Christmas tree on with a large fairy on the top, 'do yoo wan ta put some glitter on tha fairy ta make her sparkle?' Lucy's eye's widened, 'aye a doo,' she covered the fairy with glitter, when she shook off the loose glitter you could hardly make out the fairy at all,

Am Bratach Sith of Dunvegan

Lucy did not mind, 'aye that'll doo,' Anne looked impressed 'can yoo draw me a big fairy, ta have in ma bedroom?' Anne fingered through the card until she found the largest piece, she started to draw a fairy, Lucy carried on drawing green snowmen with yellow eyes and orange noses.

Iain announced he could not free the cupboard door, he would need to replace the handle, Anne told him not to worry, he went over to the table and commented how good the Christmas cards were, 'do yoo like ma fairy, she's tha fairy from tha story?' Iain commented how realistic she looked and Lucy had better look after her, if she was going to be her friend and bring her good luck.

After they had eaten dinner and cleared away Iain had an idea, 'let's go too tha woods and dig up a Christmas tree,' Lucy was so excited she could not speak, which was unusual, Anne thought it was a good idea too, Iain did not have many good idea's but this was one of them, Anne knew Iain could be called back to his squadron at any time, even so he only had a couple of days left and there was no telling when he would get his next leave.

They all wrapped up warm, you could hardly see Lucy she was covered from head to foot in her coat, wellies, gloves, scarves and a woollen hat which she said looked more like a tea cosy on her head.

Iain fetched a spade and a axe from the shed, it was bitterly cold but the winter sun was at least warming, as they walked they soon warmed up, it was not too far to the woods about a mile.

Lucy much preferred to run than walk, she would run ahead then run back, Iain always said whenever they went walking Lucy would walk or run at least twice the distance.

On the hillsides they could see deer, pheasants and sheep scratching a meal from the frozen heather and grass.

As they approached the woods Anne called Lucy to stay with them, the woods scared Anne they were dark and mysterious, 'are there any fairies in tha woods mummy?' Lucy hoped there were, she wanted to see one, Lucy looked wide eyed as a whisper of mist came out of the woods, 'a ghost' she held onto Anne, Iain laughed, 'It's only mist, as tha trees warm up in tha sun tha water evaporates to form a whisper of mist, a agree tha do look haunting, people call them willow tha wisp,' Lucy was having none of it, she held onto Anne's hand and did not stray again that day.

A short way into the wood Iain found the perfect tree, just over six foot high, the branches all hung right just over the ones below, he began to dig, it would take a while, he wanted to get as many of the roots out with the tree as possible, otherwise the tree would end up dying.

It took a good three-quarters of an hour to finally remove the tree, Lucy was really bored, she thought it would only take a few seconds, Anne was also becoming impatient, it was becoming cold, the sun was starting to go down, Iain wrapped the tree and roots in an old sheet he had found in the shed, he hoped this would protect them while he dragged the tree back home.

The walk home was cold, they tried to enjoy themselves but Iain was finding the tree hard to drag, Anne helped as much as she could but there was only enough of the tree trunk showing for one pair of hands to grab hold of, finally they reached home, Iain stood the tree up against the wall at the side of the door, 'a'll fetch it in latter when we've got warm,' Iain was exhausted, Anne had made up the

Am Bratach Sith of Dunvegan

fire before they had gone out it was roaring away nicely, Lucy was told not to stand too close otherwise she may get burnt or get hot aches, 'what are hot aches' she looked at Anne, 'they are when yoo warm up too quickly and ya fingers start ta hurt and tingle like yoo have hot pins and needles,' Lucy knew what pins and needles felt like, she moved further away from the fire, they quickly warmed up, Anne warmed up some broth she had made earlier, it was warm and welcome.

After an hour or so Iain felt a lot better, 'a'll bring tha tree in shall a?'

Anne nodded in agreement, Lucy did not hear she was too busy watching the fairies dancing in the fire, Iain put his coat on found his torch from the kitchen cupboard, he needed something to put the tree in, he knew there was a tub in the shed, he was unsure if it would be big enough.

It was pitch black out side, 'no moon,' he thought to himself as he opened the shed door the torch light was not bright but it did pick out the tub, it was larger than he had first thought, they could be in luck, he dragged the tub out of the shed, it had some thing inside it, he shone the torch into the tub, only stones, he was going to tip them out but he needed some weight in the tub to help stop the tree from being top heavy, he now needed to fill the tub with soil that was going to be less easy, his spade just bounced off the frozen ground, there was no way he would get enough soil to fill the tub, he then had an idea, there was a heap of sand round the back, they had brought it for Lucy to play in, he could fill the top of the tub with that, as long as the roots were in soil they should be alright.

Sure enough the sand did the trick, he did struggle to move the tub once he had filled it with sand, he finally managed to get the tub into the front room, he then dug out some of the sand and soil much to Anne's annoyance because he managed to spill it all over the floor, once the hole was big enough Iain brought the tree in, he stood it up in the tub, Anne and Lucy held the tree in place while Iain filled the tub with the soil and sand, once it was full they stood back, it was the best tree they had ever had.

Lucy wanted to start decorating the tree, Anne told her she would have to wait until the tree had settled, the branches would need to drop back into their natural position before they could decorate it, Anne looked at the time it was way passed Lucy's bed time, by the time Anne had got Lucy ready for bed she was already falling asleep, Anne kissed Lucy on the forehead, Iain carried her up to bed, he tucked her up in bed and said good night, half asleep she picked her head up a little off her pillow to give Iain a kiss, by the time her head lay back on her pillow she was asleep, Iain closed her bedroom door nearly shut so a splinter of light shone through, enough so she could see if she woke up.

Anne was washing up when Iain came into the kitchen, he started to dry up the washed pots, he smiled at her, 'what are yoo thinking?' he asked Anne, 'Nothing, just when will we see yoo again, it's been lovely having yoo home, a wish this damned war would end and things could get back ta normal,' Iain held out his arms, Anne moved close to him he held her tight, 'tha one thing a have learnt, is ta take every day as if it will ba your last and doon't expect too much from tha future.'

Iain looked straight into Anne's eyes, 'yoo will need ta ba strong, not only fa yoo, fa Lucy, a love yoo both, a know a will have ta leave soon, a need ta take with me hope

Am Bratach Sith of Dunvegan

and your love,' tears rose in Anne's eyes, 'yoo will always hold ma love, every time yoo look ta tha stars, they'll tell yoo how bright ma love is fa yoo, a wish yoo would stay,' Iain kissed her on the cheek, 'ma staying will nee solve anything, tha war will carry on, a would ba hunted doon like a dog fa going AWOL, imprisoned when a was caught, doon't despair sooner a later a will ba home fa good.'

Anne gently held Iain's face, their lips slowly came together, Iain put his arm round her slender waist , he bent down slowly still holding onto their kiss, he placed his other arm round the top of her legs and picked her up, he carried her up stairs still embraced in their one kiss he closed the bedroom door behind them.

CHAPTER TEN
Rory's Quest

Iain woke to the sound of silence, no birds singing, no wind blowing, it was strangely quiet, Iain had heard this noise only too often he leapt out of bed, he drew back the curtains, he knew it was snowing, it was already a couple of inches deep and still falling, 'Anne, Anne come and look, tha hills and trees look like a Christmas card,' Anne wondered what was it about, fire, snow and machines that men found so excitable, 'what's up, aye it's snowing, a good reason ta stay in bed,' she snuggled back under the covers.

Lucy pushed the bedroom door open she was still half asleep, 'what's up daddy?' Iain turned round 'it's snowing,' Lucy suddenly woke up, she ran the short distance to the window, her mouth fell open, 'can we go hoot side?' Anne just pulled the covers further over her head, 'daddy can we go hoot and build a snowman, can we daddy?' Iain looked back out the window, 'noo yet tha snow isn't deep enough, maba after dinner,' Lucy's head dropped, 'a thought yoo were going ta decorate tha Christmas tree?' Iain knew that would change her mood, Lucy raised her head with a big smile, 'a had forgot that, can we do that ta day and yoo can tell ma more of tha story at tha same time?' Iain always knew he would get the short end of the stick where Lucy was concerned, 'aye, alright, after breakfast,' Lucy went to get dressed.

Iain could hear Anne chuckling under the bed covers 'what's up we yoo lassie?' Anne moved the covers from over her face, 'Yoo find your way hoot of one thing only ta find yourself in another'

Iain started to tickle Anne, 'a'm glad yoo find it so funny,' Anne pushed Iain away, 'go and start breakfast if you've that much energy, after last night it's a wonder yoo can stand,' Anne winked, Iain smiled as he turned towards the door.

Breakfast done and the pots cleared away, Anne was peeling the vegetables for the dinner, Lucy had carried some of the Christmas decorations down from up stairs, Iain brought down the rest, 'a think that's tha lot,' Lucy began taking the decorations out of the box, Anne shouted in, 'doon't touch anything till a come in,' Lucy looked at Iain, they both laughed, 'yoo can start tha story if yoo wanta daddy, while we waiting fa mummy,' Iain sat in his chair, Lucy climbed onto his lap, 'aye I suppose so'.

Around 1290 A.D a young man, said to be the half son of Tormod MacLeod of MacLeod, with the knowledge he would never inherit any of the MacLeod lands decided to seek his fortune else where with the crusades, he left Dunvegan castle with his heart filled with sorrow, he loved Dunvegan but what would there be for him other than being second to his half brothers, he would have to rely on them to provide a home for him, what if he married, or more to the point what woman of standing would have him, no he had to get away.

On joining forces with other crusaders Rory made his way to Palestine it took them a number of months to make the journey, this gave Rory time to perfect his fighting skills as a knight, he met with many opportunities to fight along the way but nothing would have prepared him for the battle which lay ahead, like most of the crusaders Rory had listened to stories of untold wealth and lands to be gained, many of the early crusaders had indeed pillaged the wealth of the lands they had effectively conquered, some knights had stayed on and developed the lands and made good lives for themselves, what Rory did not know is the crusaders were losing the holy war, this was due to the brokered peace being shattered by so called crusaders rampaging in Palestine.

Rory was stationed in the great Bastian of Acre, life was good in Acre, much suited to Rory, him being a tall raven haired, handsome self proclaimed Knight, yes he had the right to call himself a knight as he came from a land effectively ruled by a king and he was a son of that king.

Rory's taste of the sweet life as a crusader was brought to a quick end, the Moslem army was heading towards Acre, they were still days away but other crusaders returning from the battles believed nothing would stop the Moslem army from finally reaching the walls of Acre.

There was much to be done, the Bastian was considered impregnable but they would need to fight outside the walls first, they dug trenches to be filled with oil then covered with straw, this was to burn the Moslem army as it approached the Bastian.

They placed short spears in the ground to injure the horses, most of all they had to make sure they had enough to eat and drink, there was never a doubt the Moslems would be defeated, they could not possibly take Acre.

As the hours and days passed by Rory found himself thinking more and more of Dunvegan, it was mid April the heather would be green, the last of the winter snow would be hanging onto tops of mountain peaks, the breeze would chill your heart with air as pure as angel breath, Loch Folliat would be as clear as a mirror and the bonnie lassies full of spirit, never was there such a more beautiful place, he would rather be fighting for Dunvegan than Acre all there was here is sand, dust and unbearable heat.

The morning of May 5th 1291was much the same as any other in Arce hot and dusty, the only other difference the whole of the Moslem army was now camped outside the walls, Rory looked over the Bastian ramparts, there were thousands of them, they were clearly well ordered, Rory had a bad feeling about this.

That afternoon it was decided the crusaders would fight outside the walls with a large force to give the Moslems the impression there were still many more within the Bastian, a thousand mounted knights and over another thousand foot soldiers stood outside the walls of Acre including Rory, the plan was to move closer to the Moslems giving the impression there was no fear, the plan appeared to be working the mounted Moslems looked as if they were retreating, the whole crusade army was now a good two hundred yards from the walls, things were starting to look promising when a war cry went up from the Moslem cavalry, their horses turned and started to gallop towards the crusaders lines, a cry went up from one of the knights,

'For God and England,' without really knowing it Rory found himself hurtling towards the Moslems the noise was deafening as the two mounted armies met.

Rory had his harness cut by a passing strike from a Moslem sword not only was he in the mist of battle but he could not control his horse, he slashed out at anything that came in range, the Moslems were fearless they seemed to want to die, they were queuing up by now, Rory must have killed at least five Moslems, and injured many more, then without reason his horse lunged forward straight into a Moslem who appeared just as surprised, Rory ceased the chance, he slashed hard down on the Moslems shoulder his sword cut deep into his body cutting clear though his body below the arm causing the Moslems arm to fall to the floor and the Moslem to slump over his horse, Rory pushed the Moslem off his horse and somehow managed to scramble onto the Moslems horse, Rory dug his spur deep into the horse it reared up and started to gallop towards the walls, Rory could see he was not alone nearly all of the crusaders were retreating or dead, he did not dare look back.

Behind the safety of the walls Rory now felt the tiredness of battle setting in, all he wanted to do was sleep, a kick to his legs kept him awake, 'onto the ramparts they are climbing the walls,' don't they ever give up Rory thought to himself, he forced himself to his feet and to the top of the wall, little did he know this would be his home for the next fifty days, during this time Rory had very little sleep. The Moslems were relentless, clouds of arrows were fired over the ramparts, giant catapults fired bombs over the walls, finally it was not the Moslems that beat the crusaders it was tiredness, the gallant crusaders could hardly muster enough strength to man the ramparts, the order was given to start evacuating the Bastian, as luck would have it there were some galleys moored on the seaward side of the fortress, the only problem was there was not enough room for everyone, anyone that remained faced either death or slavery.

Rory decided he was not going to die here on this day, he made his way to the seaward side of the fortress only to see the last galley leaving, he kicked open a door to the right side of the port moorings, he found a large wicker basket, it was nearly three feet across, there was also sail cloth, he wrapped the cloth round the basket and tied it inside with twine, he had to waterproof the sail cloth, he looked round, nothing, come on, come on Rory he said to him-self, he kicked a large pot jug, he removed the top it smelt so sweet it nearly made him sick, he tipped some out onto his hands, it was sticky and it started to set on his hand, he quickly poured the liquid over the sail cloth it was taking too long, he used a bit of wood to smooth the liquid over the cloth, he finally finished, the liquid had started to harden, he hoped it would be waterproof.

Rory looked at his creation, not bad, he had seen similar boats used on rivers back home, he grabbed a length of wood to use as a paddle, as he launched his boat he stopped he could hear drums, the Moslems were about to storm the fortress with little resistance they would be there in less than an hour, he tried to get into the boat, it was not easy, eventually he made it, he distributed his body weight in the boat and it floated, he started to paddle, the boat was going round and round, he thought about this and started to paddle each side in turn, he was only three to four hundred yards out when he heard arrows dropping into the water behind him, he looked round the

Am Bratach Sith of Dunvegan

Moslems had taken the Bastian and they had spotted him, he paddled harder he had to get out of range, he eventually got out to sea.

The tide appeared to be taking him further out, he was exhausted, he carried on paddling until he fell sleep, the next thing he felt wet, the boat was filling with water, he tried to bail out the water but it seemed the more he bailed the more water came in, the boat sank, he was now in the sea, he had no idea where he was and could not see any land.

Rory could swim not very well but what else could he do, the only problem was which way, he could end up swimming back into the Moslems hands, he remembered when he was at Acre the Sun rose on his left which was east as he was looking onto the land, therefore the sinking sun would have been to his right, so if he placed his body with the sun on his right side he would know the way to start swimming, the opposite way, with the sinking sun now on his left side he started swimming.

After what seemed like forever he started to get really thirsty, all this water and none to drink, he looked up in the twilight, he was sure he could see a light, a fire, he started to swim with renewed vigour the light came closer and closer the tide was with him, it looked like a small island, he scrambled up the rocks, he was so exhausted, he just had to climb a bit further, his fingers grasping at the rock to gain any kind of hold to haul his nearly dead body out of the clutches of this unforgiving sea.

Rory felt warm, comfortable he snuggled into his bed, his eyes opened wide seeing everything, taking in nothing, he looked round , where was he, he didn't remember getting here, his mind began to clear, he remembered the scrambling up rocks, then nothing, the fire, he remembered the fire, it was still burning brightly, someone had been tending it, he scanned the rest of the area, he was in a cave, the light coming in through the narrow opening in the rock was blinding, the sun must be high, how long had he been asleep.

Rory decided to get up, he rose to his knees, his arms felt heavy and lifeless, he tried to stand, his legs were numb, was it a witch who lived here, had she cast a spell on him so he could not escape, he began to get nervous, he must get out of here.

He tried to get to his feet, it was no good his legs were to weak, he fell back on the bed, breath rushed out of his mouth in a long sigh as if he gave up all hope, the warmth of the fire started to make him drowsy or was it a potion the witch had given him, he tried to fight the tiredness, there was only going to be one winner as he drifted back into a deep sleep.

Rory found himself walking through purple heather in full bloom, the smell was intoxicating, it was high summer, a gentle breeze teased his long hair blowing it across his face, mountains rose majestically all around him, showing no emotion but giving comfort of protection, this could only be one place, Skye.

His flesh tingled as the hair on his arms stood up, he was home, as he walked he could hear voices, he looked round no-one was there, he continued walking , he was becoming nervous, he was sure the heather kept moving all around him, it's only the breeze playing tricks, he stopped in the distance he could see someone, a man, he ran towards him as he got closer he could see it was indeed a man with long red hair the reddest hair he had ever seen, Rory called

Am Bratach Sith of Dunvegan

the man to stop, when he caught up with this stranger Rory could see he was a powerful warrior, his emerald green eyes were like green fire which seemed to burn straight through you, 'hello, I'm Rory from Dunvegan castle, can you tell me which way to Dunvegan ?'

The man looked at Rory, 'don't you know where you live?' the man continued walking, 'wait' Rory took a deep breath, 'I have been away a long time, I don't recognize the place, I know it's Skye I can feel that, yet I don't remember ever being here,' The man turned and walked back to Rory, 'If you have to ask the way your lost, if you know the way you'll never be lost, trust in the fairy people, they will guide you,' once again the man started to walk away, Rory could not believe what this powerful warrior had said, 'did you say fairy people?' the man again stopped, 'If you do not believe then you are truly lost.'

Rory again looked straight into the man's eyes, 'who are you?' Rory was bemused to hear such words from a warrior, 'I am Olaf, son of the King of Mann,' Rory had heard of such a place but it was a place of the past, 'what are you doing here?' Rory was becoming more and more intrigued 'I'm looking for my one true love I will only find her when the Fairy flag has been returned,'

Olaf walked off striding away.

Rory stood still looking down at the heather, he was even more confused, he looked up, 'how?' he stopped before he could say anything Olaf had disappeared, Rory ran along the same path as Olaf had taken there were no traces of him being there, he went back to where they had stood, there were only one set of foot prints, Rory tried to make sense of what Olaf had said, who was Olaf of Mann and why was he so sure there were fairies, Rory remembered his mother telling them stories about fairies and of a gift a magic cloth given to an ancestor warrior but that was hundreds of years ago, Rory thought his mother always told him never renounce the existence of fairies otherwise they will disappear taking their gift with them.

CHAPTER ELEVEN
Gregor's shame

Rory felt himself being shaken, 'wake up, wake up, you sleep too long,' Rory tried to rouse himself, he was disorientated, looking up, stood in front of him was an old man with long grey hair and a beard, he thought he was a ghost, 'am I dead?' Rory asked the man, 'nearly was, nearly was,' the man gave Rory a bowl, 'drink, go on drink it will build your strength,' Rory hesitated, 'go on it wont poison you,' the man shoved the bowl at Rory, 'what is it?' Rory did not wish to offend the mans hospitality but he was still unsure to his intentions, 'a broth man, only a broth,' Rory could tell the man was becoming agitated at his lack of trust, he took the bowl and started to drink, it was good, so good he drank the lot, 'is there any more?' he asked, the man obliged, again Rory drank all of it, 'thank-you, that makes me think of home,' Rory put the bowl on a sort of table made of drift wood.

'How did you come to be washed up on my Island?' Rory began telling his story of his narrow escape from Acre and the Moslems, 'are you a crusader?' the man enquired, 'yes, well I was, now I don't know what I am,' the man picked up the bowl, 'are you from England?' he looked back at Rory, 'No, no, I'm from Dunvegan on the Isle of Skye, MacLeod lands,' the man put the bowl down and appeared unsteady, 'are you alright?' the man sat on a chair again made out of drift wood with some sort of matting for a cushion, 'yes, yes I'm well, I never thought I would ever hear the name Dunvegan mentioned again,' surprised, Rory sat upright, 'you know of Dunvegan?'

The old man looked at Rory out of the sides of his eyes, 'yes, I know of a place they call Dunvegan,' Rory was puzzled, 'how?' the man picked up the bowl from the table, 'not now, you need to rest,' Rory was even more intrigued 'you must tell me, are you from Skye, are you a MacLeod?' sensing Rory was not going to let go, the man sat down, 'alright I'll tell you' my name is Gregor, like you I left to fight with the crusades, too many years ago to remember, I had just started my fifteenth summer, a knight called at Dunvegan Castle, he was looking for good, strong Christians to join him to fight in the crusades, his stories of battles, gold and beautiful young maidens was too much for a young man trying to make his mark in life, I joined the knight along with other's sharing the same dream, we had a great time on the way to the holy land, adventures beyond our expectations, small battles easily won, many maidens even easier to win, only when the real battles commenced did the true reality and horror of fighting for the one true god against a people fighting for their homeland and very existence.'

Gregor hesitated, 'I realized I was the impostor, I wasn't fighting for God, I was fighting so, some knight could gain riches and lands for himself, the heat was relentless as were

Am Bratach Sith of Dunvegan

the Moslems, I was becoming more disillusioned as each sunrise brought more bloodshed, during what proved to be my last battle, I was injured by a Moslem, his spear ripped into my right shoulder, my sword arm, my sword dropped from my hand as if life it's self had gone, all I remember is the Moslem standing beside me, his spear had my blood dripping from the point, he knew he could take his time to finish me off, I could not even hold a sword let alone fight, I must have passed out, the next thing I remember is lying in a tent with the wound to my shoulder dressed, the tent flap was pulled open, in the doorway stood a Moslem, a giant of a man as fearsome as you could imagine, the horror of my situation struck me, I had been taken prisoner.'

'I could not hope to escape with my shoulder being badly injured, so I had to wait and hoped I would be treated well, the Moslems were not renowned for their kindness to prisoners, if they could be ransomed the prisoner was worth keeping alive otherwise they would either be sold into slavery or left to rot in some gaol, I knew I would not be ransomed, so my future appeared to be a fate worse than death.'

'My solitude in the tent quickly came to an end, what seemed like the next day I was dragged out of the tent and thrown onto a cart , I found myself with seven others, all badly injured but alive, I could not see much in front, looking backwards we were part of a caravan, I had no idea where it was heading, we travelled for days, I lost count because I kept passing out with pain, my shoulder needed rest not the constant jolting from the cart.'

Gregor continued to tell his story, 'there was one other English speaking man in the cart with me Robyn, he was from somewhere near Nottingham, we exchanged stories to pass away the time and what we would do when we got home, he said his father held an estate, he would to go back to help his father, he had left following a disagreement which he now regretted, me I said I would just be happy to see my birth place, Skye,' Gregor's shoulders dropped as he let out a tired sigh, he shook his head, 'Now where was I, ah yes, many days of travel brought us to the coast, my shoulder was still in a bad way mainly through neglect, I tried to keep the wound wrapped but with the heat and flies it had become infected, a black man came to the cart when we stopped, he looked at my shoulder and put maggots into the wound and wrapped it tight, it felt horrible, not only did it itch like feathers up your nose but as if I was being eaten alive, he did the same to every one who had an open wound, Robyn said it was to clear the infection, you know he was right after a day or so the black man reappeared, he scraped out the maggots, pushed some stuff he had been chewing into the wound, he then started to stitch the wound together with a thin piece of bone and thread, it did not hurt that much and I was grateful in the end, the injury healed well look', Gregor pulled his ragged tunic over his shoulder exposing the scar, it was nearly invisible, Rory looked at the scar 'just how long have you been here' Gregor pulled his tunic back over his shoulder 'the truth is I don't know, it's hard to know the difference from summer and winter they are both hot, all I know I was a young man when I got here and now I'm old.'

Rory sipped from a small pot, it was chipped and cracked, which allowed water to drip down his hands, 'you were saying about reaching the coast,' Gregor looked at Rory as if he didn't know what he meant, 'ah yes, there were two galleys lying at anchor just off the coast, we were pulled from the cart and forced to get into small boats which took us to the galleys, Robyn thought they were taking us to a city to be sold into slavery, they would get the best price for us in a city rather than selling us to a local tribal chief, darkness fell as we left anchor, the gentle rocking of the galley soon lulled me into a deep sleep.'

'I was woken with a sharp pain in my legs, one of the crew seemed to take delight in kicking prisoners, the sun was, as always bright and unrelenting, shade was scarce as was water, two sips of water every now and again hardly enough to keep us alive.'

Rory looked at Gregor, 'how did you escape?' 'as the day drifted into dusk, a wind sprung up from the north, this had the crew in all sorts of trouble, they were running around tying things down, the captain was shouting orders and thrashing any of the crew who came near him, there was to say a degree of panic, all was to become clear, within the time for dusk to become night a storm had risen, the galley was being washed around waves were breaching over the sides of the galley, it was not designed to withstand this severe weather, soon the galley was in trouble, it had taken on too much water and was in danger of sinking.'

'Robyn tried to reach a knife one of the crew had dropped in all the commotion, every time he got close the galley rocked and it moved further away, until it was out of reach, Robyn slumped back against the side of the galley, the crew were far to involved in saving their own skins to be bothered if we were alright, the crew started to dump what they could into the two small boats, fighting broke out between them, the captain was by now in one of the boats, with a couple of the crew, leaving the rest of the crew and us to fend for ourselves.'

'In the melly that followed three of the remaining nine crew were killed, the others launched the other small boat and took their chances, knowing they would have a better chance than if they remained aboard a galley which was sinking fast.'

Rory was eager to hear the rest of this yarn, 'but how did you escape?' Gregor was lighting a pipe, as he puffed the smell was horrid, 'what is that?' Rory covered his nose with his hand, 'it's a herb, keeps you calm, helps the day along, don't know how I would have survived without it, the black man gave me some seeds, said smoke the flower, it eases pain, I still had them when I landed here so I scattered them on a bit of ground, short time after they grew, been growing ever since, try it.'

Gregor handed the pipe to a reluctant Rory, he took a long draw from the pipe, his face screwed up, he began to cough, 'that's horrible,' after a few seconds Rory felt his head becoming fuzzy, 'I feel strange,' Gregor laughed, 'you will, don't try to move, now what was I saying?' Rory had slumped back, 'you were in the galley,' Gregor pointed the pipe at Rory he held his hand up to say no more, 'please yourself, ah yes, the galley, Robyn was still trying to reach the knife when the galley dipped sideways, a wave washed over the side and swamped the galley, when the water drained away Robyn held the knife, he started to hack through the bindings, once he had freed himself he started to cut my bindings, with my hands free, he gave me the knife, I started to cut the binding round my feet, free at last.'

'I freed the Moslem next to me who for what ever reason was also a prisoner, he called out something and held my arm, Robyn shouted he pointed to some timbers

Am Bratach Sith of Dunvegan

he was trying to lash together, I helped as best I could, the galley was sinking, water was over the sides Robyn lashed himself to the timbers, I held onto a large wooden box, soon I was in the water the box was hardly floating, I held on, that was the last time I saw Robyn, don't know if he made it or the Moslem.'

'The next day, well I think it was the next day anyway, the box bumped against something, I was exhausted, well to cut a long story short this is where I was washed ashore, just like you.'

Rory looked at Gregor, 'you mean you've been here since and never tried to get back to Scotland?' Gregor glanced at Rory, 'you think I'm mad or a coward, you do don't you?' Rory could see a strange madness in Gregor's eyes, 'no man, I don't,' Rory was quick to reply, the last thing he wanted to do was annoy Gregor he was the only person who could help him get away from this god forsaken place.

Gregor got up, he walked towards the cave entrance without turning, 'you had better sleep now,' Rory knew he had upset Gregor, he hadn't meant too, he gave out a big sigh and slumped back on the bed, Rory's thoughts turned once again to home, he had to get home, but how, his mind turned over and over.

Rory was shaking, he woke, 'wake up lad, wake up,' Gregor was shaking him, 'you'll sleep long enough when your dead,' Rory felt dazed, as if he had too much ale, 'what's wrong?' Rory looked puzzled as if to say what could there be wrong, 'nothing, I don't think you should sleep for too long at one time, that's all,' Rory regained his faculties, he stretched his limbs as he stood up and yawned.

'So why have you stayed here, why have you not tried to return home to Scotland?' Gregor slumped his head as if in shame, 'that's a different story,' he looked long and hard at Rory, this made Rory uncomfortable, he could feel Gregor's eyes burning into him as if to read his thoughts, Gregor sat beside Rory, 'before I left Dunvegan I was given a cherished possession the MacLeod's hold very dear, I was entrusted to have it blessed by a holy man in Jerusalem, when we got to Jerusalem I was told the item had already been blessed by a saint and no-one other than a saint should carry out another blessing, I have failed in the one quest bestrode on me by the MacLeod Chief, how can I possibly return?'

Rory put his arm round Gregor's shoulder, 'I'm sure you would be forgiven that,' Gregor took some comfort from Rory's words but was adamant, 'I will never return to Scotland,' Rory became intrigued, 'just what, did the MacLeod Chief give to you?' Rory enquired, Gregor got up and went to the back of the cave, he fumbled around for a while, he had what appeared to be a wrap, he sat back down and slowly unwrapped a piece of cloth 'do you know what this is' Rory could not believe what he was looking at, 'is it the Fairy cloth?' Gregor slowly nodded his head, 'yes lad, it is, now you can understand why I have failed, not only was it not blessed but it is not in it's rightful place, with the Chief of MacLeod,' Rory touched the cloth, it was cool and soft yet appeared strong, 'you must be a MacLeod, so it as never really left the MacLeod's.'

Gregor turned his head towards Rory, 'that's the point I am not a true MacLeod by birth, my father took my mother in after she was ravaged by another man, she became with child, only the three of us know of this and now you, my true father is said to be a MacDonald, he does not know of me nor I want to know of him,' Rory held out his hands, 'can I hold the cloth?' Gregor looked at Rory, he gave him the Fairy cloth, 'you could take it back to Dunvegan for me and ask the Chief his forgiveness for my failure,' Rory could not believe his good fortune, he can return home with his head held high and present the Fairy cloth to the MacLeod Chief.

'Gregor, not only would it be a privilege to return the Fairy cloth to it's rightful place but I will ensure the Chief knows of your conviction in keeping the Fairy cloth safe until it could be returned to a MacLeod,' Gregor smiled as if a heavy burden had been lifted from him.

'The only problem now is how will I get off the island to even start to get back home?' Gregor again smiled, 'come with me,' he led Rory out of the cave, along the shoreline to a small cove, there were not so many rocks there, the sea was a little calmer, 'we could launch a galley from here,' Gregor appeared pleased with himself, 'we don't have a galley, do we?' Rory snapped back, 'you don't but I have,' Gregor pointed to another small cave, 'in there,' Rory ran over to the cave sure enough in the darkness he could make out the shape of a small galley, turned upside down, Rory ran his hands over the hull, he could not feel any holes or splits, Gregor had caught up, 'it's in fine shape, I have been repairing it for some time now,' Rory began to try and drag the boat further out of the cave, Gregor grabbed hold 'let me give you a hand, you'll never move it on your own, I never could,' they pulled and tugged at the boat it slowly started to move.

It took them a while to move the boat into the daylight, they both fell to the floor breathless, 'it's heavy,' Rory spluttered between gasps of breath, Gregor took in a deep breath, 'now you know another reason I have never been able to get away from here, galleys too heavy for one man to move.'

After Rory got his breath back he enquired, 'has it got a sail or any oars?' Gregor looked over the hull of the Galley, 'both but I don't know if the sail is any good, I have used it for bedding,' Rory dropped his head onto the hull as if to say two steps forward one step back.

CHAPTER TWELVE
Farewell to Gregor

Rory turned the galley up right, it was indeed a strong galley, small but strong, there was no mast for the sail, he walked back to the cave, Gregor had pulled the sail cloth out of the bed, he started to unfold it out side the cave, it looked sound enough, a few holes here and there but nothing that couldn't be mended, there was a few dirty stains on it, Rory thought it best not to ask.

'Where's the mast?' Rory had a bad feeling about this he was not going to get the answer he wanted, Gregor gave a shallow wince, 'I used it for fire wood, I didn't think I would ever move the galley on my own so it seemed a good idea at the time, any way there's never much wind over this sea, you will have to row most of the way,' Rory was even less enthusiastic about the prospect of rowing his way to freedom.

'You may as well keep the sail cloth, there's no ropes for rigging,' Rory shrugged his shoulders, Gregor thought it best not to mention what he had used the rigging for, 'you will need supplies of water and food,' Gregor began to collect anything that would hold water, 'Gregor wait, have you any idea just how far it would be to reach land?' Gregor looked out to sea, 'I think I saw land over there on a few days, at least clouds, which could mean land, couldn't it?' Rory gave Gregor a side ways glance, 'over there you say?' Rory pointed to what he believed to be the north, 'yes, that way,' Rory remembered what he had done when he was adrift and he did not know which way to swim. 'The sun rises over there doesn't it?' Gregor pointed towards the east, 'that way, yes,' Rory stared out to sea as if looking for some sort of a sign to say that was the right way to set sail.

'Gregor how far would you say the cloud was you seen?' Gregor looked out to sea as if hoping the cloud was there so Rory could judge for himself, 'eh, not sure two three days, hard to tell,' Gregor knew he was not being much help, 'say three days, I would not need much food or water, I need the galley to be as light as possible,' Gregor grabbed Rory's arm, 'what if there is no land, may be I hoped to see land?' Rory smiled, 'if it wasn't for you I would already be dead, anyway if the Fairy cloth is destined to return to Dunvegan, I'm already home.'

As the evening surrendered to night Rory sat with Gregor by the small fire at the mouth of the cave Gregor always kept alight, 'aren't you afraid a passing galley will see the fire in the distance, there's not many friendly galleys in these waters?' Gregor gave a rye smile, 'I used to hope the fire would be seen even by Moslems or pirates, the worst they could do is kill me, surviving here was worse than death at that time, there have been galleys who must have spotted the fire, they seem to ignore it or believe any one who lights a fire that can clearly be seen is not afraid

Am Bratach Sith of Dunvegan

or it's a trap, either way no one has ever come close enough to find out, only you,' Rory nodded his head, Gregor made a lot of sense.

Gregor and Rory finished the meal of fish, Gregor had cooked, both were full, Gregor lit his pipe, 'care to have a last smoke with me?' he held out the pipe to Rory, he did not really want to take it but as this was the last time he would share a meal with Gregor, what harm would it do, he drew the pipe and inhaled the smoke, his head started to spin, he felt calm, relaxed, Gregor took the pipe from him, he started to draw on the pipe, he was more used to it and more respectful of the effects, they both sat in the mouth of the cave under a cloudless night sky, the stars glistened like ice reflecting the bright rich moonshine, the only sounds were from the gentle crackle of the fire and sea lapping against the shore, Rory could understand why Gregor did not really want to leave this place.

Rory was up and ready at day break, Gregor was a little more subdued, 'what's the matter with you this fine morning?' Rory could see Gregor was not at his best, 'leave me be lad, I'll be all right, I've yet to wake up,' Rory laughed, 'if you take too long I'll be gone before you know it,' Gregor splashed cool sea water over his face, he shuddered, that appeared to do the trick, 'are you going to help move this galley or are you just going to stand there and watch?' Gregor could not help noticing how painfully joyful Rory was this morning.

'I think I'll stand and watch, I could do with a laugh,' Gregor promptly sat on a convenient rock, 'you said you were going to stand not sit,' Gregor looked at the rock he was sitting on and patted it, 'I thought it best to sit in case I fell over laughing at the sight of you trying to move that galley on your own, I wouldn't want to hurt myself would I?'

Rory laughed, 'come on old friend or have you not the strength?' Gregor got to his feet, 'I'll show you who's got the strength, laddie.'

Together they slowly pushed the heavy galley to the shore line, 'lets stop a while,' Rory was gasping for breath Gregor had his hands on his knees, he could not talk he was so breathless, 'you, you would never have moved this,' Rory gasped another breath Gregor just nodded his head in agreement.

When they had regained their breath they loaded the galley with the few supplies Rory agreed to take with him, 'have you got the Fairy cloth?' Gregor was making sure, 'yes,' Rory pulled a corner out of his tunic to confirm he had it.

'Right then you'll need these,' Gregor handed Rory the oars, for a moment both had their hands gripping the oars, Rory looked at Gregor, 'I know laddie, I know, now be away,' they pushed the galley into the gentle waves, Rory scrambled aboard the tide slowly moved the galley out to sea, Rory shouted, 'do you not want to come with me?' Gregor gestured with his hand as if to push Rory away, 'be gone, I've had enough of you any way,' Rory gave one last wave and started to row north, Gregor watched until the boat was just a speck on the sky line, 'god's speed Rory MacLeod, wish Dunvegan well for me.'

Rory kept his eyes fixed on the island as he rowed away, he told himself to keep a bearing on his direction, his heart told him he had left a man who he would be proud to call a friend MacDonald or not.

Rory had been rowing for half a day the sun was high and so hot he could feel it burning his hands, he kept putting them in the cool water to ease the burning but it seemed to make them worse, he thought the salt in the sea water must be stinging his hands.

He was careful not to drink too much water, he did not have much but not knowing how long it would need to last, he wanted to conserve his rations, he had to stop and rest, he had no idea if the current was helping him or driving back or even sideways, all he knew he had to keep rowing.

The afternoon sun was unbearable, he had to stop otherwise he felt he would collapse, he had a sip of water, it tasted so good he would not have traded that sip of water for knights fortune, he sat back and rested.

Rory woke to a loud splash, he was dazed he must have fallen asleep, he collected his thoughts, what was it he looked round one of the oars was missing it must have fallen over board, that was the splash he heard.

Rory stood up in the galley careful not to start tipping it over, he could see the oar behind the galley, it seemed to be going away from him or was he going away from the oar either way he had to get the oar back, he could not hope to turn the galley round with one oar, he would have to swim, he took his cloths off and jumped off the back of the galley as close to the floating oar as he could, it felt like forever until he reached the oar, he grabbed it in his right hand and turned round to swim back to the galley.

Rory could not believe it, the galley was double the distance way from when he first jumped off it, he found he could not swim fast enough to catch the galley using one hand, he decide to put the oar between his legs and use both hands, this did not work either, he ended up on his back holding the oar in both hands using his legs to swim, this was working, if he looked back over his head he could see the galley from time to time as it rolled over the waves, this way he did not have to stop swimming, by the time he reached the galley he was exhausted and the sun was starting to go down.

Back on the galley when he had recovered from his swim, Rory deduced as the sun was setting over his left shoulder he must still be heading north and the current must be helping him, he decided to rest and eat some of the berries and fish Gregor gave him to regain his strength.

After eating half of his food supplies, Rory began to feel much better, he knew he was taking a gamble on reaching land before he starved to death, he thought it was better to keep his strength and row longer than half starve and be able to row half the time, the darkness of the night brought on it's own fears.

Rory had always been fearful of the dark, he was thankful of the full moon, which gave an eerie light but it was enough for Rory not to feel so alone as he tried to put any thoughts of failing to reach land out of his mind.

Rory woke up from his half sleep as fingers of sunlight reached out over the horizon, within a few moments he was rowing northwards, the sun warming his tired body in some ways the warmth seemed to give him energy, he knew he had to find land within the next two days otherwise he would not have the strength to row any further.

The morning rolled into afternoon the sun was again unbearable, he could feel his skin burning, he used every scrap of clothing to cover his bare skin, his hands were becoming so burnt he was having trouble holding the oars, each time he pulled on the oars it was more painful than the last.

Rory could not hold the oars any longer, it was mid afternoon, he was too tired to move, he just managed to pull the oars into the galley, he did not want one of them to slip overboard again, before he fell sleep slumped over his knees, the galley was left to drift, at this point Rory could not care less, not that he had the strength to do anything about it.

Rory cried out as he woke, a sea bird landed on the side of the galley, he could not decide if it was real or his mind playing tricks, he slowly reached out, the pain from sun burn bit into his every movement, he was close to the bird, if he could catch it he could try and eat it, he was close enough to make a grab for it, as he lunged forward the bird rose into the air leaving Rory trying to regain his balance before he fell over the side of the galley, he fell back into the galley looking at the bird gently soaring away from him, it gave a shrill call as if mocking him, Rory raised his fist in a defiant gesture.

Rory sat back to start rowing again, a drink of water first, as he put the water pouch to his lips he thought, where did the bird come from, he must be near land, without taking a sip of water Rory looked all round trying to spot any sign of land, he could only see the sea and sky, his only consolation was the bird was going in the same direction as he was rowing, Rory took some comfort from that.

Rory started to believe land was only a days rowing away, therefore he could eat the rest of the food, without any further thought he started to eat, within a short time all of the remaining food had been eaten, he did stop at drinking all the water just in case.

Rory began to feel refreshed, his strength was returning, the sun was starting to cool in the late afternoon, he decided to start rowing again, his hands were still painful but he had no choice other than to keep going.

Rory rowed well into the night, it was difficult for him to know if he was rowing in the right direction, during the day he had the sun to use as a guide, it was no use using the moon because it was never constant, he decided to row towards a bright star that always appeared to be at the back of him when the sun went down, right or wrong he had to use something.

Once again Rory became overwhelmed by tiredness, he remembered to make the oars safe, then curled up in the bottom of the galley, the warmth of the morning sun gently woke him up, the sun was already well up in the sky, a few moments later Rory decided he was hungry, he then remembered he had finished off all the food last evening, he muttered to himself, what a fool he was. He reached for the water pouch, he shook it, that was nearly empty, he took a couple of sips and shook it again, there was about two good sips left, 'it's to day or never then,' he said out loud, he stretched his arms over his head as he rolled his head to ease his tired muscles, sitting down he picked up the oars and plunged then into the sea, he started to count one, two three as he beat out the oar strokes in his head, he had found this useful as it kept his mine active and took his mind off the monotony of rowing and the constant pain of sunburn.

Rory was quiet pleased with the way he kept going, it was now well into the afternoon, he was shielded from

Am Bratach Sith of Dunvegan

the sun by a line of cloud, this made the situation more bearable, toward the evening a fear came over Rory, he could not see land, with all of his food and water gone, he was in trouble, to make things worse with the clouds, he could not see the bright star he had been using to guide him.

Rory started to have all kinds of bad feelings, he found it difficult to row, may be he should just go to sleep in the bottom of the galley and pray death to come quickly, at this point that was all too much of an inviting thought, he got down into the galley, has was waited to sleep his thoughts were visited by Gregor, he reminded him of his promise to deliver the Fairy cloth and reconcile his failure with the MacLeod Chief, Rory's eyes opened, 'a canny give up, if death should come it will have to take me awake, not sneak up in my sleep,' Rory pulled himself to a sitting position, he lowered the oars into the sea, very slowly he started rowing one, two, three he began to count.

The night passed, Rory opened his eyes, had he been asleep, he was still sitting holding the oars, he could not have been asleep long, he could not remember, it was day light, the sun was as bright as ever, he surly could not make it through another day, he closed his eyes, he was too tired and weak to carry on, death was calling him, strange voices calling him, he felt the galley hit something, he looked up through sunburnt tired eyes, it was another galley, the crew were grabbing at him, he was too weak to resist, he was hauled onto the deck and dropped onto a pile of ropes, before he passed out the last thing Rory smelt was fish.

CHAPTER THIRTEEN
The voyage home

Rory felt a sudden cold wet chill as he woke up, he cleared his eyes to see a group of mean looking sailors, one was holding a pail, the cold chill he had felt was water splashing over him from the pail, each man had a knife in a waist band, their hair was long and black, most of them had a large gold ear-ring in one ear, Rory couldn't understand what they were saying, one of the men was holding what looked like a cosh of some kind, he drew his knife and moved towards him, Rory moved backwards as far as he could, the man knelt down his knife close to Rory's face, he sliced the large sausage he was holding and offered Rory a piece, the man smiled.

Rory was too overcome by relief to take the food, he was convinced he was going to be killed, the sailor again gestured to Rory to take the food, this time Rory was not going to refuse, another sailor offered Rory a drink which he gladly accepted, Rory didn't like the sausage much but it was food and he was hungry.

Rory soon found out the sailors were in fact fishermen and the ropes he had been sleeping on were fishing nets, Rory tried to talk to the fisherman who appeared to be in charge, the man couldn't speak English, Rory did make out Espanola, which he believed to be Spain, if that is the case Rory thought to himself he was way off course, no wonder he hadn't reached land he must have been drifting west instead of north, at least he was closer to home.

The Fisherman turned out to be most hospitable when he got to know them, they had even put his few belongings safe, the captain grabbed Rory by the arm and pointed west and said one word over and over, Rory did not understand, he hoped it meant home, Rory began to feel quiet pleased with himself, after all he had made it this far and there was a good prospect when they reached the fishing village, he could find a merchant galley that was going to Ireland or England.

A cheer went up from the crew, Rory looked what are they cheering at, Rory looked over the side of the fishing boat in the distance he could see land, they must be close to home, the crew began making ready, they started to bring the baskets of fish out from under cover, it was clear the fishing trip had been a success, the crew were all smiles, they appeared to be exchanging stories of what they would do when they docked the boat, some of their gestures did not need any explanation, they must have been away from home a few days.

The fishing boat moored in a small fishing village, it looked as if all the village had turned out to greet them, it was not what Rory was hoping for but at least he was alive and on dry land, as the villagers were helping the crew

Am Bratach Sith of Dunvegan

unload the fish the captain gestured to Rory to follow him, he led him to a small house, all the houses were white, the captain opened the door and ushered Rory in.

It took Rory's eyes a while to adjust to the darkness after being in the bright sunlight, he could make out two other people in the room, the captain held out his hand pointing to a large woman 'Roseanna,' the woman gave Rory a polite curtsy, the captain lowered his arm pointing to a small girl, 'Mercedes,' she copied Roseanna and gave a curtsy, Rory took them to be the captains family, Rory bowed in return and pointed to himself, 'Rory,' the girl gave out a little titter of laughter which was quickly rebuked by the captain, Rosanna gestured for Rory to sit at the large wooden table that dominated the room, she then produced a large iron pot she ladled out a kind of stew mainly made from fish, it did not smell too good but Rory thought that it tasted great, so good he had a second helping.

After the meal Rory tried to ask the captain his name at first he did not understand what Rory was asking, Roseanna said something to the captain, he nodded, 'ah, Miguel, Miguel,' Rory lifted a drink of wine he was holding into the air, 'Miguel,' and took a drink, the captain nodded and smiled, it was getting late Rory needed to be getting on his way, he tried to thank the captain and Roseanna for their hospitality, and pointed to the door trying to say it was time he left, the captain started to wave his arms in the air he grabbed Rory's arm, took him to another room and pointed to a bed, Rory did not want to impose on the captain or his family any longer, he tried to explain he had to go but the captain was having none of it, Rory finally gave in and accepted the captains generous offer of a bed for the night, Rory was tired and went to bed soon after, leaving the captain to be alone with Roseanna.

Rory slept like a log, when he woke up he lay listening to the faint noise of the village, he could hear Mercedes trying to speak quietly to Roseanna trying not to wake him, this made Rory smile, it had been a long while since he had heard children, it was a far cry from the noise of battle and death. Rory lay awake for what seemed an age, he finally got up gave out a yawn and stretched so hard it felt his body was going split, he looked into the main room, there stood Roseanna a pretty woman with long black hair and a well rounded figure, next to her hanging onto the table and standing on her tip toes was Mercedes, she wanted to take over what ever Roseanna was mixing, she eventually got her way much to her delight.

Giving Mercedes the bowl Roseanna caught sight of Rory, she smiled, then spoke, he did not understand but he replied with a nod of his head hoping he had given the right answer, she waved him to sit at the table, Roseanna then produced a wooden bowl full of all kinds of fruit and a chunk of bread across the top, Roseanna pointed to her mouth as if to say, 'eat,' she filled a goblet with wine and placed it on the table next to the bowl, Roseanna smiled at Rory and carried on with what she was doing.

Rory had almost finished the fruit and bread when the captain arrived, he patted Rory on the shoulder, after Rory had finished the captain picked up Rory's belongings and gestured Rory to follow him, Rory bowed to Roseanna in a gesture of thanks for her hospitality.

Rory followed the captain who was already out the door and a distance down the track leading to the fishing boat, the captain stopped at a house and knocked the door an old man with grey hair answered the door, they had a conversation the captain kept pointing at Rory, the old man looked at Rory and shook his head, after a while the old man allowed the captain to enter the house, before he disappeared through the door the captain gestured Rory to follow.

As Rory went through the door way he heard a voice, 'Rory,' this took him by surprise, 'yes,' he replied, 'come in,' Rory looked at the old man who was pointing with an open hand for him to sit down, 'I am Samuel,' his English was not good but at least Rory could understand him, Rory held his hand out, Samuel took it as a gesture of greeting.

The three men sat down, 'Miguel tells me he found you out at sea nearly dead,' Rory looked across at the captain, 'yes, I believe he did,' Rory nodded to the captain in recognition, the captain asked Samuel what he had said, the captain started to nod his head as he understood, he looked at Rory with a broad smile, 'Miguel wants to know what you were doing out at sea?' Rory looked at the captain, 'escaping from the Moslems,' Rory turned back to Samuel 'you are a crusader, yes' Rory again nodded his head, 'I was, all I want to do now is return home' the captain looked puzzled, Samuel explained what Rory had said, 'I need to know where I can get a galley to Ireland or England,' Samuel put Rory's question to the captain, he shrugged his shoulders, Rory did not like the way this was going.

'I must get home to Scotland,' Samuel put his hands up to calm Rory down, 'Miguel may know of a galley leaving for Ireland in a few days from Cadiz,' Rory was becoming anxious, 'how far is Cadiz?' Samuel was starting to lose patience with Rory, 'stay calm, all in good time,' Samuel carried on talking with Miguel, finally Samuel turned to Rory, 'Miguel will take you to his cousin José, he will take you to Cadiz and help you find a galley,' Rory looked at Miguel and nodded in agreement.

They all stood up, 'before we leave can you tell Miguel how grateful I have been for his help and hospitality,' Samuel passed on Rory's words to Miguel, he smiled said something and patted Rory on the back, 'what did he say?' Rory looked at Samuel, 'nothing, it was nothing,' Rory smiled at Miguel and shook his head in disbelief of how he could call what he had done for him, nothing, Rory thanked Samuel for his help, 'by the way how far is Cadiz?' Samuel thought for a moment 'about a day on horseback.'

Miguel led Rory to a stables, Miguel had a long conversation with a man who Rory believed to be the owner, Miguel and the man went inside, after a while Miguel came out leading two fine looking horses, he handed the reins of one of the horses to Rory, a sleek almost pure white stallion, a keen spirit and difficult to handle.

Rory was used to horses, he had rode many during the crusades but none with this spirit, he mounted the horse, it was now a battle of wills, which Rory was determined to win, it took him a while to calm the horse down much to Miguel's and the stable owners amusement.

Miguel galloped off, Rory could tell Miguel was as comfortable on horseback as he was at sea, Rory galloped after him, it took them about half a day to reach his cousins house, Miguel gestured to Rory to stay with the horses while he went into the house, Rory dismounted and stretched his legs, he led the horses to a trough for a well earned drink, Miguel came out of the house with José, Miguel's cousin.

Following introductions and a big hug from Miguel, Rory and José set off for Cadiz, as far as Rory could make out Miguel would stay at José house until he returned, then he would take the borrowed horses back to the fishing village.

The journey to Cadiz was uneventful for a change, they reached Cadiz during the evening, José led Rory to the port, there were three galleys lay at anchor, José went passed the first one, he gestured to Rory to dismount, then he put his finger to his mouth as if to say keep quiet, José went aboard the galley, a few moments later he appeared with another man, José took the reins from Rory and gestured he should take his things and follow the man aboard the galley, all this was done without a single word being said, as Rory boarded the galley José was already leading the horses away from the port, no time to say thanks or good bye.

On board Rory was taken to the back of the galley, to a small cabin, the sailor knocked the door, 'come,' thank god an English voice Rory thought, Rory was ushered into the cabin, the sailor shut the door behind him, the captain was standing with his back to Rory he appeared to be looking at maps or charts, 'you want to go to England do you lad?' Rory cleared his throat, 'well Scotland really sir,' Captain Jacobs turned round, he was of medium build but stocky, his outstanding feature was his face, it was covered in hair, Rory had never seen a beard like it before, all he could see was two small weasel like eyes peering through a mass of hair, you could only see his mouth when he spoke or when he smoked his pipe.

'Not going Scotland, Bristol, no further,' the captain looked at Rory for a reply, 'Bristol, aye, that will do,' the captain roared, 'aye, captain,' ' Smith,' the captain roared again, the door opened 'show,' he looked at Rory and gestured as if he had already forgotten his name, 'MacLeod, Captain, Rory MacLeod,' 'show MacLeod to his bunk, advise him of his duties,' the sailor turned towards Rory, 'aye, captain, this way MacLeod.'

Rory followed the sailor out of the captains cabin onto the deck, Rory let out a heavy gasp the sailor turned to Rory, 'don't worry his bark is worse than his bite, I'm Jim Smith,' he held his hand out to Rory, 'Rory MacLeod,' Jim carried on walking, 'pleased to meet you Rory,' they went down a few steps to a very cramped crew quarters, 'this is your bunk it's the only private place you have on this Galley, anyone found stealing from other crew will be severely punished understand,' Rory looked at the small bunk, 'aye,' Jim grabbed Rory's arm, 'next to the captain I'm in charge, don't forget it.'

Rory sat on his small bunk, 'stow your things and follow me,' Rory quickly put his belongings down the side of the bunk, 'ready MacLeod?' 'ready,' Rory again followed Jim up the few steps to the main deck, 'you will be expected to keep the deck clear of anything loose, any thing rolling around a deck is dangerous, I nor the captain expect to see any thing out of place, clear MacLeod,' Rory looked around the deck, 'clear,' Jim started to walk off, 'good, get on with it then MacLeod,' Rory began to wonder what he

Am Bratach Sith of Dunvegan

had got himself into, he wasn't a sailor, he had seen enough of the sea in the recent past to last him the rest of his life.

The galley was the largest Rory had ever seen, at least four times larger than the one's back home, he had heard stories of galleys big enough to hold small armies but he had never seen a galley this size.

Rory busied himself picking things up and securing the unsecured, the galley was a hive of activity as the small crew prepared to set sail, Jim bellowed out orders, as the galley prepared to slip anchor the captain came on deck, he didn't seem to do anything, that was left to Jim Smith, as the galley set sail orders were lashed out one after the other, Rory was bemused by it all until, 'get a move on MacLeod, don't stand there with your mouth open, there's work to do,' Jim Smith made Rory jump 'yr, yr, yes Jim,' Rory started to pick up anything lying on the deck, after the galley was out at sea, in full sail, the mood appeared less aggressive, Jim Smith was talking to the crew as if they were old mates, not so long ago he was ripping their heads off, Rory found it difficult to understand.

'Come on lad look lively,' the voice came from behind Rory, he turned round, an old sea salt was scrubbing the deck, Rory bent down, 'sorry, I don't want to get shouted at, I'm Rory,' Rory held out his hand, 'I'm Jack, put your hand down you'll get us both lashed,' Rory looked at Jack, 'lashed, for what, talking,' Rory bent down and picked up a loose galley hook, 'less than that if the mood takes them, you stick with me I'll show you the ropes lad,' Jack moved away from Rory to avoid any further contact.

As night fell each member of the crew was expected to stand watch in case of pirates or other galleys, Rory would stand the first watch as it was his first night, with him would be Jack, he had volunteered to stand with Rory, normally the crew needed to be ordered to stand watch with a new crew mate because if anyone on watch makes a mistake everyone on the same watch takes the same punishment, this is to stop the crew going to sleep or trying to skive off their watch.

Rory was to be on watch from sun set to halfway through the night, Rory hadn't a clue what he was supposed to do, Jack told him to be on deck before sun set, they were to stand on watch and watch would end when the next watch crew took over, the captain had a bell and would be sounding the bell at the start of each watch, Rory thought this was taking things too far, bells for this and that where will it end, he was just happy he was only on this galley for one voyage but was already wishing he was home.

CHAPTER FOURTEEN
Jack's destiny

As Rory was on first watch he and Jack were first to eat, Jack had previously asked Rory to meet him on the bow just before sunset, Rory had nearly finished clearing the deck when Jim Smith came up to him, 'MacLeod, how do you think you have faired today?' Rory looked at Jim as if it was a trick question, 'not bad for my first day,' Jim Smith looked round the deck, 'not bad, as you say, better tomorrow eh MacLeod, I'll be keeping my eye on you,' Rory looked out to sea, 'aye Jim,'

Jim Smith walked slowly off as if he was still looking for something to pick Rory up on, Rory took his words as a threat, he would have to watch that one.

Rory met up with Jack as planned, they went below to get something to eat, 'don't expect much but don't complain,' Jack warned Rory, Jack was not wrong the food was just about edible, Rory had eaten some awful broth in his time, he had eaten dog and horse while on the crusades but this was awful, a kind of soup with something floating on top, he was given stale bread with maggots crawling out of it, Jack told him to shake the bread, the maggots would fall out.

Rory had been hungry in the past but it was as much as he could do to eat this, Jack was right again, one of the crew who joined at Cadiz threw the slop at the cook, he was instantly flogged with a short whip by Jim Smith.

They finished the so called meal, Jack thought it would be a good idea to rest awhile before watch, Jack's bunk was three back from Rory's, before they went to their bunks Jack warned Rory not to go sleep or there would be hell to pay, Rory reassured Jack he would not let him down.

Rory lay on his bunk, most of the other crew were suffering their meal, Rory smiled to himself as he pulled out his belongings from the side of the bunk, he checked to make sure the fairy cloth was still there, he was relieved to find it was, he could not understand how a place like this, full of men who would rather cut your throat than look at you twice could be so safe, there is a respect for everyone's bunk and that's the way it was.

Rory decided to go back on deck, he didn't want to be late, he didn't want to let Jack down, neither did he want to give Jim Smith anything to have a go at him for. The deck was quiet apart from a few crew going about their duties, Rory made his way to the front of the galley, he could not understand why the front was the bow, why don't they call it the front, he waited, Jack didn't turn up, Jim Smith rang the bell, Rory didn't know what to do, if he went to look for Jack and Jim Smith found them both missing he would be in trouble yet if he stayed he would be in trouble because Jack was not there, as he was deciding the best course of action, Jim Smith walked up at the back of him, 'all quiet MacLeod?' Rory nearly jumped out of his skin, 'er, aye Jim, all's quiet,' Jim looked at Rory, 'tell me MacLeod, who's on watch with you?' he asked the question already knowing the answer, Rory didn't know what to do, Rory thought to himself, he only wants to know who is on watch, not where he is, 'Jack,' Rory replied.

Jim Smith continued to slowly walk round the deck as he got about six paces away he turned, 'and where is Jack, MacLeod?' Rory felt up against it, if he lies he's in big trouble if he tells the truth they are both for it, 'I have not seen Jack for some time, could be at the back, err stern,' Jim Smith began to walk slowly back towards Rory, by this time Rory was sweating and agitated, 'shall I tell you where Jack is, MacLeod?' Rory knew the game was up, 'aye yoo can if yoo want ta,' by this time Jim Smith was standing right in front of Rory, 'he's cleaning my boots MacLeod,' Rory's face filled with hate, Jim Smith knew Rory would be scared if Jack failed to turn up, he deliberately made him late so he could goad Rory, to see if he told the truth or lie to try and save his skin, Jim Smith looked at Rory, 'careful MacLeod don't let your temper get the better of you, I'll send him over when he's finished,' Rory could hardly speak, he knew he had to answer, 'aye, you do that.'

Jim Smith swaggered back along the deck, believing he now had the measure of Rory MacLeod.

Jack finally turned up, he was full of contempt for Jim Smith, 'that man will get what's coming to him, mark my words,' Rory grabbed Jack's arm, 'aye when he does it'll not be by your hand,' Jack looked at Rory, 'sure of that are ya?' Jack went about his duties, the watch finished without any further problems, the bell was again sounded by Jim Smith, Rory thought at last he could get some sleep, he was all in, Jack was already away to his bunk, Rory's watch replacement was slow to arrive, when he did he grunted rather than spoke, Rory did not care he was off to his bunk.

Rory was already awake when the bell sounded again, his mind in turmoil, how would he survive this hell?

All the bunks were full, the smell was awful, it was such a confined space, Rory felt he had slept in the same place as pigs, not men, no time to pass pleasantries to his galley mates, Jim Smith was already bellowing out orders and abuse, once on deck Rory started to clear anything that had fallen or been dropped on the deck, Jim Smith was in his normal pleasant mood, 'MacLeod,' Rory was quick to answer, 'aye Jim,' Jim Smith pointed to a length of rigging one of the crew had dropped while working on the mast, 'pick it up lad, not so tidy this morning MacLeod?' Rory wanted to reason with him, he knew it would only lead to trouble, 'no Jim, thank-yoo for pointing it out,' not the reaction Jim Smith was hoping for, he stared at Rory, his nose nearly touching Rory's face, 'I should not need to point it out, it should not be there in the first place, your treading a fine line MacLeod,' Rory tried his best not to look him in the eyes, he knew that would be contempt and would give Jim Smith reason to discipline him, 'thank-yoo Jim.'

The rest of the day passed without trouble, Rory felt he was beginning to get used to what was no more than a prison, he hung on to the fact it would only be for a short time, neither Rory or Jack had watch duty that night, after eating another dish of cooks best slop they sat up on the deck, the evening was pleasantly warm with a light wind just enough to fill out the sails, they shared stories, Jack of his travels at sea, Rory of the crusades, it was one of short periods of peace and humanity in a place of constant torment.

Rory asked Jack about the galley and the attitude of the captain and Jim Smith, Jack told Rory this was a new kind of galley, larger than the others, it would carry either trade goods or fighting men, this was only it's second voyage, Jim Smith had told Jack the idea was to use more sail to power the galley instead of using oars and man power, Rory looked at Jack, 'do you think it'll work?' Jack looked up at the sails and shrugged his shoulders, 'don't know, if it means I haven't got ta sit pulling an oar all day, I hope it does,' Rory nodded in agreement, rowing a galley was not the best of pass times, back ache, blisters and cramp, sail power was certainly more appealing.

Rory was still puzzled about the captains attitude and the way Jim Smith acted as if he had a god given right to treat the crew like dogs, Jack told him the galley was part of a new fleet belonging to the King, there was going to be a new approach to seafaring, bigger galleys could carry more trade goods, the King was supposed to hold a vision that England could never be conquered if his galleys controlled the seas, Jack said he had even heard the King had tried to fire a catapult from a galley, missed the target completely and scared the crew to death by nearly capsizing the galley, Jack could not help but laugh, 'I don't think firing rocks from galleys will catch on, do you,' Rory laughed, 'not in our life time anyway, I hope.'

The next day started as the previous with Jim Smiths tongue lashing anyone for no real reason, Rory thought Jim Smith was definitely not at his best first thing in the mornings, Jack and Rory were ordered to swab the decks by Jim Smith, a job normally given as a punishment, it was hard work and painful to their knees, Jack really found this type of work hard, Rory had to help him to stand.

'The old knees are not what they used to be,' Jack joked, 'just how old are yoo?' Jack smiled, 'dun no, can't be that old, still got most of me teeth,' Jack opened his mouth wide exposing two lines of teeth as black as tar, 'I see what yoo mean,' Rory looked impressed, Jack started to laugh. 'MacLeod,' Jim Smith was standing close by, 'aye, Jim,' Jim Smith glared at Rory, 'what's going on, why are you not swabbing the deck?' Rory looked at Jack, 'Jack needed a rest,' Rory's comments enraged Jim Smith, 'needs a rest does he?' Jack knew this was leading to trouble, 'no Jim, I knelt on a nail that's all, I'm alright now,' he tried to defuse the issue, 'I was not talking to you Jack, who gave you the right to say Jack could rest, think you know better do you?' Rory sensed he was in deep trouble, 'no Jim, it's as Jack says, I didn't know about the nail,' Rory hoped that would pacify Jim, 'your not here to know anything, you're here to take orders and work, is that clear MacLeod?' Rory was quick to answer, 'clear as day,' Rory closed his eyes praying that would be the end of it, 'you Celt's are all the same, not worth the ground you stand on,' Rory was starting to lose any fear of punishment, Jim Smith kept goading him, Rory had to keep calm and take the abuse, he could not possibly win and Jim Smith knew it, 'worthless Celts, all of them,' Rory snapped, he grabbed Jim Smith round the neck and threw him across the deck, before Jim come to his senses enough to call out Jack plunged a knife into his throat, Jack stood back, looking at Jim Smiths blood dripping from his hands, Rory stared in disbelief as the last flickers of life drained from Jim's body.

Jim Smith made no movement, 'stand back I say,' second in command to Jim Smith, William Dorset stood pointing a sword inches away from Jack's heaving chest, Rory knelt on one leg beside Jim's lifeless blood soaked body, he shook Jim as if to shake life back into him, there was no reaction.

William Dorset had one eye on Jack and one on Jim Smith's body, 'call the Captain,' he ordered, Captain Jacob had already heard the shouting and for once ventured out of his tiny cabin only to find Jim Smith's body lying in a pool of blood, 'who is responsible Mr Dorset?' he looked at Jack 'Jack, captain, you can see he has blood on his hands, I found him standing over Jim,' Rory could not let Jack take the blame, 'Captain,' Rory called out,' 'No Rory, I done the animal, it was me.' Jack's words would surely hang him, he was clearly proud of what he had done, Jack was taken to his bunk and tied up, Jim Smith's body was quickly prepared for a burial at sea, Rory was ordered to clean up the blood from the deck.

Rory was still dazed from both Jack's speed in killing Jim Smith and his willingness to take all the blame, after a while he remembered their conversation when Jack said Jim Smith would get what's coming to him, Rory was sure they must have had a past he was not aware of.

Later that evening Rory stood on the deck, still wondering what Jack held against Jim Smith, what hate he could hold enough that he was willing to hang for.

The crew talked about little else, to a man they were saying, Jack was right to kill him, Rory wanted to see Jack, he was being held in the small bunk area, Rory was standing looking out to sea, his mind clearly elsewhere when William Dorset came and stood beside him, Rory looked at him, 'can I have a word Mr Dorset?'

William Dorset was very different from Jim Smith a real gentleman, he was tall and from a good background, 'what is it MacLeod?' his tone took Rory by surprise, 'can a see Jack, I need ta speak with him?' William looked Rory in the eyes and shook his head, 'no MacLeod, you may not, Jack's a condemned man, God help him,' Rory turned away, 'a wanted too know why he did it,' Rory turned his head towards William, 'why he murdered Jim Smith is irrelevant MacLeod, he did and he will hang,' Rory nodded then walked towards the stern of the galley.

While he was looking out to sea, Tom, one of the crew came and stood next to him, 'I hear you want to know why Jack done Smith?' Rory looked at Tom, 'do you know?' Tom looked round the galley as if he was making sure no-one could hear him, 'Jack had a daughter, a real beauty, be about sixteen at the time, Smith abused her, left her fa dead, Jack found her, she told him what Smith done, she later died in Jack's arms, from that day Jack vowed ta kill Smith, he's bin waiting fa his chance fa over a year, he'll go in peace.'

Rory began to understand, he looked at Tom and nodded as if to say thanks, Tom started to walk off, 'don't ya go tellin the captain now or they'll not hang him, Jack'll not thank ya if ya did' Rory again nodded in agreement.

The next morning would be Rory's last morning at sea, the galley was due to dock in Bristol that evening, the crew was called together to witness Jim Smith's burial at sea, it was a simple affair a few words from the captain followed by a short prayer, then his body was cast to the deep and that was that, not much to say for a life.

Am Bratach Sith of Dunvegan

The Captain ordered the crew to stay as they were, Jack was brought from his bunk, William Dorset read out the charges Jack was being tried for, the Captain asked Jack how did he plead 'guilty, I done him good I did,' Jacks words, showing he had no remorse, angered Captain Jacob, 'you stand before the crew of this galley, you have admitted your guilt, do you have any reason for the murder of Jim Smith?' Jack thought for a moment, 'God will be me judge not you or any of ya.'

Captain Jacob rose to his feet, you leave me no option, by the power vested in me by the King of England you are sentenced to death by hanging for the murder of Jim Smith, the sentence will be carried out immediately, Jack did not struggle, he was stood blindfolded on a small casket, a rope had already been threaded through a metal loop fastened to the main mast, William Dorset tied a noose and placed it over Jacks head, the rope was pulled tight and secured to the mast, William Dorset was ordered by the captain that on the count of three he would kick the casket from under Jack's feet, Dorset stood in position, he asked Jack for his forgiveness, Jack obliged, 'one, two, three' William Dorset kicked the casket so hard it spun across the deck, Jack's body fell his feet dangling just off the deck, his body twitching at first, then still.

Captain Jacob ordered Jack's body to be cut down and cast to the sea without ceremony, the crew did not like it, the captain was in no mood for compromise, Rory volunteered to help cut Jack's body down, two of the crew helped, as they lifted him from the deck his limp body wrapped with weights to make it sink, Rory started saying a prayer under his breath so no-one other than the two crew helping could hear, the other two men nodded at

Rory and smiled, they lifted Jack's body over the side of the galley, Jack's body dropped into the sea hardly making a splash.

Rory stood looking as Jack's body slowly sank, 'see yoo again Jack,' the mood of the crew was sombre as the galley docked into moorings down river from Bristol, William Dorset allowed Rory to leave the Galley as he was not a regular member of the crew, Rory went to his bunk to collect his belongings, he pulled them up from the side of the bunk, wrapped in the Fairy cloth he found a gold cross and chain, Rory took it to William Dorset, he told him where he had found it, William took Rory to one side, 'the cross belonged to Jack's daughter, he wanted you to have it, he asked me to put it in your things it was his last wish,' Rory looked at the cross, then at William, 'yoo knew, yoo knew didn't yoo, why did yoo let him hang?' William grabbed both of Rory's arms, 'I got him on the galley, if the captain found out I would be done for, Jack was on my last galley when his daughter was butchered by Smith, when he told me what Smith had done, I wanted to kill him myself, I couldn't tell the Captain or both of us would be found out,' Rory could see the turmoil in Williams eyes, he knew he was telling the truth, 'aye best left, dun's dun' Rory put the cross back in the Fairy cloth, nodded to William, Rory slowly walked towards the gang plank and off the galley, he didn't look back until he was leaving the dock, he looked across at the galley it was just as he had first seen it in Spain, he smiled and thought to himself, 'what did yoo get ma inta Miguel?'

CHAPTER FIFTEEN
Return to Dunvegan

After the long journey from Bristol Rory sat in a small fishing galley, he had talked a local fisherman into taking him across the sea to Skye, the fisherman lived on Skye anyway, so it was not like he was making a special trip, the distant Cuillin hills stood proud veiled in cloud, Rory was glad to be home.

The fisherman was curious, he kept asking questions, too many for Rory's liking, Rory gave one word answers or plainly ignored him, much to the disgust of the fisherman, the small galley grounded on a pebbled beach, Rory jumped out as far as he could to avoid getting wet, his feet crunched onto the pebbles, he was back on home soil, his heart lifted, he looked around nothing had changed since he left, only him, he was older.

There was still quite a walk to Dunvegan and no point in dwelling on the past, Rory had a spring in his step, it would take him a day or two to get home, Dunvegan castle was on the other side of Skye.

Rory would have to sleep under the stars tonight, he didn't mind, he was used to it , he thought what's better than lying on the ground looking up at the stars while the sweet smell of heather on a gentle summer breeze lulls you to sleep.

He was making good progress along a well trod track towards Drynoch, Rory knew this track well, most of the islanders either lived near to Dunvegan or Armadale for safety, Armadale is a MacDonald stronghold at the southern end of Skye.

Rory knew there was not many places he could ask for shelter along the way, the afternoon began turning to evening, a mist was spreading it's cool fingers over the burns and small lochs, Skye without mist is like the sea without fish, you can't have one without the other, he thought to himself. In the distance Rory could see a wisp of smoke, he first thought it was mist rising from the trees, as he got closer he could see a small croft, the smoke was coming from a hole in the turf roof.

Rory decided to ask if they had room for him to stay the night, as he approached the croft he was curious, he could not remember a croft around here, still he had been away a while, he knocked the door, no-one answered, he knocked again, still no answer, he pushed open the door enough to see if anyone was home, he couldn't see anyone, 'hello' he stood in the doorway, he had a bed feeling about this, 'what would yoo be after laddie?' the voice startled Rory, he turned round, behind him stood an old woman, she had a shawl pulled over her head, Rory could not see her face, 'err, it dose nye matter, a'll be on ma way,' Rory tried to push by the woman, 'yoo must a wanted something or yoo would nee be here now would yoo?' the woman

Am Bratach Sith of Dunvegan

pushed Rory into the building, she shut the door, 'noo sense letting tha cold in is tha?' the woman removed her shawl, she was an old hag if ever there was one, Rory was becoming anxious, 'what da yoo want laddie?' Rory was not sure what else he could say, 'a err, a was wondering if a might stay tha night, it does nye matter a'll be on ma way,' the woman placed her shawl on the back of a large chair, 'yoo can stay.'

Rory went to the door, he tried to open it, 'what have yoo done, tha door will nye open?' the woman walked to the door and pushed it open, 'see, yoo doon't nor what your doing laddie,' Rory went to go out the door, the woman refused to let him pass, 'a yoo a witch?' the woman looked at Rory, her steely eyes cold and lifeless, 'some say a am, what da yoo think?' Rory had heard stories of witches on Skye, he didn't know what to do, she could turn him into a sheep or worse, 'a, a canny say, a don't know any witches,' the woman laughed, 'yoo can stay or go,' she opened the door, Rory pushed by the woman and looked into the night, even if he does go, if she is a witch, what's to stop her following him or putting a spell on him, he thought it best to humour her, 'aye a'll stay a while,' the door shut banging against the stone wall, Rory watched the woman's every move as she shuffled towards the fire, she bent down and started stirring a large metal pot warming on the fire, 'broth?' she said without looking up, Rory was unsure but he was hungry and the broth did smell good, 'aye, a will,' the woman reached for a wooden bowl, Rory could see her hand was old and wrinkled, curved claw like nails extended her long thin fingers, Rory shuddered, his mind conjured up all kinds of things, all of them horrid.

She ladled the broth into the bowl, muttering to herself all the time, Rory tried to hear what she was saying, was it a spell of some kind or the ramblings of an old woman, she slowly stood up holding the bowl in both hands, 'there yoo arr, get it while it's hot,' she placed the bowl on the table and pulled a chair out, 'sit here.'

Rory moved round the table towards the chair, his eyes firmly fixed on the woman, as he sat down he closed his eyes as if expecting her to turn on him and reveal her true self, nothing happened, he picked up a wooden spoon from the middle of the table and gingerly dipped it into the broth, he stirred the spoon round, 'eat up laddie,' Rory sensed the woman was becoming impatient with his lack of enthusiasm to eat, he lifted the spoon, liquid dripped off splashing into the bowl, his mouth opened to receive the spoon, he held the liquid in his mouth, he could feel it draining down his throat until he either had to swallow or spit it out, with one gulp he swallowed the broth, he took another spoonful, turning to the woman who was standing over his shoulder he smiled, 'good broth.'

Rory did not really notice what the woman was doing after that, he was too busy finishing off the broth, dropping the spoon into the bowl he sat back on the chair and held his stomach, 'ahh, that was good,' the woman pulled a stool round and sat beside Rory, 'where would yoo be going?' Rory was still unsure if she was a witch, he figured telling her would make little difference, 'Dunvegan castle,' she picked her head up, 'Dunvegan castle, MacLeod, tales of fairies an magic I hear, what da yoo know of such tales?' Rory became more uneasy, 'nothing,' her head moved closer to him, he could smell her breath, it wasn't rancid as he expected more like spring flowers, surely a witch could not have breath that smelt of flowers, 'yoo must know a tale ta tell?' Rory conceded, 'aye a do, it's said a fairy gave a cloth ta tha MacLeod ancestors, it would bring them victory when facing defeat in battle.'

The woman started to laugh, more of a shriek than a laugh, 'yoo noo believe that da yoo?' Rory became incensed by her ridicule, 'a know it ta be true, woman,' he answered back sharply, before he could think Rory pulled out the Fairy cloth, the woman stopped laughing, her long fingers reached towards the Fairy cloth, her face became full of purpose, 'give ma the cloth laddie.'

Rory pulled it out of her reach, 'noo, it's for tha Chief,' the woman stood up, 'a want ta hold the cloth,' Rory pushed his chair away and stumbled backwards as he fell his head hit the corner of the table, he held his head, he felt dazed, suddenly he thought, the Fairy cloth, he reached for it, it was gone, he looked round the witch must have taken it.

Rory struggled to his feet, he picked up a wooden staff, still dazed he stumbled out the door, he could see nothing at first, as his eyes became more used to the darkness he caught a glimpse of the witch running down towards the burn, he ran after the hag, he ran as if he was being carried by the wind, he called out, the witch stopped, she started to cast spells to halt his progress, nothing she did stopped him.

Rory was soon standing in front of the witch, she was wearing the Fairy cloth round her waist, 'yoo canny kill ma noo,' she stood as if inviting Rory to try to kill her, he drew back the staff and plunged it into her stomach, the look on her withered old face was more disbelief, she truly believed the Fairy cloth would make her invincible.

Rory pulled the staff from her as the last flickers of life drained from her body, she cast one last spell, 'a curse on MacLeod's unborn,' Rory removed the Fairy cloth and tucked it in his tunic, he had to get far away from the witch, he still didn't trust she was dead, he had heard tales of witches reincarnating as wolves or bears, he started to run it was not easy in the darkness, he followed the burn until he found a place to cross, as he stepped into the shallow water he was startled by a voice 'yoo have ta fight ma ta cross.'

He looked round, across the burn stood a young woman, she looked strong and full of purpose 'this is ma Burn.'

Rory was too tired to fight again, 'a'll go farther doon the burn' he started to walk away 'a'll ba waiting, when yoo cross,' Rory stopped he really didn't need this but he had to cross the burn somewhere.

'Who are yoo?' the woman asked, 'why?' Rory replied, 'a want ta know who a beat,' Rory found himself smiling, the cheek of the woman as if she would beat him in a fight, 'Rory MacLeod' she nodded, 'and who are yoo?' Rory thought it was only fair he should know her name, 'maidioun Sitte she replied, 'what will yoo give ma when a beat yoo?' Rory only had the Fairy cloth, he had left his few other belongings at the witches house, not that they were worth anything, 'a have nothing ta give yoo,' he felt the cross around his neck Jack had left him, he could not give that as a payment to cross a river but he had nothing else and anyway he would not lose a fight with a woman, 'a have this holy cross, it's gold.'

Rory held it up so the woman could see, 'aye that'll doo,' the woman splashed into the burn, Rory jumped as far into the middle as he could, the woman shoulder charged Rory, he was not expecting her to be so strong, he fell face down into the burn, he was soaked.

She grabbed him round the neck and held his head under the water, he struggled but could not break her grip, the cold water numbed his senses, he rolled onto his back and brought his knee up into her groin, she loosened her grip enough to allow him to throw her to the side, he seized his chance, it was his turn to hold her down, with her head and body almost submerged under the water she kept struggling, Rory was in no mood to let her go, she clawed at Rory's skin and tunic for anything to grip, after a while she began to lose strength, she was drowning.

Rory was not going to let her off lightly, she may be pretending, as soon as he let go she would take advantage, this time he may not be so lucky, the woman stopped clawing at Rory, he slowly released his grip, he pulled her head out of the water, she was close to death, he dragged her to the bank, she was still breathing.

Rory was tired, the fight with the witch then with Maidioun Sitte proved too much he lay on the bank and fell into a deep sleep.

Rory gasped, his eyes opened wide, he had fallen asleep, next to him sat Maidioun Sitte, he looked towards her, 'yoo beat ma fair, a give yoo this,' she handed Rory a box, 'there are many boxes only open in times of trouble an not fa a year an a day or consequences will be calamitous,' Rory looked puzzled, 'what's in the box?' the fairy held his hand, 'the Bratach Sith' Rory felt in his tunic, 'yoo stole the Fairy cloth?' Rory grabbed the box, 'Noo, ta protect tha MacLeod unborn from tha witches curse, remember not ta ba opened fa a year an a day.'

The fairy disappeared as quickly as she arrived, Rory could hardly believe what had happened, he began to wonder if he had fell asleep and dreamt it all, he looked at the box, no it hadn't been a bad dream, he was about half way to Dunvegan, if he made haste he would reach Dunvegan by nightfall. He started to run at first but soon settled for a fast walk, as evening fell Rory was again tired and hungry, he was close to Dunvegan but every step was hard going. As he dragged himself to the top of yet another high hill he could see in the distance was Dunvegan Castle standing every bit as proud and noble as he remembered it to be, he stood for a moment while he caught his breath, he could hardly believe he had finally made it back home.

Rory felt the tiredness lift and the spring returned to his step, before nightfall he was standing on the edge of Loch Dunvegan, he called out, he heard a voice asking who he was, 'Rory MacLeod,' after a short wait the voice asked him his business, Rory was hardly expecting a welcoming party but this was ridiculous, he thought of the one thing they wouldn't turn away, 'a hold treasure fa Chief MacLeod.'

Rory had just about given up when a small boat appeared with three men aboard, as it got close one of the men asked Rory what treasure he held, Rory refused to disclose he told them it would only be revealed to Chief MacLeod himself, the men discussed what to do, the boat turned around, one of the men told Rory to go away.

Rory shouted after them, 'if yoo don't take me ta MacLeod when he finds hoot he'll hang your heads off tha castle walls,' again the three men held a discussion, finally the boat turned around, as it moored by a large flat

Am Bratach Sith of Dunvegan

rock one of the men got out first he had a sword in his right hand and a burning torch in the other.

'Rory MacLeod yoo say, last a heard he wa dead,' Rory looked at the man through the torch light, 'is that yoo Fergus?' the man stepped forward to gain a better look at Rory, 'aye, Fergus,' a broad grin came upon Fergus, 'Rory MacLeod a did nye expect ta see yoo agin, come on laddie, lets get yoo inta tha warm.'

The three men continued to question Rory about the treasure, coming to the conclusion he was making it up just to get into the castle, Rory jumped from the boat as it moored at the sea gate, he ran up the steps to the main castle rooms.

Chief MacLeod was entertaining a representation from the MacMillan and MacLean's clans, no doubt plotting against their bitter enemies the MacDonald's.

Rory begged a word with the Chief, Rory waited, he could hear laughing coming from the main hall, Rory was getting fed up, he was tired and hungry, the door opened, there stood Chief MacLeod of MacLeod, 'Rory, laddie come an join us,' Rory entered the main hall, the single table was covered with half eaten food, he could feel his stomach rumbling at the thought of all that food, 'come laddie eat,' Rory didn't need to be asked twice.

CHAPTER SIXTEEN
The Witches curse

Rory ate until he was stuffed, he had drank too much, it was as much as he could do to keep his eyes open, he fell asleep at the table.

When he woke in the morning he had a terrible hangover, he staggered to the castle walls to get some fresh air, as he stood taking in gulps of icy cold morning air, 'ah yoo alive then laddie?' MacLeod slapped him on the back, it was the last thing Rory needed, he was having trouble keeping last nights meal in his stomach as it was, without being slapped about, 'aye Chief just aboot,' Chief MacLeod looked as if he had woken from a full nights sleep, how could someone who had ate and drank as much as he had look that lively in the morning, Rory wished he knew the secret.

'Come laddie yoo have treasure fa me?' Chief MacLeod would not be put off, Rory pulled his-self together as best he could, Rory handed the box to the chief, he went to open it, 'noo,' Rory raised his voice, the Chief looked at him with surprise, 'yoo give me treasure in a box an yoo doon't want me ta open it?'

Rory took a deep breath he really did not want to do this now,' if yoo open tha box before a year an a day, terrible things will happen, it holds tha Bratach Sith, a curse was put on the MacLeod clan by a witch,' Chief MacLeod sat back in thought.

Rory began explaining about Gregor and his promise to return the Fairy cloth to the chief, then he went on to tell about the witch and the Maidioun Sitte, 'yoo add a bit of an adventure laddie? Gregor should a come back, he's a MacLeod as far as I know, yoo done well, a'll need ta keep this hidden.'

Chief MacLeod gently patted the box, Rory later left the castle, going to his mothers home, the chief told him he was welcome to stay after what he had done for the MacLeod family, there would always be a home for him at Dunvegan.

Chief MacLeod promised Rory lands in recognition for his loyalty and courage, Rory smiled to himself, he had travelled across the world to make a fortune and lands, only to receive lands as a gift on his return, he thought how strange life can be.

Autumn became winter and winter turned slowly to spring, Lady MacLeod was joyful, she was to announce to her husband she was with child, this was not their first child, they had three fine strong sons already, Chief MacLeod longed for a large family, she knew he would be delighted, she had to contain her delight for a few days, as her husband was away sorting out affairs on the mainland.

Am Bratach Sith of Dunvegan

Lady MacLeod was busying herself by clearing out the bed chamber, it needed a good clear out, the chief would hoard anything, she didn't normally touch any of his things but with a new baby on the way things needed to be sorted, Anne a local girl, one of the servants was helping Lady MacLeod, they were careful not to remove or break anything

Anne opened a small cupboard to put a few of the smaller items away when she found a box, 'Lady MacLeod,' Anne held up the box, 'noo idea what's in it, best put it back,' Anne placed the box back in the cupboard, after they had finished Lady MacLeod looked at the room, 'a fine days work,' Anne agreed.

Lady MacLeod was worn out, she had done too much that day, she decided to retire to the bed chamber to lie down, she lay thinking about what life would be like with a new baby and how their sons would spoil it, especially if it was a lassie.

After a while her mind turned to other things, she looked at the small cupboard, she began to wonder what was in the box, she hadn't seen it before, her husband did not hold any secrets from her, that she knew of anyway.

Finally her curiosity took the better of her, as she jumped up from the bed she felt a stabbing pain in her lower stomach, it took her breath away, she sat on the bed until she regained her breath, she suddenly remembered about the box, she bent down, opened the cupboard and removed the box, placing it on the bed, she opened the lid very slowly, she thought it might be a present for her, that would be the reason she didn't know about it.

Inside was another box, she was even more curious, she opened the second box only to find a third, she opened the third box, inside lay a forth box, as she was removing the forth box, she heard someone running up the stone stairs.

Lady MacLeod hesitated, a knock at the door, 'aye,' the door opened, Anne stood with a broad smile on her face, 'Lady MacLeod, tha Chief, he's here, at tha sea gate,' Lady MacLeod started to panic, she did not want her husband to know she was going through his personal things, it would be bad enough when he found out they had tidied up, she was relying on the fact he would be so delighted in her good news he wouldn't mind what they had done.

She hadn't time to put all the boxes back, 'Anne come here, come here lassie, put tha boxes inside each other an put them back in tha cupboard,' Anne looked at Lady MacLeod, 'a was curious,' 'hurry,' said Lady MacLeod, as she rushed out of the bed chamber and down the stairs to greet her husband.

She was just in time, she held her arms out, they embraced, the Chief gave her a strong hug, 'careful yoo big oaf, yoo might hurt your child,' a broad grin filled the Chief's face, he picked her up and kissed her, he slowly let her feet touch back on the floor.

'A feel faint,' Lady MacLeod fell in the Chief's arms, 'Anne,' he shouted, 'come on lassie, hurry,' Anne came running down the stairs, 'what's wrong, what's happened?' Chief MacLeod carried his wife up to the bed chamber, pushing the door open with his foot, instantly he saw to his horror, the open boxes with the Bratach Sith lying unfurled on the bed.

'No, No, what have yoo done?' he lay Lady MacLeod on the bed, her dress was covered in blood, Anne tended her, she was as close to a nurse there was in Dunvegan,

Am Bratach Sith of Dunvegan

Chief MacLeod folded the Fairy cloth and placed it back in the box, hoping the curse would end, Lady MacLeod miscarried.

A Physician was sent for from the mainland, he confirmed her miscarriage was so bad she may never conceive another child, during the days following Lady MacLeod's miscarriage, a large number of other woman and animals either miscarried or suffered premature births.

The months that followed no other babies were born alive in the shadow of Dunvegan castle until one year and a day had passed since the return of the Bratach Sith to Dunvegan.

Lady MacLeod didn't have anymore children.

Chief MacLeod kept the Bratach Sith locked away, after a while he sent for Rory MacLeod, on his arrival Rory begged forgiveness from the Chief for his part in returning the Fairy cloth with the witches curse.

Chief MacLeod blamed only himself, Rory told him of the conditions surrounding the curse, it was he who did not take heed he should have locked it away and told everyone at Dunvegan of the curse.

Chief MacLeod granted Rory three lands near Bracadale, two for bringing the Bratach Sith back to Dunvegan and a third on the condition Rory's family, now and in future years would take trust of the Bratach Sith until it was needed by the Chief of MacLeod.

Rory believed the Fairy cloth should always remain at Dunvegan, but took it as an honour to hold the Bratach Sith on behalf of the Clan MacLeod.

Lucy was lying asleep on Iain's lap, Anne looked at him, 'she's been like that fa tha last couple of hours, she hasn't heard a word you've said, it's a good thing too, from what I heard she would have nightmares, yoo filling her wee head with murders, hangings an witches.'

Iain shrugged his shoulders, 'only story telling, yoo would want ma ta tell her tha truth wouldn't yoo?' Anne shook her head, 'she is only six, noo sixteen,' Iain started to try and rouse Lucy, 'come on lassie, if yoo don't wake up noo, yoo wont want ta go ta bed latter,' Lucy tried to make herself more comfortable, 'come on Lucy, a need ta stand up, ma legs have gone stiff,' Lucy rubbed her eyes, she stood up, Anne held her hands, she could tell Lucy was still half asleep, 'do yoo want ta help me put tha decorations on tha Christmas tree?' Lucy gave a tired nod of her head, 'a'll tell yoo what shall we go ta tha bathroom an wash ya face, that'll help yoo wake up?' Lucy gave another nod of agreement.

Lucy skipped out of the bathroom, a good face wash in cold water soon had her wide awake, 'daddy, are yoo going ta help?' Iain looked across at Anne, 'noo lassie, a think it best if yoo help mummy, daddy will only get in tha way,' the rest of the afternoon was spent decorating the tree, Iain decided he was going to catch up on some reading, he had borrowed a novel off Jonny, one of the pilots in his squadron, he told him it was about a spy who ends up saving the world.

Lucy did not normally like it when Iain sat reading, he never listened or played with her, today was different Lucy had plenty to occupy her mind, so Iain took his chance, pipe lit, a roaring fire, a good read and his family around him, what could be better, Iain felt like a clan Chieftain.

Anne decided not to make any lunch, so they had a big breakfast and she would prepare an early dinner so they could sit round the fire, Iain could carry on telling Lucy her story.

Anne needed Iain to spend as much time with Lucy as he could, he was due to go back in a couple of days, although she did not want to admit it, Lucy may never see him again.

Anne had another surprise up her sleeve, Iain was unsure if he would make it back home until after Christmas, she had prepared cakes, mince pies and ordered a large chicken from a farm by the village, they would have Christmas dinner tomorrow.

Lucy was everywhere, she wanted to hang all the decorations on the tree, at times it was as much as Anne could do to stop Lucy falling into the tree, Lucy stood on tip toes trying to reach the top.

Knowing Lucy wouldn't stop, Anne fetched a milking stool from the kitchen, 'here Lucy, stand on this,' after a couple of hours the tree was finished, the last decoration to be placed on the tree was always the fairy.

'Look daddy, look,' Iain slowly raised his eyes from his book, 'what's that lassie?' Lucy could not believe he had not noticed the tree, 'tha tree, daddy, tha tree,' she pointed to it as she jumped up and down with excitement, 'och aye, very nice,' Iain started to read his book again much to Lucy's annoyance, Anne smiled, she knew Iain was teasing Lucy, she falls for it every time, Lucy pulled at Iain's arm, 'daddy stop reading, come an look at tha tree,' Iain placed an old leather bookmark in the book and closed it sharply placing it on the arm of the chair.

Iain allowed Lucy to pull him up from the chair, he removed his pipe holding it by the bowl, he used it to point to different decorations continually teasing Lucy about where she had put them, 'alright yoo two, that's enough,' Anne could see Lucy was close to tears, she needed her daddies approval. Iain knew what Anne was really saying, he picked Lucy up, Anne handed him the fairy, 'she's lovely isn't she?' Lucy touched the fairies golden hair, 'a wish ma hair was golden,' Iain gently placed the fairy on the top of the tree, 'do yoo believe in fairies Lucy?' Iain looked down at Lucy, 'oh aye daddy, they're ma friends,' Iain smiled, 'a think it's tha best Christmas tree a've ever seen, tha decorations are bonnie,' a big grin rose from Lucy's tiny mouth lighting up her face like the morning sun, she flung her arms round Iain's neck and rested her head on his shoulder, 'a love yoo daddy.'

It had always been a tradition in Iain's family to toast the Christmas tree once it had been decorated, Iain stood Lucy on the milking stool she had been using earlier, he always kept a bottle of cream sherry in the sideboard for such occasions, he poured a large glass for Anne and himself and a very small glass for Lucy, this was a real treat for Lucy, she felt like a big girl when her daddy gave her the glass, 'noo don't drink it fast or yoo'll ba sick,' Lucy hung onto her daddies every word.

Iain raised his glass towards the Christmas tree, Anne and Lucy quickly followed suit, 'God bless this bonnie Christmas tree, God bless this family an all MacLeod's wherever they may be,' Iain and Anne took a mouthful of sherry, Lucy did the same, her face screwed up, 'err, that's horrible,' Iain laughed, 'not all it's cracked up ta ba lassie,' Lucy handed her glass to Anne, she tried to wipe the taste from her mouth with the sleeve of her jumper, 'doon't do that, use a towel in tha kitchen.' Lucy ran to the kitchen, she came back with a tea towel, all the while rubbing her mouth, 'that's enough now, yoo'll make your mouth sore,' Anne took the tea towel from Lucy, 'go an get a drink of water,' Anne pointed to the kitchen, 'a'll get it,' Iain went to the kitchen with Lucy following behind, Lucy finally removed the taste of the sherry from her mouth, it would be a long time before she would try drinking sherry again.

Anne started to prepare the dinner, Lucy helped as usual, Anne liked Lucy to help but she always wanted to do everything, if it went as normal Lucy would end up in a mess, Anne wondered how Lucy would ever learn to cook.

Iain took the opportunity to read some more of his book, he had just got to an exciting bit when Lucy made him put it down, after half an hour or so Anne called from the kitchen, 'Iain, if you are not doing anything would yoo lay tha table?' Anne knew he was reading but she wasn't going to let him get away without doing something towards dinner.

'I'm just at a good bit, a canny put it doon now or a'll lose tha plot,' thinking that may have done the trick he continued to read, 'if tha table isn't laid soon a wont be serving dinner,' Iain sighed 'alright then,' he reluctantly placed the bookmark in the book, he put his pipe out, then removed the tobacco by tapping the bowl of the pipe on the hearth of the fire.

After dinner, with all the pots and pans washed and put away, they all sat round the fire, Iain reading his book while Anne sat knitting a jumper for Lucy, a big thick one for the winter, it was a good job it was nearly finished with the first snow already falling.

Lucy was also trying to knit, she kept dropping stitches and getting in a mess, Anne would have to sort it out, she didn't mind at least Lucy was having a go and persisting with it.

Lucy looked across at Iain, 'what aboot tha story daddy?' Iain peered over the top of the book as if he was hoping Lucy would have forgotten about it, 'noo ta night lassie, a'm reading this, may ba tomorrow, how's that?' Lucy shrugged her shoulders and carried on knitting, Anne looked at them both, Iain reading, Lucy knitting, she thought how cosy and serene, not a worry in the world, she smiled to herself, that's how it should be on Christmas eve.

CHAPTER SEVENTEEN
David's secret

Anne was up early the following morning, before six o'clock, she had arranged for the chicken to be delivered early, there was a lot to do, she wanted to finish most of the vegetables before Lucy and Iain got up otherwise they might suspect something.

Anne caught sight of the farmers horse and cart coming up the lane, she slipped on her Wellington boots and coat and went to meet him, he pulled the horse up at the side gate to the house, 'morning Anne, tis a cold un,' Anne nodded, 'aye it is tha Angus,' he passed her a large bag, 'careful it's heavy,' Anne wasn't expecting a chicken to weigh so much, she was beginning to wish she had let Angus bring it in, 'thank ya Angus bye,' Angus gave the horse a slap with the reins, 'aye see yoo enjoy ya meal,' Anne smiled and nodded as if to say we will.

Anne lifted the chicken onto the kitchen table, as she removed the various pieces of cloth the chicken was wrapped in, she could tell Angus hadn't disappointed her, it wasn't until she had removed it completely, to her surprise Angus had gave her a goose, how and more to the point where did he get a goose from.

Anne was delighted, this would make dinner even more special, she had no time to waste, she filled the breast cavity with stuffing after she had removed the giblets, then placed it in the range to cook, she was pleased she had got this far without Iain or Lucy knowing what she was up to.

Just after eight o'clock Lucy came down the stairs, 'mummy, where are yoo,' Anne poked her head round the kitchen door, 'a'm in here lass,' Anne was really pleased with herself, not only had she prepared dinner without anyone knowing, it was cooking as well, 'mummy what have yoo been doing,' Lucy knew some thing was going on, she looked round the kitchen, 'what's cooking?' Anne looked at Lucy, she could not contain her surprise any longer, she knelt down in front of Lucy, 'yoo know daddy might not be here fa Christmas dinner doon't yoo?' Lucy's face dropped, 'listen, Lucy what if we have Christmas dinner today?'

Anne looked for Lucy's reaction, 'yoo mean cakes an trifle an presents?' Lucy started to understand what was happening, a smile soon turned into a broad grin of excitement 'is Santa been?' her eyes were wide open, 'noo Lucy Santa won't come till tha real Christmas day, but we can have everything else.'

Lucy was a bit less enthusiastic because there would not be any presents, 'yoo'll have ta wait an see, if Santa knows what we're doing he might ask tha fairies ta use their magic fa us,' that did it as far as Lucy was concerned the fairies would never let her down, she gave Anne a big hug, 'thank yoo mummy,' Lucy pulled back from Anne, 'what aboot daddy?'

Anne smiled, 'that's tha best bit, he does nye know yet,' Lucy's feet began to twitch with excitement, she ran up the stairs, 'daddy, daddy,' she burst through the bedroom door and threw herself onto the bed, 'daddy, daddy wake up it's Christmas day,' she began to pull at the bed clothes trying to get Iain out of bed, Iain was still a half-sleep.

'What yoo on aboot lassie, it's nye Christmas fa a couple of weeks,' still pulling at the bed clothes, 'nor daddy we're having Christmas ta day,' by this time Anne was standing by the bedroom door, Iain looked at her as if asking what was going on, her face was full of delight and mischief, she nodded her head to conform Lucy was right 'aye tis Christmas day in this hoose,' it all began to sink in, 'Christmas dinner?' again Anne nodded her head, 'how, we doon't have a bird.'

Iain was still some what confused, 'aye we doo, it's in tha range, can ya noo smell it cooking?' Iain smelled the air, 'aye a can, a think a add better get up, afore it's Easter,' Iain got out of bed trying to pull on his dressing gown while Lucy insisted on pulling him towards the bedroom door, 'steady on lassie,' Lucy carried on pulling, ' come on daddy, come on.'

When they reached the kitchen the full impact of Anne's playful deception was clear, Iain scratched his head, 'a canny say what this means, a thought a would miss all this,' Iain reached out to Anne she moved into his arms, 'thank yoo lassie, happy Christmas,' he gently kissed the top of her head.

They decided to skip breakfast because of the large dinner they would be having, Anne was still busy in the kitchen, she had a trifle and other bits and pieces to finish.

Iain thought he would take the opportunity to read some more of his book, Lucy had other ideas, 'daddy yoo said yoo would tell ma tha story, yoo promised yesterday,' Iain looked at Lucy, 'a doon't remember making a promise, but yoo are right, a did say, didn't a?' Lucy gave definite nods of her head, 'come on then,' he lifted Lucy on his lap he gave a brief run down of the bits she missed while she was asleep the day before.

Some years after there was a different Chief MacLeod, these were troubled times, there was a lot of feuding between the clans, some clans were bitter enemies, it was like this between the MacLeod's and the MacDonald's, like most clans who boarded each other's land there were disputes over land ownership and cattle rustling was common place, many small fights broke out, then on all too many occasions there were full clan battles, many good men would lose their lives or suffer appalling injuries.

Lucy looked up at Iain, 'but daddy tha MacLeod's had tha Fairy flag,' Iain nodded, 'aye they did, remember tha Fairy flag could only ba used ta save tha clan three times, therefore each MacLeod Chief was reluctant to use tha Fairy flags magic unless they were in dire need, any way tha MacLeod's fear no other clan, so they did not need ta use magic ta win battles.'

Angus Macdonald held lands south of Glen Coe, he had a large heard of cattle, he wasn't normally an aggressive man, what he lacked in stature he made up for in strength and cunning, he only hated people who stole his cattle, that was normally the clan MacFarlane.

Am Bratach Sith of Dunvegan

Fate would change his destiny, by chance he met a lass from Lochleash, while treading cattle in Argyle, she was staying with her uncle following the death of her mother, her father was killed in a battle with the clan Fraser a year or so before.

Megan MacLean had long golden hair, skin, white as fresh snow, a real beauty, Angus couldn't believe his luck, Robert Argyle, Megan's uncle, had the responsibility of finding her an appropriate suitor, a man to marry, Angus MacDonald was prime marriage material as far as Megan's uncle was concerned, a land owner with a degree of wealth, what more could a woman want.

They were introduced with the intent of courtship, Megan didn't really take to Angus, he wasn't one of life's romantics, his idea of showing a woman a good time would be getting drunk or talking about cattle farming, Megan wanted to love the man she married, after a few days of fighting off Angus, she decided to return to Lochleash much to her uncles annoyance, really he was glad to see the back of her.

Megan's uncle was not one to give up, he arranged for Angus to accompany her as far as Glen Coe, he thought it was an opportunity to get to know her better, or more like persuade Megan to marry him, Megan left Angus at Ballachulish ferry, she agreed to think about his offer of marriage.

Megan met with a small group at Fort William travelling back to Skye, among the group was a young man with bright red hair and green eyes, he was quiet shy for a man, Megan spoke to him as they walked along, she came to the conclusion he was not interested in her, he didn't really take any notice of her.

It wasn't till she spoke to another woman travelling with them, she understood why he was so shy, the woman told Megan the lad was called David, he was deaf and dumb, the Chief MacLeod sent David to a Physician in Edinburgh, to see if he could help the poor sole, later that evening they stayed by Invergarry castle, in a hay store, it was at least warm and offered a degree of comfort.

Megan looked for David, he was not there, she decided to look for him, outside the summer evening was pleasantly warm, the only problem was, the warm air brought out the midges, Megan was used to the midges, they were a discomfort more than a problem.

Megan found David sitting by the Loch, he was talking, she could not make out what he was saying or who he was talking to, she crept closer, she stood on a twig it gave a sharp crack as it snapped under the weight of her foot, she closed her eyes.

David must have heard her, she opened one eye slowly, David was looking straight at her, how could he have heard if he's deaf, David stood up, 'what da yoo want?' Megan walked up to him she put her soft white hands on his face, 'I want ta be a friend, do yoo understand?' David looked at her, 'aye of course a doo,' Megan was the one finding it difficult to understand how could he hear what she was saying, 'how can yoo hear ma?' David dropped his head as if in shame, Megan picked his head up in her hands, 'tell ma,' there was a tear in his eyes, ' a'm cursed, as a wee lad a saw witch tryin ta kill a fairy, a yelled at her, she dropped the fairy an cursed ma never ta ba able ta tell what she did an a would never ba able ta hear a yell again, later that night a fairy come ta ma an told ma the fairies add cast a spell fa helping one of them, tha witches curse would stay

Am Bratach Sith of Dunvegan

but only during daylight, if a told anyone not pure in heart the fairies spell would ba undone, tha witch would have her way' Megan put her arms round David, 'a will nye tell a soul.'

Megan sat and talked with David for most of the night, David knew Megan was pure in heart otherwise the fairies spell would have lifted and the witches curse would stop him from talking to her.

The next day Megan found it difficult not to talk to David, the others thought she was mad even trying, Megan smiled at David, the other's didn't know what they did, Megan and David spent most nights together, they would find a place well away from the others so no-one overheard, they became good friends, by the time they reached Eilean Doran castle Megan held strong feelings for David, so strong she did not want to leave him.

The night before David was to catch the ferry to Skye from Lochleash, Megan returned home, it was cold and damp, she lit a fire to warm it up, she sat thinking mainly of David, out of nowhere a fairy appeared, the fairy thanked Megan for showing kindness to David, the fairy told Megan she could not grant her a wish but she could bring a dream true, the fairy told Megan she would dream of the man she would marry, the fairy also warned Megan that for every foretold dream there is an unforetold dream, which the outcome is opposite, the fairy also told her if she bore a child the fairies would protect the child.

Megan shivered the fire was still lit, she looked round, had she just dreamt or did the fairy really appear, she lay down thoughts of what the fairy said going through her mind she fell asleep.

When she woke the next morning she had to find David, she ran to the ferry, she was too late the ferry had already left for Skye.

Megan knew she had to find David, she was not prepared to wait until the next day to catch the ferry, she knew a local fisherman in Lochleash, Andrew, he might agree to take her across to Skye. When she arrived at Andrew's house, his wife answered the door, Megan explained she needed to talk to Andrew on a matter of importance, the woman shook her head, 'he'll noo ba takin yoo anywhere, he's doon with a fever tha noo,' Megan had no-one else to ask.

She decided she would have to wait for the ferry after all, walking back home she passed the small fishing boats all lined up waiting for the next tide, as Megan walked by she spotted Andrew's boat, she knew it well, she had been out fishing with Andrew many times, she thought if Andrew was ill, he would not be using his boat, without thinking of the consequences, she decided to take the boat and row to Skye herself.

The boat was only a few feet from the water, she tried to push the boat, it was more difficult than she had first thought, she had seen Andrew push the boat easily, after an hour or so of trying to move the boat she gave up, she needed a rest, she decided to climb into the boat and sit on the dry nets.

Megan thought how nice it was to feel the swaying of the boat, she sat up the water had risen, she must have fallen sleep, she clambered out of the boat, the water had risen up to the middle of the boat, she pushed the front of the boat with as much strength as she could muster, it slowly started to slide into the water, she found herself

Am Bratach Sith of Dunvegan

standing up to her ankles in water, it's now or never she said to herself.

Megan scrambled into the boat, she had to hurry some of the other fisherman would be here soon to catch the high tide, she pulled the two oars up from the bottom of the boat, they were heavy, one after the other she dropped the oars into the wooden rowlocks, Megan had never rowed a boat before, she had sat by Andrew years ago when she was a young girl, she held one of the oars while he was rowing but nothing else, Megan started to row, the oars hardly touched the water, then she put them too deep into the sea, when she tried to row the weight of the water on the oars nearly pulled them out of her hands.

Megan was too preoccupied to notice the boat was being carried by the strong sea current that runs between the mainland and Skye, Andrew had told her about the strong current, by the time she noticed she had drifted down into Loch Aish, she was determined to get to Skye, she was rowing better now, she was desperately trying to row with both oars at the same time to keep it going in the right direction, she pulled at the oars with all her strength, although she had drifted the current had also taken the boat nearer to Skye.

Megan was tiring fast she could hardly pick the oars up from the water, she gritted her teeth and told herself to ignore the pain of her over tired muscles, from somewhere she found the strength to keep rowing, looking over her shoulder Megan could see she was so close to reaching Skye it hurt, she could hear the highland cattle baying.

One last effort she kept on urging herself on, finally the boat was close enough to the shoreline for her to start looking for somewhere to land, she spotted a piece of land sticking out into the Loch, that'll do she thought to herself, as she guided the boat towards the spit of land the boat grounded, she could not believe her misfortune, there must be rocks just below the surface of the water.

Megan tried to row backwards to free the boat but the current was working against her, if anything the boat was becoming more trapped, she decided there was only one thing to do, get wet, she climbed out of the boat, the boat was jammed between two rocks, either side the water came up to her waist, she swam to the shore and she crawled up onto the stony beach she was so exhausted, she collapsed.

CHAPTER EIGHTEEN
Megan's search

Dougall MacDonald had decided to stroll along the beach on this fine afternoon, he felt good about life, he and his cousin Angus had increased their wealth during their recent trip to Argyle.

Dougall spotted Megan's stranded boat, he walked closer to have a better look, his eyes were so fixed on the boat, he hadn't seen Megan lying face down on the beach, Megan began to stir, her hair and clothes still soaked, she pushed herself up.

Dougall still looking at the boat caught a movement through the corner of his eye, he was so surprised to see Megan he just stood there looking at her, Megan stumbled as she tried to get up, this brought Dougall out of his trance, he ran up to her stumbling over the pebbly beach, Megan still trying to get to her feet was grabbed by Dougall under her arms just below her shoulders in an effort to stop her falling over.

Megan hadn't noticed Dougall, when he grabbed her it startled her, she went to pull away but she was so weak

Dougall had little difficulty preventing her from moving, 'it's all right lassie, a will nee harm yoo,' Megan stopped struggling in response to Dougall's soft reassuring voice, he led her up from the beach to a grass bank and helped her to sit down, he sat beside her, 'was yoo in tha boat lassie?'

Megan turned her head, she looked at Dougall, 'aye,' she looked for his reaction, 'where are yoo going lass?' still looking at him Megan pulled her hair from her face, 'Dunvegan castle,' Megan knew if she had drifted down the loch she would be on MacDonald lands, she would soon know if Dougall would help her, 'MacLeod eh?' he looked for conformation 'noo, a'm noo MacLeod,' Dougall smiled at her, 'then we'll have ta get yoo dry won't we, come with ma, can yoo walk?'

He helped Megan to her feet, she was still weak and unsteady but with Dougall's help they made their way to Dougall's house.

'Take ya dress off so a can dry it fa yoo,' Megan was not going to do anything of the sort, she glared at Dougall, 'noo lassie ma wife will help, ya noo think? noo, noo lassie,' Dougall was clearly embarrassed by what Megan was thinking he went out of the house.

'Flora, Flora' he called, Flora a short round woman came half walking, half running, her dress wrapping round her legs preventing her from going any faster, catching her breath, 'What's up Dougall?' she looked puzzled, he was still red faced from his recent embarrassment 'there's a wee young lassie in tha hoose, help a ta dry a clothes a'm going fa a wee stroll,' Dougall set off leaving Flora without any further idea of what had happened.

Flora found Megan sitting by the fire, she was staring into the flames, Flora could see she was shivering, 'here

Am Bratach Sith of Dunvegan

lassie let ma help yoo hoot a them wet clothes' Flora wasn't going to take no for an answer, 'stand up lassie,' Megan did as she was told still gazing into the fire, Flora found a warm blanket and wrapped it round Megan, she sat back down, Flora wanted to know how Megan came to be in her house, 'where yoo from lass?' Megan carried on staring into the fire, 'Lochleash,' Flora nodded, 'an what are yoo doing over here?' Megan still didn't move, 'ta find David.'

Flora was by nature a nosy woman, she was becoming agitated by Megan's lack of information, 'come on lassie, yoo could have tha courtesy ta tell ma what happened,' this broke Megan's fascination with the fire, for some reason, whether it was because Flora was another woman and she would understand or just to stop all the questions, Megan started telling Flora the whole story right from her mother dying and having to stay with her uncle in Argyle.

Flora was a good listener, you miss too much gossip if you interrupt some one in full flow, Flora didn't give any reaction when Megan mentioned Dougall's cousin Angus, she knew it could be no- one else, how many Angus MacDonald's could there be trading cattle in Argyle last week.

Megan finished her story, 'would yoo like a bowl of broth lassie?' Megan nodded and smiled, 'aye, a would, thank yoo.'

When Dougall came back he poked his head round the door, 'helloo can a come in?' Flora pushed him out the door, 'a want a wee word with yoo,' she told him what Megan had said, 'yoo need ta get word ta Angus,' Dougall looked at Flora, 'an how doo yoo expect ma ta do that, we canny keep her here till he can ba bothered ta turn up.'

Flora always knew men were hopeless in a crisis, she let out a deep long sigh, 'go ya self mon,' Dougall had only arrived home yesterday, the last thing he wanted was to ride all the way back past Glen Coe, 'a'll send word with a runner, that'll ba quicker,' he hoped this would satisfy Flora, she looked at him with that, don't you let me down look, which Dougall knew only too well, 'doont worry lass, a'll see ta it tha noo,' Dougall set off to send a message to Angus.

Flora pushed open the door, 'Megan ma poor lassie, can a get yoo some more broth?' Megan shook her head, 'noo thank yoo it was fine broth, who was that at tha door?' Flora was always quick thinking in these situations, 'a fishermon asking if a wanted any fish, a thought it best tha less people noo yoo was here tha better, eh,' Megan began to get suspicious, 'where's ya husband?' Flora didn't even stop what she was doing, 'gone fa a walk, he can ba gone fa hours,' Flora played her part well, Megan's suspicion faded, the only thing Megan found strange was Flora would not stop talking as if she was nervous.

The door opened, in walked Dougall he made a point of saying what a good walk he had been on and he was sorry if he had stayed out too long, Megan thought it strange how someone who had been so concerned about her wellbeing a few hours ago didn't ask how she was when he came in, he seemed to preoccupied telling Flora who he had seen while walking.

Dougall poured himself a drink and sat in a chair covered in deer skin by the fire, 'ahh, things a'll ba fine, lassie,' Megan smiled at him, what did he mean, his words were said as if he knew something.

'Yoo can sleep here ta night lass,' Flora had already made up a make shift bed for Megan, 'noo, it's alright a'll ba on ma way shortly,' Flora gave Megan a stern look 'you'll do nothing of tha kind, you'll stay here,' Megan thought it best not to upset them after all they had been kind enough to dry her clothes and feed her.

Megan smiled at Flora, 'aye, of course a will, very kind of yoo,' what was left of the evening passed quickly, they were soon all in bed, suspicious thoughts began creeping into Megan's mind, while she was drifting off to sleep, these thoughts worried her enough, she decided to leave early before Flora and Dougall were awake.

Megan opened her eyes wide as if someone had woken her, she slowly got up, the fire had died down but it was still giving off enough light for her to see, she quietly gathered her dress which was left in front of the fire to finish drying, her shoe's were still damp but she had no choice, they would have to do.

The door was only a few feet away from her, she gently opened the door it creaked every time she opened it a bit further, she was sure Flora would hear her, Megan squeezed through the door she dare not open it any further, she closed the door behind her making sure it closed without too much noise, the sun was just starting to rise, she walked up the stony track, she had to stop to put her shoes and dress on, she did not know why but she knew she had to get as far away from Flora and Dougall as possible.

Megan made good time, she felt refreshed after her long sleep, by the time Flora and Dougall realized she had left she was a good couple of miles away, she headed back towards Breakish, Megan wasn't sure how to get to Dunvegan, all she did know is the further towards Dunvegan she got the safer she would be.

Flora shook Dougall, 'wake up mon, wake up, she gone,' Dougall was never at his best first thing in the mornings, the last thing he needed was Flora bellowing in his ear, while he was still half asleep. 'What's up wee yoo woman,' this was too much for Flora, not only had Megan gone but she had to rely on Dougall to try and find her 'git ya self up mon n find her' Dougall finally got the picture, he started to dress.

Flora was helping him which made things worst, she kept getting in his way, 'hoot a ma way woman,' he grabbed his hat and went outside, he looked round as if Megan may be just out enjoying the morning air, he shook his head, no such luck he thought to himself, Dougall started to walk down the track the same way as Megan had gone, 'why don't yoo take ya horse mon,' Flora wondered sometimes how ever Dougall made any money, she didn't think he had an ounce of common sense.

Dougall went back and saddled his horse, he began to ride towards Lochleash just in case Megan had decided to head back home, Megan had received a piece of luck, a horse and cart had come up the track behind her the farmer was going to Portree.

He had been on the mainland to buy cattle and he was heading home, Megan sat in the back of the cart, this was better and quicker than walking, she could also see anyone coming up the track behind her.

They made good progress, at about midday the farmer pulled up the horse at a junction in the track 'Sligachan yoo want a ba going that way lassie,' Megan was sorry to lose her carriage, she thanked the farmer for his kindness,

Am Bratach Sith of Dunvegan

he gave the horse a slap with the reins, the horse gave out a surprised 'nay' and started to canter off towards Portree, Megan gathered her thoughts, after looking back down the track, she started the long walk towards Dunvegan.

Megan was delighted she had got this far, she kept looking back down the track, each time no-one was there, she started to believe no-one was following her anyway, why should they, she could not get it out of her mind Dougall and Flora were deliberately trying to keep her from leaving.

She started thinking about David, he hadn't told her where he lived, only Dunvegan, she supposed that was as good a place to start looking for him, she slowly walked away the miles, that night she slept between a grassy knoll and a large rock this kept the wind from her.

The next morning she woke quite refreshed, she was soon on her way determined to reach Dunvegan before night fall.

Dougall returned home, he tried to explain to Flora, he had travelled as far as Sligachan and Megan could not have walked that distance in a day, Flora still thought he had not looked long enough, she even doubted he had even gone to Sligachan, Dougall just waved her away, 'leave ma alone woman a did ma best, now leave it ta Angus if he wants her he can get her.'

Two days after Megan had left Dougall's house, there was a thump at the door, in walked Angus, 'where is she? a want ta talk ta her,' Flora got up out of her chair, 'an helloo ta yoo Angus, aye, a suppose yoo do want ta talk ta her, she ran off two days ago,' Angus appeared distraught.

Flora and Dougall had ever seen him like this before, he was normally so quiet, 'where did she go?' Dougall tried to calm him down, telling him to let her go, if she wanted to marry him she would be back.

Angus was having none of it, 'where did she go, come on mon tell ma?' Flora could see there was no reasoning with him, she thought if she told him it would calm him down, he wouldn't dare follow her to Dunvegan, he wouldn't be safe, 'Dunvegan,' Angus was pacing the house as Flora spoke , he stopped in his tracks, he looked at Dougall, 'a'm going after her,' Dougall grabbed Angus, 'don't be mad mon the MacLeod's a'll kill yoo,' Angus shrugged Dougall to one side, 'a'm noo afraid of any MacLeod.'

Angus opened the door, 'a thank yoo kindly fa ya message, a'll come back afor a go back ta tha mainland,' he shut the door behind him, mounted his horse and rode off towards Dunvegan castle.

Megan had reached Dunvegan to be told by Chief MacLeod that David was the grandson of Rory MacLeod and he lived near Trumpan.

The Chief ordered one of his clansman, to escort Megan safely to a croft a short distance from Trumpan, it wasn't too far, Megan soon found herself standing at the croft of Rory MacLeod, he and David had moved to Trumpan from Bracadale some years earlier, sadly Rory had died a few months ago.

A man was outside chopping wood, when he saw Megan he stopped, 'canna help yoo lassie?' Megan walked nearer to him, 'a'm Megan a wanta speak with David,' the man stared at her his face changed, he looked mean, 'a yoo being cruel lass, David canny speak or hear,' realizing what she had said Megan quickly altered 'a would like ta see him, if a can, a have come a long way,' the man was still unsure of Megan's intentions.

Am Bratach Sith of Dunvegan

'Aye, lassie yoo'ad better come in,' Megan followed the man inside the house, David sat by a large wooden table with his back to the door, the man tapped him on the shoulder, David's head spun round, he immediately saw Megan, their eyes met, a broad smile rose up David's face, he jumped up from the table walked over to Megan and picked her up in a tight hug, this caught Megan by surprise, she hugged him back, after a while she tapped him on the back to let her go.

Megan gestured to David, she needed to talk to him, he nodded and pointed to a dark corner of the house, Megan nodded, she understood he was saying tonight when it's dark, the man coughed, 'a see yoo know each other, a'm Alex,' Megan shook his hand, 'a'm Megan a good friend of David's, tha Chief MacLeod told ma a would find David here,' Alex went outside and thanked the clansman for escorting Megan.

Later that evening, David took Megan to his special place, it was beautiful, a small loch, like a mirror, the moonshine lit up the loch like daylight, Megan told David of the fairy and the dream, she told him he was the man she was destined to marry, she told him of her love for him, a tear formed in David's eye, he held her, 'a have been waiting fa yoo, a had the same dream,' David removed a gold cross and chain from round his neck 'ma grandfather Rory gave ma this ta give ta ma wife,' David placed it round Megan's neck, 'it belongs ta yoo now.'

Angus arrived at Dunvegan castle, the Chief MacLeod refused to tell him where Megan was, Angus would not be put off and started making threats of what the MacDonald Clan would do unless Megan was handed back, this was too much for the Chief MacLeod too bear he had Angus pulled from his horse and stoned out of Dunvegan.

A MacDonald clansman found Angus near to death, Angus had just enough time to say he knew Dougall of Ornsay before he passed out, the clansman took Angus to Dougall's house, Angus made a full recovery and vowed to kill every MacLeod he laid his hands on.

CHAPTER NINETEEN
A Fairy lullaby

Megan married David, their secret stayed with them, the only other person they would tell, would be their only child Bess, born with her mothers beauty and her fathers hair and eye colour, Bess was a playful child, full of mischief, she would often be found playing in the heather near to burns, she said that's where the fairies hide, Megan just smiled at her, 'of course they do lassie.'

Bess had a favourite place, she called it the Fairy bridge, the bridge was a distance from their home, Bess visited the bridge at every opportunity, David would take Bess to Dunvegan, the Fairy bridge was on the way, they would stop near the bridge, Bess spent hours talking to the fairies.

David and Megan now lived in Lusta, they moved there after they were married, Chief MacLeod thought it best, he didn't trust the MacDonald's, they may come looking for Megan.

Lusta was close to Dunvegan castle, Bess was born a year later, life was hard on Skye but Megan and David remained happy, they lived in a small croft with a few cattle and sheep, they managed to breed enough to sell.

David would also help out at the castle, he received oat meal or grain in payment, their diet was supplemented by fish and venison, there was an abundance of Red Deer roaming on Skye, as the years went by, Bess grew to be a tall, beautiful auburn haired woman with deep green eyes that sparkled like ice in moonlight.

Bess also helped out at the castle, she proved to be exceptional with babies and young children, her main duties was to take care of three of Chief MacLeod's five children, the youngest being a new born baby boy.

The castle was in the mood for a celebration, the Chief's eldest son was to come of age, he had already proven his guile and bravery in catching and killing a prime Red Deer stag with only a knife, he had also accompanied the Chief into battle with the MacDonald's, both Clans were not above rustling cattle, if that lead to a skirmish with the owners of the cattle, all the better, his biggest test was to spend the night in the woods armed only with a derk and his courage, everyone held a fear of the woods especially at night, it was believed witches, goblins and demons roamed the woods, no man who had a choice, would be found in the woods after dark.

Tonight would be the celebration of a boy becoming a man, the last test would be for him to drink wine from the horn of a highland bull, normally the horn would hold enough wine to make most men drunk, this was to be no exception, the boy managed to drink three quarters in one go before he fell to his knees spilling the rest on the floor, much to the enjoyment of the rest of the guests, a boy entered the hall, a man would leave.

Am Bratach Sith of Dunvegan

During these festivities, Bess was looking after the Chiefs youngest children as usual, Bess longed to be at the party, the noise of the celebrations proved too much for her, she checked the children were asleep before going to a room with a window that overlooked the hall.

Bess arrived just in time to see the Chiefs eldest son drinking from the horn, a great roar went up from the guests when the boy slumped to his knees spilling the wine, Bess looked on with a broad smile, she liked the Chiefs son he was everything she longed for in a man, good looks, brave and he had a cruel sense of humour which always made Bess laugh.

Bess had been watching events unfold in the hall for sometime when she heard singing, she looked round, it appeared to becoming from the rooms where the children were asleep, Bess listened, it was like a lullaby, one she had never heard, her stomach began to feel heavy, someone was with the children, someone who shouldn't be there, she rushed back to the children's rooms, the gentle singing was even more clear.

'Ho-ro veel-a-vok, bone and flesh of me, ho-ro veel-a-vok, blood and pith of me, skin like fallen snow, green thy mail coat, live thy steeds be, dauntless thy following.'

Bess eased open the door slightly, she could see a small woman dressed in a green kirtle, she was leaning over the cot, wrapping the child in a silken cloth, Bess was so engrossed with what she was seeing, she didn't hear Lady MacLeod coming up behind her, 'what a yoo doing lass?' Bess gasped, she became frightened, what would the

Chief do to her knowing she has aloud a stranger near his children.

Bess put her finger to her lips as if to tell Lady MacLeod to be quiet, Bess pushed open the door, Lady MacLeod could not believe her eyes, 'God save us, I am the mother of this child,' at the sound of Gods name the woman smiled at Bess looked down at the child sleeping soundly then vanished. Lady MacLeod rushed over to her baby, 'what curse has been laid on ma child?' Bess was calm, 'noo curse ma Lady, she was making sure tha baby is safe and warm, look this is noo tha babies wrappings,' Lady MacLeod unwrapped the baby, he started to cry, 'wrap him up again ma Lady.' Bess held Lady MacLeod's arm, she started to wrap the baby in the silken cloth, as she did the baby stopped crying and returned to sleep, Bess repeated the rhyme the woman was singing, they both looked on the baby he was so contented he would hardly stir during the rest of the night.

Lady MacLeod ushered Bess out of the room, 'who was she, a witch?' Bess smiled, 'noo ma Lady a fairy, she did no harm,' Bess told Lady MacLeod how she had left the children to look over the celebration and her fondness for her eldest son.

Lady MacLeod decided she would have to tell the Chief what had happened, but not till the next morning, Bess didn't leave the children all that night, the next morning Lady MacLeod asked Bess to go with her to explain the events of the previous evening.

Chief MacLeod was not feeling too well, he had indulged himself a little too much during last evenings celebration, Bess was holding the silken cloth the baby had been wrapped in, she handed it to Chief MacLeod, 'tha

Am Bratach Sith of Dunvegan

Fairy cloth, who made it inta a banner?' he looked at Bess, she looked at Lady MacLeod, 'a don't noo, was nee me,' Bess looked anxious, Chief MacLeod looked over staring at Bess, 'your family were trusted ta keep tha Fairy cloth safe, how did tha fairy get hold of it?' Bess hadn't any answers, she shrugged her shoulders, 'ma be she took it back' Chief MacLeod had to know the truth, he decided to go to the family home of Bess MacLeod and see for himself.

Bess and Lady MacLeod went with the Chief, when they arrived at Lusta, David MacLeod removed the box containing the Fairy cloth, he carefully open the box, he was fearful, he had been told what happened the last time the Fairy cloth had been removed, 'don't worry laddie, noo harm a'll come ta yoo,' Chief MacLeod stood next to David, as the lid was pulled back Lady MacLeod let out a gasp, 'it's noo there,' hearing her comment David opened the box fully, it was indeed as Lady MacLeod said, the box was empty.

David shook his head, as if to say no-one had touched the box, Bess knew no-one else knew it was here, David looked at Chief MacLeod, looking for him to acknowledge that he believed him, Chief MacLeod nodded his head, 'aye laddie it's true, tha fairies have taken the cloth an returned it ta it's rightful place, Dunvegan castle.'

During the following years the clans battled between them-selves, the more they battled the more hatred grew between the clans.

Angus MacDonald was by now more a warrior than a cattle farmer he never lost his hatred for the MacLeod's.

Angus blamed everything that happened on the MacLeod's, his own lands boarded on MacFarlane country, the MacFarlane's renowned for their cattle rustling activities during night time, they would venture miles into MacDonald country to steal cattle, including Angus MacDonald's cattle, on one occasion a neighbour of Angus told him he saw the MacFarlane's stealing cattle but they were too close to their own lands to raise the alarm, Angus refused to believe it was any other clan other than the MacLeod's.

Angus had waited years to gain his revenge on the MacLeod's, one autumn day a small raiding party of MacLeod clansmen landed on the Isle of Eigg, the men folk were out on the hills tending their livestock, the raiding party attacked a small croft, three of the MacLeod's found four woman hiding near by, they ill-treated the woman and left them injured, before the raiding party could get to their galley, they were ambushed by a group of MacDonald Clansmen.

As punishment for their crime, they were bound, hand and foot and set adrift in their galley, no oars or sail, one of the party had managed to hide a derk from the MacDonald's, when they were out of sight of the MacDonald's, they managed to use the derk to cut their bindings, when free they used their hands as paddles, slowly they managed to steer the galley back to Skye.

On hearing of their treatment at the hands of the MacDonald's of Eigg the MacLeod Chief ordered a full war party to sail to Eigg and avenge his Clansmen, the war party was easily spotted by the Islanders of Eigg, they hid in a cave which had a very narrow entrance, so narrow you would fail to see it even if you were standing close by, the islander's had used the cave on other occasions, when they knew they were out numbered, so why fight a battle you could not win, the war party searched everywhere, it was if

Am Bratach Sith of Dunvegan

the MacDonald's had disappeared, some of the MacLeod Clansmen started to become uneasy, they began to think it was the work of a witch or demons, finding no-one, they pillaged the crofts, killed any livestock they could find and set light to anything that burned.

As the MacLeod war party set sail back to Skye the weather started to close in, it was starting to snow, one of the Clansmen spotted a figure running over the skyline on Eigg, on seeing the figure Chief MacLeod ordered the war party to return to Eigg.

The footprints they found in the light covering of snow lead them to the cave, Chief MacLeod demanded the clansmen guilty of setting his men adrift should be handed over for punishment, the MacDonald's refused, knowing the MacLeod's could not enter the cave without being killed, Chief MacLeod ordered his men to gather dry heather and brushwood and place it in the entrance to the cave.

Chief MacLeod again demanded they hand over the men responsible, again they remained defiant, MacLeod was by now so angry he ordered the brushwood to be set alight, the smoke was dense and choking, within a short time all of the people in the cave had suffocated or burned to death, Chief MacLeod returned to Dunvegan knowing there would be retaliation for the massacre.

Chief MacLeod made sure the clan was on alert, he was expecting a full war party to come from the south of Skye, MacDonald's lands, Chief MacLeod positioned clansmen on high ground over looking the Island, he was determined not to be taken by surprise, they waited, days turned to weeks, Chief MacLeod could not believe the MacDonald's had not attacked them, the bodies in the cave on Eigg must have been found by now, so why didn't they come.

Chief MacLeod could tell the clansmen were becoming restless, either they were going to fight or return to their crofts and families, Chief MacLeod decided the MacDonald's must be too frightened to attack the MacLeod's, there was no other answer, the clansmen were stood down, the MacLeod's was still uneasy, why did the MacDonald's do nothing, it was not like them they were usually the first spoiling for a fight, although Chief MacLeod hated the MacDonald's, he held them in quiet high esteem when it came to a fight.

MacDonald's always gave a good account of themselves, if the clan's were not so bitter enemies, Chief MacLeod believed they would make good neighbours, the MacDonald's were as shrewd in business has they were fearsome in battle, may be that's why there were so much bad blood between them, fighting was the only way they could settle their differences.

Angus MacDonald had neglected his cattle, as a result he had lost about half of his small herd to rustlers, the MacLeod's got the blame as usual, he decided to sell the rest, his heart was no longer in raising cattle or business, making money seemed less important these days, with the help of a couple of his neighbours he took the cattle to Stirling to sell them.

Angus would have preferred to sell them to a MacDonald but everyone was struggling against rustling, they appeared to spend most of the time stealing cattle from a rival clans, to make up for what they had stolen previously.

Am Bratach Sith of Dunvegan

Angus had even brought some of his own cattle from a MacFarlane, Angus was told they had found them while raiding MacLeod lands, Angus would never believe anything other, not for one instance would he think the MacFarlane's had stolen his cattle in the first place.

They reached Stirling at mid afternoon the sun was low in the sky, it was by now early spring, a good time to sell cattle, some of the cattle were in calf, they would normally fetch a higher price, two for the price of one, Angus had mixed feelings about selling all his livestock, on one hand cattle had been his life, on the other he felt he had more pressing matters to resolve, killing MacLeod's.

The next morning started off with bright sunshine, there was a cold bite in the air, Angus felt it was a good day for business, he hadn't told his brother what he was doing, Dougall would only try to talk him out of it, telling him what a fool he was to let a feud take over his life, Dougall was the common sense part of their team, that's why Angus decided not to tell him of his decision until the deed was done, besides Dougall wouldn't do bad out of any deal,

Angus was going to give him a quarter of the sale price as compensation for dissolving their business partnership, Angus went into Stirling, he asked round if anyone was interested in buying a small herd of cattle, to his surprise he didn't get any realistic offers, Angus was beginning to despair, he didn't want to take the cattle back with him, walking back to the cattle, he had left on good grazing land on the outskirts of Stirling, a tall, grey haired man, dressed in brown kilt and a Red Deer cloak was herding three head of cattle towards Stirling, Angus exchanged a greeting with the man as they passed each other, Angus wondered what the man was doing, he was either selling or buying cattle, Angus called to the stranger, 'Aye, a yoo just bought tha wee beasts or a yoo selling?' the man stopped, he turned to Angus, he looked Angus up and down, 'a ma be buying, what's it ta yoo?'

Angus could not believe his luck, 'am selling a wee herd if ya interested?' the man stood silent, what was he thinking about, the man had been caught out before, he would be lead to a remote place where he would be ambushed and his cattle stolen, 'aye thanks fa ya interest, a'll be on ma way,' the man carried on walking, Angus walked after him, 'will yoo wait mon?' again the man stopped, Angus walked up to him, 'a'm Angus MacDonald a well known cattle dealer, a have a wee herd ta sell, a ya interested?' this time the man didn't think at all, 'a am interested at tha right price?' Angus was relieved, he may have a buyer.

CHAPTER TWENTY
Angus plots revenge

Angus looked at the man as they were walking back to his cattle, 'yoo did nye say your name?' they walked a little further, 'Robbie,' came the reply, Angus raised his eyebrows, this was a man of few words if ever he had met one, they were soon amongst the cattle Angus had for sale, Robbie began to examine the beasts, looking in their mouths, picking up a front leg to look at the hooves, he gently patted the beasts along the back as if to show he knew the difference between a beast in prime condition and one that was not, Angus was becoming a little impatient with Robbie, 'do yoo like what yoo see, orr noo?' Angus hoped his comment would urge Robbie to make him an offer, Robbie stood back, he looked at Angus, 'how much are yoo asking?'

Angus wanted the highest price he could get but he didn't want to go too high in case it put Robbie off, Angus told Robbie the price, which was below the top price for such prime beasts, Robbie smiled at Angus, 'come on Angus, yoo'll have ta do better than that, a was thinking more of,' Robbie gave Angus a very low price, it didn't take much to build a temper in Angus these days, Robbie was certainly succeeding.

Angus told Robbie the beasts were prime cattle and the price should reflect that, Robbie knew Angus needed to sell and fast, he didn't know why nor did he care, he saw the opportunity to steal a good profit, what he didn't bargain on was Angus.

Angus half drew his sword, Robbie hadn't taken much notice of the sword Angus was carrying, otherwise he may have been less inclined to annoy him, 'a orrta cut yoo in half, yoo nothing less than tha cheating, lying MacLeod's, yoo wanta steal ma beasts do yoo?'

Angus had by now completely removed his sword from it's scabbard, he was holding it towards Robbie's throat, 'A may have been a wee bit hasty,' Robbie raised his offer to just below the amount Angus wanted, slowly Angus placed his sword back into the scabbard, Angus held out his hand to clinch the deal, Robbie was hesitant, 'come on mon, deals a deal' Robbie grasped hold of the out stretched hand, 'aye, tha deal is done,' Robbie didn't trust Angus, he decided to spend the night with the cattle, just in case they were to disappear during the night.

A fire was lit to keep out the cold, the night was drawing in, with it came a sharp spring frost, the fire was both warm and comforting, Robbie wondered why Angus held such a hatred for the MacLeod Clan, Angus told him what the Chief of MacLeod had his men do to him, left him for dead, all he wanted was Megan, the woman who was to be his wife by right.

The next morning was cold, the spring sun was watery, on these early spring mornings the sun had to rise high in

Am Bratach Sith of Dunvegan

the sky before any real warmth could be felt from it's rays, Robbie went to a nearby burn to splash cold mountain water over his face to wake himself , while he was gone Angus ceased the chance to look at some documents Robbie was carrying.

Angus felt his temper rising as he read the words, he threw the documents to the floor, picking up his sword, shaking it from it's scabbard, he ran towards Robbie who was kneeling by the side of the burn splashing water over his head.

At first he didn't notice Angus standing over him, his sword raised, Angus kicked him in the side, 'prepare ta make ya peace we god,' Robbie could not move, he closed his eyes tight anytime expecting to hear a sword cutting through the still cold morning air, 'a told ya a would pay the money Angus,' hoping Angus would relent, 'ya didn't tell ma yoo was a snivelling, lying, cheating MacLeod did ya, noo ya would rather deceive ma an have a wee laugh we the other rotten MacLeod's,' Robbie knew he was not going to get out of this alive, this gave him more courage to speak out, 'do what yoo have ta, yoo'll get tha same as tha MacDonald on Eigg,' Angus was ready to unleash revenge, something stopped him, 'what aboot Eigg, come on mon tell ma?' Robbie slowly rolled onto his side, he looked up into a cruel, screwed up face that was Angus, 'MacLeod slaughtered all of tha MacDonald's on Eigg before tha snows.'

Robbie began to laugh at Angus, he felt the heavy sword raise in his hands, within a second Robbie laughed no longer, Angus stood over Robbie's lifeless body, he removed the blood soaked sword, holding the sword up watching the blood drip slowly off the edge as it glistened in the sunlight, only the sound of the water in the burn breaking the silence, until the two clansmen helping Angus with the cattle came to see what was happening, 'what have yoo done Angus?' he looked at the men 'killed ma a MacLeod, yoo sell tha beasts, a'm looking fa a fight.'

Angus picked up his few belongings, 'what aboot him,' one of the men stood pointing at Robbie's lifeless body, 'a did it, tell em, Angus MacDonald killed the MacLeod,' he started to walk back towards Glen Coe and home.

Angus had lost all interest in his cattle, he stole a horse from a crofter to get back to the MacDonald chief, he had no time to waste, on arriving he demanded to speak with the Chief MacDonald, Angus was told not to try and avenge the massacre, it would be dealt with in good time, nothing Angus could say would alter Chief MacDonald's decision.

Angus was not prepared to let this settle, he had at last found plenty of justification to attack the MacLeod clan, he knew there were other clansmen who would support him, he would have to travel across to Uist to gain the element of surprise, the MacLeod's would still be expecting any attack to come from the land, a small war party could sail to Skye and get ashore without being noticed.

Angus arrived on Uist with a few other MacDonald clansmen who shared one common interest to heap revenge on the MacLeod's, they were joined by local clansmen, some of whom had relatives who died on Eigg in the massacre.

Angus was told how the massacre happened from a MacDonald point of view which was at least third or forth hand to the actual events of the fateful day, Angus was told how fifty of MacLeod's most trusted clansmen raided Eigg with the intension to rape and pillage the Isle, a party of MacDonald clansmen were waiting for them, the surviving MacLeod's were set a drift with their hands and feet bound, the intension was they would be found dead, that would serve as a warning to the MacLeod's and other clans intent on taking on the MacDonald clan.

The problem was the MacLeod's in the galley survived, they hid their humiliating defeat behind lies of how bravely they had fought before being overwhelmed by hundreds of MacDonald's who lay in wait for them, the MacLeod Chief then ordered a full war party to crush the Islander's of Eigg and any other MacDonald's on the Island, Angus was then told how the MacLeod Chief had discovered the cave, instead of allowing the trapped Islanders the opportunity to escape and fight as men the MacLeod Chief ordered the fire that killed all, including women and children.

As much as Angus wanted to believe the story and the events which lead up to the massacre, he made a decision to go to Eigg to see the site of the massacre for himself, he was told the bodies still lay inside the cave, there were too many to remove through the narrow entrance, now the stench of rotting burnt bodies is overwhelming.

Angus didn't truthfully know the reason he had to see the aftermath of the massacre for himself, whether he held doubts about the story and wanted to be sure they were true or if he held Chief MacLeod in better esteem as an enemy, that he would have given the people trapped in the cave the opportunity to surrender especially the woman and children, either way Angus would make his own mind up how the massacre came about.

Angus set sail from South Uist, the sea journey would take them most of that day, Angus knew the journey would be perilous, they might run into MacLeod's at any time, they would need to pass by the Island of Rum to get to Eigg, if they were spotted by MacLeod's clansmen, they might be mistaken for a war party.

The sea journey passed by without incident, Angus was not the best sea traveller, he preferred to be on dry land, he felt a certain vulnerability while in a galley, the journey gave Angus time to ponder on what he was going to find and what he was going to do if his worst fears were confirmed, he felt cold as if a death shroud had wrapped round him, he shivered trying to shake it off, Angus believed his destiny was in Gods hands, belief in making his own future had long since disappeared.

The small galley approached the Island of Eigg, Angus raised the MacDonald banner to let the Islander's know friends were approaching, as the galley crashed up onto the shale beach there were no signs of life, they slowly made their way to the nearest croft.

Angus didn't like it there was something wrong, he pushed open the door of the first burnt out croft they came to, it was deserted apart from a few livestock roaming around, every croft was the same, Eigg is only a small Island with few inhabitants, Angus was becoming increasingly edgy, were his worst fears about to be proven true.

One of the clansmen Angus took along with him to Eigg said he knew where the secret cave was, he had been there before when he lived on Eigg as a child, Angus looked at the man and nodded, 'aye we add better go an find hoot the truth,' the cave was a distance from the crofts, located at the remotest part of the Island, no wonder it was difficult to find Angus thought to himself.

The clansmen leading the way stopped, turning to Angus he pointed to a crack in the rock, it was on a steep hill just away from the cliffs which dropped straight into the sea below, Angus looked at the man, 'a don't want ta see.'

Angus gave a nod of understanding, he slowly walked to the cave, as he got closer he could smell the cold stench of death and damp remains of burning, the entrance to the cave was chard from the fire, the remains of the fire lay scattered over the ground, they had been moved away from the cave, Angus knew someone else had been inside, was it the MacLeod's checking to make sure everyone was dead or his own clansmen, first finding the massacre.

Angus handed his shield and Red Deer cloak to one of his men, he wouldn't get through the narrow gap with them on, as he pushed through the gap the stench was horrid, nothing like he had smelt before, it was pitch black inside, he reached out through the entrance and was handed a flaming torch, pulling it back into the cave, his eyes began to adjust to the twilight the torch gave out, only then did the true horror of what happened here on that fateful day come to him, up to now he had listened to the accounts of what had happened with a degree of scepticisium, now he knew the truth.

One by one three other clansmen riddled through the cave entrance, they stood silent, the torch crackled as the flames sent shadows dancing over the bodies lying on the cave floor, 'bear witness ta what yar see, ba sure yoo tell it true.'

Angus turned, he handed the torch to the man standing next to him, he pushed his way back through the narrow entrance, the other's followed, outside the light was fading, Angus knew there was nothing they could do this day, they would need to take shelter for the night.

One of the crofts was a short walk away, they decided to camp there for the night soon after reaching the croft they had a large fire going, taking the chill out of the night air.

Angus lay looking up at the stars, clouds moved through the sky like ghostly galleys, he was uneasy, this place made him nervous, Angus decided to block up the cave as a lasting tomb instead of trying to remove the bodies.

The entrance would be closed up, he lay pondering over what to do next, a calmness had come over him, he no longer felt anger towards the MacLeod's, the feelings he held went beyond any human feeling, cold and merciless, he longed to avenge his fellow clansmen.

At first light the next day the cave entrance was being blocked up, first they piled in small rocks and smashed them into the narrow entrance, then larger rocks were wedged in, finally peat was pushed into every nock and cranny, this would allow heather to grow, over time the roots would bind the rocks together making it more difficult for anyone to discover, after they had finished their sombre task, a short prayer was said for the souls of the dead, their first task was over.

Angus wasted no time, it was as if he had stopped to carry out a duty that had to be done before he could carry on with his quest for vengeance, the events of the last few hours since he first landed on Eigg had certainly fuelled his vengeful lust, he was now more single minded than ever, even the other clansmen were taken back by his eagerness to fight the MacLeod's.

With the galley ready to sail, Angus wasted no time arguing with two of the clansmen who said they were going

Am Bratach Sith of Dunvegan

to stay on Eigg they wanted to try and rebuild the small community.

Angus agreed to send word to their families of their decision, the galley made good time back to South Uist, a stiff breeze pushed the small galley along, Angus believed it was Gods will, the galley grounded on the beach, Angus jumped off, as he was striding up the beach he yelled back orders to the other clansmen, what he wanted them to do and to meet him later at Tobha Mor.

He made straight for the small community of Ludag, Angus knew of a giant of a man who lived at Tobha Mor, a MacDonald to his very core, it didn't take long for Angus to encourage a crofter to loan him his horse, Angus was very persuasive when angry, usually the point of his sword cut out the need for debate.

Angus rode hard to Tobha Mor, the horse had never galloped for so long, just outside Howmore the horse stumbled and fell to the ground throwing Angus over it's head, Angus landed with a thump, by luck he landed in a dense clump of heather which broke his fall.

Angus rose to his feet, shaken but not hurt, he looked back at the horse, it's front leg was broken, Angus had no alternative, he drew his sword, walked slowly to the front of the horse, he held the sword in both hands, gripping the hilt as if praying, with the blade pointing down he pulled the hilt high over his head and plunged the blade deep into the horses neck between it's front legs, the horse let out a low roar of pain has it's head rose upwards, then in a moment the horse lay still.

Angus pulled the sword blade from the horse, he used the horses back to clean the blood from the blade, he stood looking at the horse for a moment then shrugged his broad shoulders and started to walk the short distance to Tobha Mor.

It didn't take long for Angus to find Murdo MacDonald, Angus arrived at his croft, 'Murdo a yoo in?' a reply came after what seemed an eternity to Angus, a low deep voice, 'who's asking?' 'Angus MacDonald,' the door was wrenched open, in the doorway stood Murdo MacDonald, his head stooped to get through the door, outside he stood up, his head was covered in long matted brown hair, a beard covered his face so much it was difficult to see any of his features, Angus wasn't a little man but Murdo made him look like a dwarf, this made Angus slightly nervous, 'walk we ma a ways will yoo?' Murdo gave one nod of his powerful head.

Angus told Murdo of the massacre on Eigg and how he had seen the remains in the cave, Angus wanted Murdo to be part of a small war party, the idea was to hit deep into MacLeod lands showing the MacLeod's once and for all if they attack the MacDonald's revenge would be hard and swift, Murdo being the sort of person he was, jumped at the chance of a fight especially with the MacLeod's.

CHAPTER TWENTY-ONE
Revenge of the MacDonald's

The day after Angus arrived at Tobha Mor, the other clansmen joined them, they set off on their quest, Murdo carried a large double bladed battle axe, a fearsome weapon it surely was.

They travelled to Loch Skinport, Murdo had friends there who would loan them galleys, as they crossed country the stiff breeze that had helped them back from Eigg was now biting into them, it carried with it cold rain, they were glad to reach Loch Skinport.

Murdo, true to his word, was greeted warmly, as they all were, that evening Angus discussed with Murdo what would cause the MacLeod's the most harm, they agreed an outright attack on Dunvegan castle would be out of the question, they agreed to land on the north west coast close to Waternish point, then they could attack crofts all the way down to Dunvegan, Angus thought it was a great plan because not only could they attack hard into MacLeod lands but they could cover their back allowing them to escape the same way as they arrived.

The mood was buoyant that night, strong drink loosened tongues, tales of past battles with other clans and other heroic deeds filled the cold evening air, grossly exaggerated of course, raising laughter from those who knew better, that evening ended all too soon, it had been a long time since Angus had felt so relaxed.

In the cold morning air Angus looked over the loch towards Skye, 'soon MacLeod, very soon,' his eyes transfixed as if he was looking straight into the heart of Dunvegan castle, Murdo slapped him on the shoulder, 'come on mon, we have a fight ta pick.'

Angus smiled to himself, 'don't worry, yoo'll noo ba away we hoot me,' they packed up their few belongings and stowed them into the small galleys, before going to Skye they were going up the coast to Loch Nam Madadh, Murdo had a cousin there he would not forgive Murdo if he went with out him.

Angus didn't mind there might be others willing to join them, he didn't want too many because a number of galleys might be spotted, where as a few may get through unnoticed.

The journey to Loch Nam Madadh seemed to take forever, the wind had dropped, the Minch became unerringly calm, in all his days Angus had never seen the Minch this calm, each man took turns in rowing the galley, they kept close to the coast of North Uist so their sails could not be seen from Skye.

Murdo laughed at Angus, 'do yoo think they can see us from Skye?' Angus was not taking any chances, he wasn't afraid of the MacLeod's, he just didn't want to run into

Am Bratach Sith of Dunvegan

a reception party when they landed, finally they reached Loch Nam Madadh, it was agreed they would rest there for the night and set sail for Skye in the morning.

Murdo managed to rally ten more MacDonald clansmen, his cousin included, to join their adventure, things were looking good, they were now forty strong, enough to cause havoc and enough not to be seen until it is too late.

Angus woke to the wind howling through the narrow windows, he went outside the rain was falling in sheets, he looked to the heavens as if thanking God for this fine weather, Murdo joined him, 'we'll have ta wait mon,' Angus gave a nod of acknowledgement, 'aye a guess we will.'

Murdo went back into the croft closely followed by Angus, all they could do is wait, the mood was quiet, as the day went on tempers began to fray, at least later on during the late afternoon the rain stopped, it was too late to set sail, they would have to wait until tomorrow.

Murdo woke Angus, 'come on mon do yoo want ta miss tha fight?' Angus woke quickly he was soon outside looking at the sunlit morning, before he really woke up he plunged his head into a water filled trough, as he pulled his head clear he sent water splashing over anyone standing close by including Murdo who was not best pleased, Murdo and water didn't mix too well.

With the galleys ready and set to sail, they were hoping the early start would get them to Skye before many of the MacLeod's were up and about, less chance of being spotted.

Angus had a good feeling about this, he was sure they would have a day to remember, as the galleys sailed ever nearer to Skye, the MacDonald clansmen became increasingly more edgy, they knew they had the element of surprise but you never know with the MacLeod's, the galleys drew closer and closer, they were now so close they could here the cattle bellowing, the wind had knocked them off course instead of beaching the galleys around Waternish point, they were sailing down towards Loch Dunvegan, that was the last place they wanted to be, they decided to beach the galleys at Ardmore point, a narrow spit of land but easier to defend, they jumped from the galleys as if expecting hoards of MacLeod's to come charging towards them, it was silent, they had got away with it.

They pulled the galleys up out of the tide, each man made himself ready for the coming fight, it was fair to say they didn't expect much opposition for a time after they had landed, if the MacLeod's knew they were coming they would have attacked them on landing as they were beached the galleys.

The war party rested a while behind a Dyke before slowly setting off towards Dunvegan, it was mid morning when they reached Trumpan, on the way they had already killed a few MacLeod's who they happened to bump into.

Trumpan was quiet, hardly anyone about, as they crept through the small community voices were heard coming from a small fane, it was Sunday, the MacLeod's from around the area had gathered in the Trumpan fane for Sunday service.

Angus could not believe his luck, God had surely delivered retribution, he gestured to Murdo, he came over, 'burn tha fane,' Murdo looked at Angus as if he was mad, 'I'll noo burn the hoose of God,' Angus shook his head,

Am Bratach Sith of Dunvegan

'don't yoo see, God has delivered them ta us, wa can avenge tha MacDonald's of Eigg.'

Angus picked up a wooden staff which was laying beside one of the crofts, he tied dry heather onto it with a piece of MacLeod plaid he found, some of the others did the same making torches out of whatever they could find, most of the crofts had fires burning, a MacDonald clansmen brought out some burning peat from one of the crofts, they approached the fane from the side where the door was, when they were close enough Angus wedged the door to stop anyone from escaping.

Inside the fane the people were oblivious to what was going on outside, until a voice was heard shouting, 'death to the MacLeod's.'

The People inside the fane began looking through the narrow windows, some of them could see Angus standing with a flaming torch in his hand, 'death ta tha MacLeod's, vengeance fa tha MacDonald's,' the people in the fane began to panic as they realized what was about to happen, they tried to push the door open, it was wedged shut, there was no way out, the windows were too narrow to escape.

Angus took great delight in setting light to the wooden fane, it burned slowly at first, he could hear the screams of the people inside, this is what he had waited months for, his revenge on the MacLeod's and there was still more to come, they left the fane to burn and all inside to perish in the flames.

Everything was going to plan, they decided to stack up everything they had looted and press on to Hallin, Stein and Lusta, they made good progress towards Hallin they again wreaked havoc killing any MacLeod they could find, there was little resistance, the MacDonald's were right no-one expected an attack from the Minch.

When they had destroyed Stein and Lusta, they decided they could not hope to go on much longer before the MacLeod's realized what was happening and mounted a counter attack, Angus wanted to push on further as far as Bay, Murdo tried to talk him out of it, 'tha MacLeod's a'll come, we need ta ba ready ta fight, better still take what we have an sail back ta Uist.'

Angus could see the logic in Murdo's words, he still wanted to kill more Macleod's, reluctantly he agreed to make their way back to the galleys, they were loaded up with loot and they still had the pile of loot at Trumpan.

When they arrived back at Trumpan the fane had burnt to the ground, they could see the chard remains of the people trapped inside, Angus thought to himself this had been a triumphant day for the MacDonald clan, when news of this reaches the other clans they will be in fear of the name MacDonald.

There was too much loot for them to carry back to the galleys, it was decided half of the men would take what they could, then return to Trumpan to help carry the rest back, all was going well, so far they had not lost a man unlike the MacLeod's, there were at least a sixty MacLeod's slain on MacLeod land.

Murdo heard a shout, he nudged Angus, in the distance they could see a party of MacLeod's, 'now yoo'll get ya fight,' Murdo said softly to Angus, 'we can take them, there's only a handful,' Angus gripped his sword turning his knuckles white, 'a think we should get back ta tha galleys Angus.' Angus looked at Murdo, for the first time he could see fear in his eyes, 'don't ba daft mon there's only a handful, wa can take them easy.'

Murdo eased back as if to start retreating, 'a sense something bad is going ta happen,' Murdo started to make his way back, they had to cover quiet a distance to get back to the galleys, all the time the MacLeod's were gaining, they tried to move quicker but the weight of the loot was holding them up, Murdo dropped his loot, 'if a'm going to fight I'm noo carrying this lot,' Angus dropped his loot as well, 'aye we can pick it up later.'

They began to run much quicker, as they approached the beach they were joined by the rest of the war party, 'now lets see who's going ta run?' Angus turned round and started to charge the MacLeod's, the others followed, the MacLeod's stopped, seeing they were out numbered they retreated, seeing the MacLeod's retreat the MacDonald's stopped and started jeering, they watched the MacLeod's disappear into the distance.

Angus decided they should stand a couple of men on guard while the others carried on taking the loot to the galleys, with all the loot on the beach they only had to launch the galleys and load the loot then they would be away.

As they were trying to launch the galleys a shout went up from the guards, the MacLeod's were making another attack, Angus looked across at Murdo, 'there must be more of them,' they all left the galleys, 'let's finish this,' Murdo glanced across to Angus, 'aye, it's time,' as they got to the top of the beach Angus could see the same number of Macleod's as before running at them, 'ma be they got courage all of a sudden?'

Murdo shrugged his heavy shoulders, 'let's noo disappoint them then,' they started to charge the MacLeod's, this time they would not back down, as the MacLeod's were running towards them their numbers seemed to grow, the Macdonald's stopped, they were now clearly out numbered and in trouble, they retreated back to the beach and started trying to launch the galleys into the receding tide, the tide had gone out further than they thought it would, leaving the galleys too far up the beach.

'Angus, look' Murdo pointed towards the skyline at the top of the beach, there stood over one hundred MacLeod clansmen, Angus drew his sword, 'we'll have ta fight are way hoot of this one lads,' Murdo stretched over the side of the galley, picking up his battle axe he started to swing it menacingly above his head, 'aye we will that Angus,' the MacLeod's took their time, they knew there would be only one outcome to this fight.

Angus was not about to die easily, he charged up the beach, his heavy sword held high above his head, Murdo close behind, the other MacDonald clansmen started to charge, in one voice the MacLeod's roared, 'MacLeod, MacLeod death ta tha MacDonald's,' the two sides clashed near the top of the beach, Angus smashed into a MacLeod knocking him over, without hesitation Angus brought his sword down plunging it deep into his rivals chest, no sooner had he dispatched one MacLeod, a sword came swinging towards him, he blocked the blow with his shield and swung his sword into the side of his opponent almost cutting him in half.

Angus was then set upon by two MacLeod's, one with an axe the other carrying a sword, they struck blows on Angus at the same time, he managed to block the axe as

Am Bratach Sith of Dunvegan

it swung towards his head, the sword dug deep into his left shoulder, he felt it smash into his collar bone, the pain didn't stop the swing of his own sword reaching it's target, cutting so deep into the MacLeod neck removing his head, his opponent slumped to the ground, his head and sword dropping beside him.

Angus again managed to block the flight of the axe as it rained down on him, this time he struggled to fend off the powerful blow, his left arm was almost useless, the axe dug into his wooden shield, the blade of the axe going clean through, it's edge cutting into his forearm, with the axe imbedded in his shield, Angus had time to stab the MacLeod in the chest, Angus was badly hurt, his left side covered in blood, he carried on fighting.

Murdo was doing much better, he had killed over ten MacLeod's without suffering any injury, his size and power made him difficult to fight, he kept swinging his battle axe round decapitating, heads, arms, anything it made contact with, he was slicing his way through the MacLeod clansmen when a spear plunged into his leg, causing him to drop onto one knee, his mighty axe fell clattering onto the blood soaked stony beach, before he could regain his defence a sword struck him on the side of his head splitting his skull in two.

The force of the deadly blow sent Murdo sprawling sideways, he fell dead on the beach, the battle was all but over, MacDonald's lay dead or dying along with a large number of MacLeod's, one body that wasn't there, was the body of Angus MacDonald, badly hurt he had witnessed Murdo being cut down, he knew he would not be killing any more MacLeod's this day, he managed to slip away from the melly, finding a place to hide, he remained there until night fell only then was he able to try and escape.

After the battle the bodies of the dead, MacDonald and MacLeod were laid side by side in a long row beside the turf dyke the MacDonald's had used for cover when they first landed on Skye, the dyke was thrown over them to form a giant tomb, from this act the battle would always be known as Blar Milleadh Garaidh or the battle of the spoiling of the dyke.

It was believed all of the MacDonald's had perished during the battle, some years later a band of MacDonald's carried out another daring raid on the MacLeod lands, they came to rustle MacLeod's cattle, this time the MacLeod's had been warned and were waiting for them at the same spot on the beach, the battle was even more bloody than the last, losses were heavy on both sides, nearly all the MacDonald's lay dead or badly injured, among the dead lay an old man, it was never proven but one clansman thought his name was Angus MacDonald.

CHAPTER TWENTY-TWO
Fairy flag unfurled

Bess MacLeod had grown into a bonnie lass, now twenty-two years old, she had not yet married, her true love, the Chief's son, who was still more interested in holding onto his youth than to contemplate marriage, even through he was now twenty-six.

Bess knew he held strong feelings for her, she was prepared to wait for him, she had more than enough to occupy her time helping her family and working at Dunvegan castle, she was staying at the castle more and more, she didn't mind because she could be close to the Chiefs son and she enjoyed looking after the Chiefs other children who were growing up fast.

Chief MacLeod had taken his children to a gathering at nearby Roskill, Bess took the opportunity to visit her family in Lusta, she left Dunvegan on the Saturday afternoon, it wasn't far but she wanted to spend some time by the Fairy bridge, it seemed ages since she had visited the bridge, it was still as it always was, the burn sparkling in the afternoon sun, which was welcome as it had been raining hard most of the day

The stiff breeze whistled through the heather and under the arch of the Fairy bridge, to Bess it sounded like gentle music, she lay on her cloak staring under the bridge, were the fairies still there, she found herself talking to them, telling them all about the Fairy flag and the fairy she found in the babies room on the night of the Chiefs sons coming of age.

Time passed slowly, Bess was becoming tired, her eyes heavy, she kept on talking, when she noticed five bright lights under the bridge, she couldn't believe her eyes, one by one the lights came from under the bridge and formed a circle round her head, one of the lights started to fade, it faded enough for Bess to see it was a fairy, Bess held out her hand, the fairy settled in the palm of her outstretched hand.

Bess drew her hand closer to her face, the fairy greeted Bess by name, 'Bess, you have always respected and never denounced the fairy people, in return for your belief, you will be protected in times of your greatest need,' the fairy bid Bess good-bye and returned to being a bright light, the fairies then disappeared back under the bridge, moments later Bess shivered, her eyes opened, she looked round, the burn was still playfully dancing under the Fairy bridge as it made it's way to the loch.

Had she fallen asleep and dreamed about the fairies, no she couldn't have they were real, they always were, she rose to her feet still puzzled, picking up her cloak she noticed it was quite dry yet the ground was wet from the rain, Bess said her good-byes to the fairies under the bridge and carried on with her journey.

Am Bratach Sith of Dunvegan

She reached her parents home as the sun was disappearing over North Uist, the weather at the end of the day was better than at the start, David and Megan were naturally always pleased to welcome their daughter back home, David didn't go to the castle that often these days, he was slowly going blind, he believed it was part of the witches curse laid on him all those years ago.

Megan would tell him not to talk rubbish he was getting older that's all, Bess told them what happened at the Fairy bridge and what the fairy had told her, David and Megan were as puzzled as Bess, what could they mean by, 'at the time of her greatest need,' the conversation soon changed.

David was as always only too happy when darkness fell so he could talk, Megan often remarked to Bess he would talk so much she believed he was trying to cram everything he had to say in a few short hours especially during the summer when the days were long and nights short, Bess talked to David for hours, Megan decided to go to bed, she reminded David not to be up too long they had to be up early as they were going to Trumpan.

As Megan had warned David, she was up at the crack of dawn, David wanted to carry on sleeping, she ended up pulling him out of bed much to the delight of Bess, she was happy to see her parents were still full of the fun and mischief she remembered as a child.

With breakfast out of the way it was time to start off for Trumpan, Megan wanted to visit friends in Trumpan, they had been going to visit for ages but never got round to it, Megan had baked some bread and cakes to take with them, it was a fine day for walking, they reached Trumpan at mid morning, Megan taking great delight in exchanging the bread and cakes she brought with her, for the pies her friend had made.

David and Bess tagged along, no-one really tried to talk to David because he couldn't hear them, they would nod in a form of greeting, he would nod back in return and smile, David didn't mind he said he would watch people, it was surprising how easily he could tell if they were being honest or not by how they looked and moved.

Megan often asked him at night what he thought about things that had happened during the day, she had said to Bess before how intuitive David was.

It was time to go to the fane, a small church, there was a priest visiting from the mainland, they did not want to miss his service, the local priest was alright but his services had become boring, many of the Islanders were starting to believe they were better served by the old gods rather than Christ and the almighty, at least the old gods didn't stop you having fun, in fact some of the pagan celebrations were the highlights of the year.

They walked to the fane with their friends, inside the small fane it was packed, MacLeod's had come from all over the area to hear the service, the local priest accompanied his visitor.

The service was well under way, when there appeared to be some kind of disturbance outside, people were trying to see what was going on through the small windows, David was standing at the back of the fane against the door, he couldn't hear what was being said anyway, he would wait till tonight.

Megan would tell him all about it, David felt the door push against his back as if someone was trying to get in, he tried to push the door open it was jammed, he pushed it

Am Bratach Sith of Dunvegan

hard, it still wouldn't open, people began to become uneasy, outside a voice was heard, it wasn't clear, someone said it sounded like, 'death ta tha MacLeod's,' and something about the MacDonald's, the Islanders who could see out of the window saw Angus MacDonald standing with a blazing torch, a cry went up in the fane, 'tha gonna burn tha fane.'

Panic started to consume the Islanders trapped in the fane, the men were trying to push the door open, it was so full of people they couldn't get a good push on it, soon smoke started to fill the fane people were being trampled under foot as they dropped to the floor choking from the smoke and fumes, the smoke was so thick David could not find Megan or Bess, they had been standing at the front.

David was pushed against the door, he began to suffocate from the smoke and the weight of people pinning him against the door in their vein efforts to escape, the smoke started to give way as flames began to engulf the wooden building, within minutes the fane was a ball of fire.

Outside the MacDonald's having carried out their deed were in agreement no-one inside the fane would survive the flames they decided to move to the next village to seek more plunder and kill more MacLeod's.

Bess found herself kneeling on the floor holding the body of her dead mother, she could not see David or anyone else alive, out of the flames came a bright light, as it faded, a fairy spoke to her, 'you must escape through the window,' at first she was reluctant to leave her mother, let alone climb through a burning window, the fairy spoke again, 'you must warn the Chief or others will die it is your destiny,' Bess gently placed Megan's body on the floor, she kissed Megan on the forehead.

As Bess approached the window she felt a cold wind blow, it blew out the flames from around the window, as she gripped the hot wood it gave way, she began to pull the wood to make a hole big enough for her to escape.

As soon as she started to climb through, the wood began to burn again, she fell from the burning window to the floor, there was burning all around her as bits began to fall away from the fane, she had to get help, she began to run towards Dunvegan castle, her legs began to tire, telling herself to keep going, tears filled her eyes thinking about David and Megan, as she ran over the Fairy bridge she blacked out, a few moments later she came to, she was lying beside the sea gate in Dunvegan castle.

How did she get there, she snapped out of her thoughts, 'tha fane, tha MacDonald's,' she ran up the stairs to the castle shouting for the Chief, she suddenly remembered the Chief was not there, no-one was, even most of the clansmen had gone to the gathering with the Chief, she told the few men who were left guarding the castle what had happened.

Leaving the minimum of men behind to guard the castle about fifteen MacLeod clansmen headed off towards Trumpan to hold off the MacDonald's, while one rode to tell the Chief and gather reinforcements.

Bess stood thinking, surely there was more she could do, what could she do, 'tha Fairy flag,' she ran up the stairs to the Chiefs main room, she knew he kept the Fairy flag somewhere in this room but where, she pulled open draws, opened chests, where was it, as she was pulling trying to open a stiff draw in a dresser, the dresser rocked forward, one of the small doors in the bottom of the dresser opened.

Bess was so amazed she had the strength to move such a heavy dresser, she didn't notice the door of the dresser had opened until she hit her shin on the open door at first she grabbed her shin, it was so painful, she went to slam the door shut in temper, as she did there in the opening was the box she remembered seeing at her father's house, when the Chief went to find the Fairy cloth.

She grabbed the box in both hands, the pain of her shin was forgotten, the lid to the box was tight she clawed at it so hard she broke her finger nails so low down they started to bleed, finally the lid came open, she gently removed the Fairy flag, she unfurled it exposing the bright yellow colour with a delicate red berry pattern, Bess ran back to the sea gate, the boat had gone, the clansmen had taken it to the shore, she could swim but not that well, 'come on Bess,' she said to herself, 'the keep,' she could wave the banner from the tower if it was magical surely it would work from there, it had too.

Lady MacLeod was having the Fairy tower built following the appearance of the fairy at the side of her youngest sons cot, five years previous, although the tower was not yet finished Bess was sure she could climb to the top, and then onto the keep, the highest point of Dunvegan Castle.

It only took her a few minutes before she was standing on the top of the keep, she could see the smoke in the distance still bellowing up from the fane, she didn't know what else to do other than to stand there and wave the Fairy flag over her head, she found a length of wood at the top of the tower, it looked like a flag pole.

Bess tied the Fairy flag to the pole using a tie from round her skirt, she began to lift the heavy pole, holding it upright was not as easy as she thought it would be, the breeze held the Fairy flag out for all to see.

The clansmen who had first left Dunvegan castle to challenge the MacDonald's were in some disarray, when they confronted the MacDonald's, they hadn't expected to find so many of them, they decided to retreat and make a stand if they came any further, otherwise wait for reinforcements to arrive, thinking it would be sometime before the Chief got there they settled down for a long wait.

Suddenly out of nowhere dozens of MacLeod clansmen were running through the heather towards them, all with a cry of, 'MacLeod, MacLeod, death ta tha MacDonald's,' stunned at first the small group picked up their weapons, the clansmen swept passed them, then they knew they weren't dreaming, they ran after them catching up with them on the top of the beach, the MacLeod's stood shoulder to shoulder in a long line, no words were uttered, they just stood looking at the small band of MacDonald's busy trying to launch their galleys.

Soon the MacDonald's realised they would not escape, first one of them charged at the MacLeod line, followed by a giant of a man wielding the biggest battle axe you could imagine, without any order the MacLeod line shouted, 'MacLeod, MacLeod, death ta tha MacDonald's,' as they began to charge forward, the fight was brutal no quarter asked for or given.

When the MacLeod Chief arrived the battle was neither won or lost, he had brought another hundred clansmen

Am Bratach Sith of Dunvegan

with him, they soon joined the melly, the numbers were too much for the MacDonald's, they were soon defeated.

At the end of the battle the MacLeod Chief reported none of the MacDonald's had survived, the original fifteen MacLeod's who had first confronted the MacDonald's all survived with minor injuries as did the clansmen with the Chief, as none of the MacLeod clansmen who had died in battle appeared to be known which seemed strange at the time, it was decided to line the bodies up with the bodies of the MacDonald's and bury them using the earth from a nearby dyke.

Bess finally gave up waving the Fairy flag, she was too tired to hold the flag pole any longer, it dropped bouncing on the edge of the Fairy tower, as the pole bounced it jarred the Fairy flag loose, the flag floated gently through the air, after a while, still dejected the flag hadn't produced the magic it was supposed to and her efforts had counted for nothing, she thought she had better replace the flag to the box before the Chief returned other wise she would be in a lot of trouble for going through his personal things.

She looked at the end of the pole the Fairy flag had gone, the fairies must have claimed it back because she had used it without just cause, she looked round, the flag was nowhere to be seen, the reality of what had happened began to dawn on Bess, she could not believe her mother and father were dead, burnt to death for nothing, she went to the Chiefs room and started to tidy up, placing the empty box on the top of the dresser, she knew she had to tell the Chief what she had done.

It was nearly dark before the Chief returned, Lady MacLeod had returned earlier, Bess had told her what a fool she had been losing the Fairy flag, Lady MacLeod told her she had done it for the best reasons and she would be with her when she told the Chief.

Bess was waiting nervously in the great hall, Chief MacLeod entered the hall along with Lady MacLeod following close behind, he stared at Bess, 'tell ma lassie what have yoo been up ta?' Bess started to ramble, 'noo, noo lassie start from tha beginning,' the Chief interrupted, Bess started to tell him everything that had happened.

She was fighting back tears as she told her story, 'a'm truly sorry aboot tha Fairy flag,' the Chief started to laugh, 'it was a'll down ta yoo, was it lassie?' he then told Bess about the unknown clansmen and how her actions had saved many MacLeod lives, he pushed his hand inside his shirt and pulled out the Fairy flag, Bess could not believe it 'where did ya find it?' the Chief looked at her and winked, 'tha fairies gave it ta ma' he handed the flag to Bess 'better put it back lassie, till next time.'

CHAPTER TWENTY-THREE
Christmas in November

Much to Lucy's disappointment Iain stopped telling the story, 'a think we add better help ya mother don't yoo?' Lucy reluctantly agreed, she eased herself off Iain's lap for a moment and stood staring into the fire, Iain broke her gaze, banging his pipe on the hearth, 'come on Lucy,' he held her hand as they went to join Anne in the kitchen, 'what can we do ta help?' Iain asked hopefully, without looking up Anne replied, 'yoo can lay tha table.'

Iain removed the table cloth from the kitchen draw, he took hold of the end and in one movement he unfolded the cloth and bellowed it across the table, Lucy grabbed the other end as it flapped in front of her, she straightened it and pulled it tight across the table to remove any creases.

One of the kitchen draws was full of cutlery, Iain began to count out three knives, six forks and three spoons, he handed them to Lucy, she banged them on the table in one heap before starting to lay them in place order.

The knives and forks were the wrong way round but that didn't matter, she had tried, while Lucy was doing that Iain was putting out the condiments, pepper, salt and home made raspberry jelly. Raspberries grew wild around the cottage, Anne had found a patch where the biggest sweetest raspberries she had ever seen grew, this year had been a very good year for raspberries, she had made lots of jam, jelly and chutney, the table was set.

Anne had taken the goose out of the oven, it smelt gorgeous, Lucy wanted to eat the crisp skin, 'noo lass, it's ta hot,' Anne tapped Lucy on the hand as she tried to remove part of the goose skin, much to Lucy's disgust, 'oh mummy,' she cried, Anne smiled at her, 'yoo can have some in a wee while when it's cooled doon,' the compromise seemed to appease Lucy.

With the potatoes and carrots strained and ready to be served, Iain was ready to carve the Goose, not before Lucy had got her piece of skin, Iain gently removed a large piece of crisp skin from the goose breast, he gave it to Lucy, she folded it into a cone shape before beginning to eat, the goose grease dripped from the corners of her mouth, she wiped it from her chin with the back of her hand, 'use a tea towel,' Anne insisted, Iain began to carve the breast of the goose, he carved enough for their dinner and left the rest to cool.

Anne had done them proud, their plates were piled high with the best Christmas dinner they had ever seen, before they started to eat, Iain said grace, he thanked the lord for their meal, for their good health and for blessing him with such a loving family, Lucy could not wait for Iain to finish.

Anne looked across the table, her eyes meeting with Iain's, she smiled at his words and wrinkled her nose in acknowledgement, Lucy was by now tucking into her

Am Bratach Sith of Dunvegan

dinner, Anne received compliments on how tasty the dinner was which she accepted in her own good grace.

Iain suggested they should go for a walk after dinner across the moor, Anne and Lucy both thought that was a good idea, 'don't forget you've ta finish tha story daddy,' Lucy looked at Iain 'a will nay forget, a'll finish it latter.'

With the plates almost clear of any food, dinner was over, Lucy knew what was to come next, Christmas pudding, she loved Christmas pudding, not only did it taste good but the fairies may have put a farthing in the pudding, she liked farthings because they had a robin on them.

Anne removed the pudding from the range where it had been steaming most of the morning, it was covered with a cloth, in a large pot basin, Anne unwrapped the cloth from the top of the pudding and placed a plate over the top of the basin then holding the basin and the plate she turned them over and removed the basin, she then unwrapped the pudding, it was dark and piping hot, Anne placed a sprig of holly in the top of the pudding, Lucy smiled, she thought her mummy was so clever, Iain started to pour whiskey over the pudding, he struck a match and held it close to the pudding, in an instant the pudding was ablaze, Lucy's eyes were wide open in amazement, the flames soon died down, 'who wants pudding?' Anne was of course kidding, she already knew the answer, 'a do mummy,' Lucy bit at Anne's suggestion that one of them may not want any.

Iain smiled and shook his head, he was not going to rise to her comment, the pudding was so rich it hurt their teeth, the whiskey and rum in the pudding cut through the sweetness like a knife through butter, this was indeed a king of puddings, seconds was the order of the day, leaving them all well and truly stuffed.

'Who's going ta wash up then?' Anne looked at Iain and Lucy, they both groaned, 'in a wee while' Iain sighed, after a few minutes Anne got up, 'a suppose a'll have ta do it?' Iain reluctantly followed her into the kitchen carrying the pudding dishes.

'Lucy come an dry tha dishes,' Iain was not going to let her get away without helping, 'daddy must a?' Lucy began to walk slowly to the kitchen, 'aye, if we all help it'll get done quicker,' Iain handed her a tea towel, Lucy reluctantly accepted.

While Anne washed the pots, Iain and Lucy dried them, it didn't take long before everything that could be, was cleared away, Anne made a cup of tea, Iain went and sat by the fire and lit his pipe, Lucy was on the settee half sitting, half lying, she was too full to know what to do for the best.

Anne came through with the tea and a cup of sweet hot milk for Lucy, they sat in silence for a few minutes, Iain gently puffing on his pipe, Anne sitting back in her chair holding her cup in both hands as if warming herself, Lucy was staring into the fire, 'drink ya milk afore it gets cold,' Anne's words broke Lucy's day dream, 'aye, mummy a will,' she began to drink.

Iain placed his empty cup on the hearth in the spot where he always did, he gave a puff on his pipe releasing a cloud of smoke into the room, 'what aboot a walk then?' the response from Anne and Lucy was at best half hearted, 'aye come on will yoo, get ya coats on,' Iain was not going to take no for an answer, he tapped his pipe on the hearth and got up, he pulled Anne to her feet and started to tickle

Am Bratach Sith of Dunvegan

Lucy until she agreed to go for a walk, she giggled so much it hurt and she nearly wet herself. After she had been to the toilet, they soon had their coats, hats, gloves, scarves and boots on and were ready to venture into the cold freezing afternoon, 'we must ba mad leaving a warm hoose ta walk in this cold,' Anne looked at Iain, he smiled back, he knew there was nothing she liked better than to walk in the snow.

The early afternoon sun hung low in the sky, like a big orange, it's strength hardly enough to feel in the bitter cold, they decided to walk up through the old lane to the devils cauldron, it wouldn't take them long, Lucy as always went running off in front, the snow came to the top of her wellies, so she found walking difficult let alone running, Anne held on to Iain's arm, she felt she needed to be close to him.

When they reached the waterfall, known to locals as the Devils caldron, Lucy was already throwing stones into the deep pool at the bottom of the falls, it was said if you throw stones into the pool the devil would rise up and take you into the underworld.

Iain shouted to Lucy, ' ba careful tha devil will take yoo,' Lucy let out a cheeky yet shrill laugh as if she half knew the devil would not appear but still was not sure, Iain sat down beside Anne on a flat rock at the top of the falls, she rested her head on Iain's shoulder 'It's beautiful here, a wish ta day would never end.'

Iain knew she was thinking about tomorrow, when he would be leaving to return to his squadron, he put his arm round her shoulder, 'don't worry lassie a'll ba back afor ya noo a've gone,' Anne looked up at Iain, 'a hope so, a'm frightened a losing yoo,' Iain squeezed her tight 'a noo lassie, a noo,' the water poured over the falls crashing into the pool at the bottom in a constant rumble, a steam rose from the water into the cold air causing a mist that hung like smoke from the cauldron. 'Come on Lucy afor tha devil gets yoo,' Lucy didn't need telling twice, as soon as she thought she would be on her own she ran back towards Iain and Anne, "better ba making tracks afor it gets too dark,' the walk home was enjoyable.

Lucy was as always out in front not to far as the late evening sun was quickly being replaced by one of those mysterious twilights that played tricks on your eyes, it had you imagining you could see things that were not there.

Iain talked with Anne all the way home, they talked about what they would do after the war, Anne wanted to redecorate the lounge, Iain thought about moving to one of the cities, he believed jobs would be plentiful and the money good, Anne wasn't keen on that she liked the cottage and the solitude, Iain was concerned Lucy would not have many friends to play with.

Anne went quiet, she thought Iain was referring to her not being able to have any other children, he reassured her he didn't mean that, he just thought that's all.

Lucy had done well they were nearly home, she was tiring fast, Iain picked her up and put her on his shoulders, she giggled constantly as Iain jogged like a horse bumping her up and down, Anne took the opportunity to throw snowballs at both of them, knowing it was difficult for Iain to throw any back, just before they reached home Iain put Lucy down they both made snowballs and threw them at Anne, she didn't stand a chance, one after another hit her on the head, side and back until she lost her footing and fell backwards into a snowdrift.

Am Bratach Sith of Dunvegan

Iain held out his hand to help her up, she was laughing so much she couldn't get to her feet, he bent down to pick her up, as he did Anne grabbed him and pulled him head first into the snow, they both lay laughing, Lucy decided to join in by trying to cover them in snow, Iain grabbed her leg and pulled her over she landed with a bump on the soft snow.

They were all covered in snow, the late evening had turned to an eerie darkness, the snow made everything visible yet ghostly, a fat moon shone beams of light across the virgin snow, like magic it glistened like millions of sequins scattered over the moors, Lucy ran round trying to collect some of the magic twinkles, every-time she got close they disappeared, 'come on Lucy time ta get inside,' Iain called as he was helping Anne to her feet, they dusted off the snow and walked the short distance to the cottage.

Stamping their feet at the back door to remove the snow off their Wellington boots, Lucy was almost running on the spot, 'steady on lassie, a think that'll doo,' Anne tried to calm Lucy down, inside the cottage the warmth hit them like a furnace, Iain had made up the fires before they had gone out, they were roaring away.

Lucy shrugged off her coat and wellies, leaving them for Anne to pick up, she ran towards the fire, standing in front of the fire she began to slowly remove her hat, scarf and gloves, one by one she let them drop to the floor, 'Lucy pick them up at once,' Anne was not amused by Lucy's behaviour, Lucy was transfixed by the fire, it's flaming fingers reached out to her as if to coax her nearer, Anne shook Lucy's shoulders, 'a will nee tell yoo again, pick them up,' this startled Lucy, she quickly bent down to pick up the items she had dropped, she took them to the hall cupboard and hung them up as she was told.

Iain had cleaned off the rest of the snow from their boots, he placed them in a row by the back door, he stood back looking at them as if thinking what a good job he had done, Anne soon served up large mugs of hot milk, they sat by the fire, recalling their latest adventure.

Iain maintaining he had won the snowball fight, Lucy was having none of it, she was pulling at Anne's dress, 'tell im mummy we won, we won,' Anne held her arm, 'he's only teasing, stop it Iain yoo'll make a cry,' Iain held his arms open, Lucy didn't need any other encouragement she pulled herself clear of Anne's grasp and jumped onto Iain's lap, she snuggled into his thick warm woollen jumper, after a while she looked up at Iain, 'don't go daddy, please doon't go.'

Iain slowly took his pipe from his mouth, he held it at arms length over the side of the chair towards the fire, he was thinking of what to say, 'a have ta go back tomorrow lassie or the policeman a'll take ma away ta prison, yoo would nay want that now would yoo?' Lucy snuggled back into Iain's jumper, 'noo daddy,' Anne had been holding her mug of milk on the arm of her chair, she took a sip, it was cool enough to drink, 'drink ya milk Lucy while it's still hot,' she bent down to pick up Lucy's mug, Lucy held out her hands to receive the mug of milk, 'thank yoo mummy,' she smiled at Anne and started to sip the hot milk.

After they had finished their milk Lucy took the mugs into the kitchen and carefully placed them on the draining board, she came skipping back into the lounge, 'daddy can yoo tell ma more of tha story?' Iain peered over the top of his book, 'a suppose a'll have ta orr you'll have ta wait till

Am Bratach Sith of Dunvegan

a come home next time,' he placed his bookmark carefully in the book and put it down by the side of the chair, Lucy climbed back onto his lap, she wriggled to make herself comfortable, 'right noo were did a get ta?' Lucy was quick to put Iain on track.

CHAPTER TWENTY-FOUR
Dark days of Dunvegan

Following that fateful day at Trumpan the Fairy flag has never been unfurled again as a battle banner, having been used twice the next time the Chief MacLeod asks for the assistance from the fairies it would need to be for the most extreme need, the third and last time it may be used would be to secure the very existence of the clan or Dunvegan castle.

When unfurled again the Fairy flag will once again provide the necessary assistance to the MacLeod Clan, then the person who unfurled the Fairy flag will disappear forfeiting their human existence, returning the Fairy flag to whence it came.

There have been many occasions the Fairy flag could have been used, one such incident also proved to be one of the darkest periods in the clans turbulent history when the very existence of the MacLeod Clan was under threat from within the clan.

In 1552 William the ninth Chief of MacLeod died, his two brothers Donald and Torquil were absent from

Dunvegan and Skye, Ian the fair-haired was chosen by the clansman to be Chief of the MacLeod's, as he was a descendent of the sixth Chief, this arrangement was to be good until Donald or Torquil returned.

Donald the eldest brother returned to find Ian the fair-haired as Chief, Donald called a meeting of the clansman at Lyndale, he had called the meeting in order to instate himself as Chief of the clan. In Donald's absence Ian the fair-haired had wooed enough of the clansmen with inducements of rank within the clan they again chose Ian to be their Chief.

His short time as Chief has since never been recognized as legitimate by the clan as an heredity claim, following the meeting at Lyndale, Donald decided to retire to Kingsburgh rather than cause unwanted trouble within the clan.

Soon after his exile in Kingsburgh Donald was sort out by Ian Dubh, his attentions were not particularly welcomed by Donald but he managed to worm his way into Donald's circle of friends. Ian Dubh found out as much as he could about Dunvegan castle, after a few weeks Donald was enticed to a meeting with Ian Dubh at midnight, on the grounds that Ian had vital information that would help Donald regain his true status as Chief of the Clan MacLeod.

Donald arrived at a secluded croft along with six MacLeod Clansman, as they approached he could see a at least two figures in the dimly lit croft, he felt something was wrong, he knocked the door, as it opened, standing in the doorway was Ian Dubh, he nodded in recognition and held out his hand in greeting, Ian Dubh did not move.

Am Bratach Sith of Dunvegan

Donald was suddenly struck from behind by at least one of the clansman, he fell to his knees, his first instinct was to feel the back of his head with his hand, as he drew his hand back it was covered in blood, he pulled a dirk from his boot, his eyes were blurred from the first blow, he slashed out as one of the figures moved in front of him, who ever it was received a deep gash to their side.

Donald was attacked again, this time the weapon was steel, he felt the blade sink deep into his back and emerge through his chest, the blade was twisted to inflict further damage, as quick as it was plunged into him it was withdrawn, he fell to his side gasping for a breath he would never take, his last vision was that of Ian Dubh grinning at him while holding a blood drenched sword.

On hearing of the circumstances that surrounded Donald's death Ian the fair-haired ordered the arrest of Ian Dubh, who happened to be his own son.

Ian Dubh proved difficult to arrest, he evaded capture on numerous occasions, before he could be arrested Ian the fair-haired died, this again left the MacLeod clan without a Chief and in disarray.

On hearing of his father's death, Ian Dubh could not believe his luck; he headed towards Dunvegan castle with a small body of clansmen, with the intention of proclaiming himself Chief of the Clan MacLeod.

Tormod the eldest son of Ian the fair-haired was already dead, he had left three young sons who would hold the right to claim the next in line to be Chief of the Clan MacLeod, Donald Breac, brother of Ian Dubh was their guardian, on their arrival at Dunvegan castle following the funeral of their father, they found Ian Dubh already in residence.

On the young sons behalf Donald Breac pressed their claim to be Chief of MacLeod, Ian Dubh allowed them to enter Dunvegan castle in order to discuss their claim, Donald opened the sea gate, he stepped from the boat and tied it securely.

While the boys were getting out of the boat Donald decided to find Ian Dubh, he started up the narrow stairs towards the doorway to the castle, the door opened, Donald stopped, in the doorway stood Ian Dubh wearing full armour, Donald tried to reason with Ian, telling him he had no rights to Dunvegan or to be Chief of the Clan MacLeod, Ian said nothing.

Donald looked back at the boys, he felt for his sword, he knew one way or another history would be made this day, he ran up the steps toward Ian, his sword already slashing through the air into the attack, Ian did not move, he knew Donald was a better swordsman, that's why he had put on the armour, despite Ian's advantage the first strike went to Donald, his sword banging into Ian's right thigh splitting the armour and gashing Ian's leg, this caused Ian to step backwards allowing Donald to get to the top of the stairs,

Ian had lost the height advantage, Donald was spurred on by his success, with Ian in retreat Donald rained blow after blow onto Ian's armour, all Ian could do was defend himself, without the armour the fight would have been over but what Donald held in sword skill and power, Ian matched in cunning.

He knew he would get at least one chance, all he had to hope was it came early enough to make the difference, just in case Ian had made sure his loyal clansmen were at hand to defend him if he looked like being defeated, after all if Ian was beaten they would lose their recently gained power.

Donald became more confident as the fight went on that was to be his downfall, he caught Ian with one powerful blow to the side knocking Ian against the wall, Ian appeared to have lost the strength to defend himself, as Donald raised his sword above his head to bring down on Ian's undefended head and neck, he was distracted by one of the clansmen close by moving in to join the fight, this was the opportunity Ian had been waiting for, he brought his sword round in a one swiping movement, the blade hit Donald just above his waist cutting into him like a scythe through dry golden corn, the fight was over.

Donald fell to the ground, Ian showed no mercy to his brother leaving him there to die an agonising death, Ian Dubh wasted no time, he looked over to the stairs leading to the sea gate, the three brothers looked on in disbelief, one of them snapped out of the gaze and started to run back down the stairs to the boat, the others quickly followed, closely followed by Ian Dubh, he cut down one of the brothers half way down the stairs cutting off his head in a single swipe of his heavy sword, the decapitated body fell withering down the stairs onto the legs of the next brother knocking him over and banging his head onto the stone steps.

Ian stepped over the two bodies to reach the last brother who was desperately trying to untie the boat from it's mooring, Donald had moored the boat well, the last brother looked up to see Ian standing over him, at the back of Ian lay his two brothers one, clearly dead, the other groaning from the injuries he received during his fall down the stairs, the last brother stood up in defiance of Ian Dubh, the boy said nothing not even a plea for his life.

For a moment this took Ian by surprise, he stared at his nephew, his cold steely eyes showed no sign of mercy, the boys eyes moved down and became fixed on Ian's sword as it slowly raised, the point level with his chest, Ian drew back the sword and thrust it so hard into the boys chest it went straight through him and knocked him back into the boat at the same time.

The boy was dead before his body crashed into the boat, the boat slowly started to drift away from it's moorings, the untied rope slipping through the metal mooring ring, Ian Dubh hadn't spotted this he was more concerned about the other brother who lay dazed on the steps, this time there was no hesitation, with one skull splitting blow of his sword, the last boy lay dead beside the feet of his brother, with no other boat available Ian Dubh could only stand and look on as the small boat drifted down the loch towards the sea.

Ian Dubh was now in a position of strength, not only had he dispatched his main rivals but he held the wives and children of the other leaders of the clan, within Dunvegan castle and dungeons, who by his good fortune were already in the castle when he arrived, this ensured he would not be opposed by any of the Clan leaders.

The MacLeod clan was now to be helped by an unlikely source, the only remaining child of the ninth chief was Mary, she was under the guardianship of the Clan Campbell, Ian Dubh hadn't really considered Mary to be a threat, he misjudged the Campbell's thirst for power, if Mary became Chief, they would gain control of the MacLeod Clan and lands through Mary, the Campbell's

Am Bratach Sith of Dunvegan

landed a large war party at Roag in Loch Bracadale, south of Dunvegan, this alone was an act of defiance towards Ian Dubh.

History shown there were not many times any other clan had taken on the MacLeod Clan on their own doorstep, knowing he was out numbered and unable to rely on the assistance of the MacLeod Clansmen outside of the castle, Ian Dubh decided to take the initiative and arrange a meeting to discuss terms with the Campbell's, the meeting was to be held in a church at Kilmuir, Ian Dubh had spent his time at Dunvegan looking for the Fairy flag, he had heard the stories of it's power and that it could be only used once more, his intention was to persuade one of the MacLeod leaders by using the threat of death of his wife and children, to use the Fairy flag against the Campbell's, knowing if the prophecy was true the person who used the Fairy flag the third time would disappear leaving the Campbell's defeated and himself in a stronger position, to take control of the Clan MacLeod.

None of the prisoners held, either knew or would tell Ian Dubh where the Fairy flag was kept, he had searched everywhere, he became more anxious to find the flag, he started to torture the children in front of their mothers who pleaded with Ian, they didn't know where the Fairy flag was.

Time had run out, Ian Dubh had to meet with the Campbell's at Kilmuir church, he decided to agree to relinquish his claim to be MacLeod Chief in favour of Mary, in return, he wanted lands to secure his new status as a Clan leader, this was agreed on Mary's behalf by the Campbell Chieftain's, in return Ian Dubh invited the Campbell Chieftain's to a feast at Dunvegan castle.

All appeared well, the Campbell Chieftains arrived as planned, Ian Dubh acknowledged as a mark of the new friendship between the Campbell's and the MacLeod's, he placed each of the Campbell Chieftain's between two MacLeod Clansmen, the feast went without problem or confrontation, towards the end of the feast a cup of blood instead of wine was placed in front of each of the Campbell Chieftains, on a prearranged signal given by Ian Dubh each of the Campbell Chieftain's was held first by one MacLeod clansman while the other stabbed the Chieftain in the throat, their bodies were returned to the Campbell's camp at Kilmuir, without their Chieftain's the Campbell clansmen had no option other than to return back to their own lands, leaving Ian Dubh again in control of Dunvegan.

Over the coming years Ian Dubh's power grew stronger to the point he began to believe he would not be challenged for Dunvegan, in 1559 the brother of the Ninth Chief, Torquil MacLeod had other ideas, he arrived at Dunvegan to press his claim as the rightful Chief of the Clan MacLeod, instead of confronting Ian Dubh he decided to carry out a covert attack on Dunvegan.

Ian Dubh had made numerous enemies within the MacLeod Clan and Dunvegan castle, Torquil MacLeod didn't find it difficult to persuade one of the castle wardens by the name of Torquil MacSween to ensure the sea gate was open in order to allow his fellow clansmen access to the castle during the night.

The plan was set, all was ready for a small number of MacLeod clansmen loyal to Torquil MacLeod to take over Dunvegan castle, Torquil MacLeod chose a moonlit night so they didn't have to use torches, the small war party

Am Bratach Sith of Dunvegan

approached Dunvegan from down the loch, as arranged, the sea gate was open, quietly the war party made it's way into the castle and one by one they overpowered the castle wardens.

Everything was going to plan until one of the war party stumbled over a small iron cauldron left in a passageway to cool, the passageway was dark, the cauldron made enough noise as it rolled down the passageway to wake the whole castle including Ian Dubh.

He looked out of the window, he could see a number of people moving around in the moonlight, it soon dawned on him the castle was under attack, he quickly dressed and made his way to the ground floor avoiding any contact with whoever was attacking the castle.

His galley was moored just off the castle, he decided to try and get to it, he would take stock once aboard, his luck held once again, no-one was guarding the sea gate, he slowly rowed one of the boats left by the attackers to his galley, once aboard he could see all was lost, the rest of his men were fleeing from the castle, some of them in the two remaining boats by the sea gate, he called for them to join him, with no boats to give chase, Torquil MacLeod called to Ian Dubh warning him never to set foot on MacLeod lands again or he would be killed.

The wives and children of the clan leaders were released from the dungeons and Dunvegan castle to rejoin their kinfolk, once again succession of the MacLeod Chieftains had been restored, one of the wives who had been held prisoner had hidden the Fairy flag to stop Ian Dubh getting hold of it, she returned the flag to Torquil MacLeod before leaving Dunvegan.

Ian Dubh managed to escape, making his way to Harris, he was soon again in fear of his life, news spread to Harris about what had happened at Dunvegan, he again decided to make an early escape, this time to Ireland.

He tried to raise a war party in Ireland, promising the Irish Chieftains lands on Skye if they helped him attack Dunvegan, news of this reached the Chief of the O'Donnell's, he agreed to meet with Ian Dubh.

On entering O'Donnell castle Ian Dubh was confronted by the Chief who was a past friend of the Ninth Chief of MacLeod, fearing the worst Ian Dubh tried to lie about the events that had happened on Skye, the O'Donnell Chief was not a very forgiving man, Ian Dubh's luck had finally run out, he was beaten and put to death by having a red hot iron pushed into his stomach through his bowels.

CHAPTER TWENTY-FIVE
Fight for freedom

Apart from defending their own lands and interests the Clan MacLeod has remained loyal to the sovereignty of Scotland, as a country in it's own right or when applicable the sovereign of Britain, this, over time caused even more conflict with other clans and along with other clans caused the MacLeod's to lose many of it's brave clansmen in battles where they have been on opposing sides. On many occasions the inability of the clans to stand together because they were not prepared to recognise and show loyalty to one heir to the Crown of Scotland, only resulted in Scotland being ruled by an English Monarch, who have in turn bribed the Clan Chieftains with lands in England to ensure the clans remain divided and the Scottish people to remain weak as a nation.

On the few occasions when the majority of the clans have been prepared to bury their differences and stand together they have succeeded in bringing a Scottish Monarch to the throne of Scotland.

The MacLeod clan fought along side Robert the Bruce, James 3rd and Charles 2nd after supporting Charles 2nd at the battle of Worcester, in 1651 it was acknowledged by the rest of the clan's because the MacLeod Clan had lost so many of it's clansman, they would not be expected to field clansmen in any further conflict until the Clan had recovered it's losses.

It has always been suspected many of the MacLeod Clansmen became part of the uprising along side William Wallace in 1297 bringing freedom to Scotland from English rule.

Following the execution of Sir William Wallace for treason by Edward 1 (the Longshanks), king of England, who himself died soon after, leaving a weak son to take the field against Robert the Bruce for the throne of Scotland.

Facing a well armed English army at Bannockburn in 1314 which far out numbered his own army of battle weary half starved countryman, Robert the Bruce won the right to restore a Scottish Monarch to the throne of Scotland.

Over generations the MacLeod Clan has suffered sacrifice, after sacrifice of it's clansmen in the cause of reinstating a Scottish king to the throne of Scotland, it was only at the start of the Jacobite rebellion of 1745 did the Chief of MacLeod decide not to formally field the MacLeod Clan in support of Prince Charles Edward Stuart.

Many of the MacLeod Clan did however take up arms in the ill-fated rebellion again showing their worth to any Scottish army.

Following the Jacobite defeat, 'Bonnie Prince Charlie' made his escape to France through the Highlands and Islands, the Chief of MacLeod was one of the Chieftains

Am Bratach Sith of Dunvegan

who had visibly been seen by the English King not to support the Prince and was tasked to apprehend the young pretender, this proved a difficult task, many of the MacLeod's own clansmen gave the fugitive Prince refuge.

As Bonnie Prince Charlie was consistently moved from safe house to safe house, Island to Island, while he waited for a ship to be sent by the King of France to take him back into exile, it became clear informants were scarce and any information the Prince's pursuers received was intentionally old or false.

It remains unclear just how much the Chieftains really wanted to capture the Prince, the repercussions within the clans could have been devastating if any one Chieftain had captured the Prince and handed him over to the English where he would be tried for treason and most likely executed, this would certainly have opened up old wounds and feuds, which were better left buried.

During the cat and mouse pursuit of the Prince, there were many acts of heroism, one of the most famous was from an unlikely source which did add some spice to the story as it involved a MacDonald, a MacLeod and the Chief of MacLeod.

Bonnie Prince Charlie was desperate to escape from the Island of Uist, by chance the whereabouts of the Prince became known to the English army, they blocked every ferry point on the Island with English troops and Officers in a desperate attempt to capture the Prince once and for all, it would only be a matter of time before the Prince would be in English hands.

Flora MacDonald a most trusted friend to the Prince had the idea of dressing the Prince in the clothes of a woman, she believed the Prince could carry this off because of his fair face and slim build, he could be passed off as her sister or maid.

When they approached the English soldiers, who were questioning everyone, Flora stood firm, the soldiers didn't suspect anything as she and the Prince boarded the ferry.

Once underway Flora found out the ferryman was Donald MacLeod of Galtrigal, she looked back towards Uist, the deep cobalt blue waters of the Styx rose up and down, each wave topped with a turquoise and white crown, had Flora unwittingly lead herself and the Prince into a trap?

In the distance they could see the Isle of Skye, as ever covered in a grey mist, as they approached

Skye, Flora became more nervous, they were landing deep into MacLeod lands, it was only then she knew they had nothing to worry about, Donald made sure their escape to a safe house went without any further incident.

In recognition of his loyalty the Prince sent the 'Amen glass' to Donald MacLeod, on it is inscribed 'To my faithful Palinurus.'

This glass along with the spectacles worn by Donald MacLeod of Galtrigal are held to this day at Dunvegan castle along with other Jacobite relics once belonging to Flora MacDonald, including a lock of 'Bonnie Prince Charlie's' hair, these item were left at Dunvegan castle by a descendant of Flora MacDonald's who stayed at the castle for a number of years following her marriage to the son of the MacLeod Chief.

The Prince finally made his escape to France, never again to step foot on Scottish soil, during his efforts to evade the English soldiers and the Chieftains tasked with his capture, no-one on the Islands, whether they supported

Am Bratach Sith of Dunvegan

the Jacobite rebellion or not gave up the Prince to the English, despite the large rewards offered, showing the high affection held by the Scottish nation for their Prince, Charles Edward Stuart, 'Bonnie Prince Charlie.'

Following the failed Jacobite rebellion many of the Scottish nobles crossed the sea to Ireland seeking refuge from English retribution, most of them knowing they would lose everything if they left, but in keeping their lives they could start over again, as many of them did until the English Kings again caused the exodus of thousands of Irish to the New World.

The main catalyst for this emigration was the potato famines, the staple diet of the Irish people was potatoes, when the crops failed year after year leaving a nation starving but still hounded to pay rents to English Kings and landowners, something had to change.

Many Scot's also emigrated to the New World again seeking refuge and a new life, they settled in Oregon and the Southern States, their respect, sense of honour and love of Scottish tradition soon integrated them into their New World.

Life was hard at first but soon the Southern States became known for it's generous hospitality and was fast becoming a wealthy part of the New World, each State tended to be self governing, some prospering better than other's until the Republicans under Lincoln decreed each State would forfeit it's sovereignty and be governed by a powerful central government.

This meant only one thing to the Scot's of the Southern States, a return to the same tyranny, false promises and stripping of their wealth, they had endured this over the last 700 years at the hands of the English Kings, they were not about to let it happen again.

The American civil war started not as a war against slavery but following an attack on Fort Sumpter by a small army of Scots from South Carolina trying to defend their right to live as free men, governing themselves in their Land.

Once again history would show the MacLeod's along with fellow Scot's far away from their beloved Scotland were prepared to stand 'Hold Fast' and die if necessary in the defence of their right to live as free men.

During these turbulent times it would have been easy for the MacLeod Chief to use the Fairy flag to try and ease the suffering of the clan, if anything, knowing the Fairy flag can only be used once more, has helped the MacLeod Clan to stiffen it's resolve in order to overcome any difficulties by using the power held within the beliefs and traditions of the Clan MacLeod.

As for the fairies, not much has been heard from them in a number of years, it is said if you are out on the moors of Skye day or night you just may bump into a fairy, if your lucky, or even a witch if your not.

Many people say they hear someone calling them as they cross the Minch on the ferry from Armadale to Mallaig, which always makes them look back over the deep blue water with its white topped waves to Skye.

They say you can feel a shiver run down your spine and you feel your feet leaving the deck of the ferry as if you are flying or is it the magic of Skye burying it's self deep within your soul, ready to draw you back someday.

It could of course just be the cold wind blowing down the Minch and sea birds cawing in the distance, would you

Am Bratach Sith of Dunvegan

be prepared to denounce the existence of fairies, witches and magic if you crossed the sea to Skye?

'So yoo see lassie it's nee good having power an magic if yoo don't noo how ta use it,' Lucy looked up at Iain, 'a noo what tha fairy told ma,' Iain frowned, 'an what was that then lassie what did tha fairy tell yoo?' Lucy jumped off Iain's lap she stared at the flames as they leapt from the fire, 'she told ma ta noo ba frightened,' Anne gave out a loud 'tut' and looked over at Iain, 'now look what you've done, her heads filled we all sorts a rubbish,' Lucy carried on staring into the fire, 'noo mummy tha lady told ma at tha loch,' Anne shook her head, 'come on lass, a think it's time for bed,' Lucy didn't move she was transfixed by the flames, even when Iain got up Lucy remained motionless, in one swift movement Iain bent down and scooped Lucy up in his arms, she started to giggle as Iain tickled her, 'stop it daddy, stop it' she started to cry with laughter, Anne brought Lucy's night clothes down from her bedroom to warm by the fire.

Anne then went to the kitchen and brought out a wet flannel and towel, she knelt down to wash Lucy's face and hands, Lucy didn't like having her face washed, sometimes soap got in her eyes and made them sting.

Lucy quickly drew back from Anne, she reached for the towel to dry her face, Anne looked at Lucy, 'a suppose that'll have ta doo,' Iain was busy holding Lucy's bed clothes up against the fire, Anne helped Lucy undress, 'a think there'll have ta go to tha wash lass,' Anne showed Lucy how dirty her cloths had become during their walk in the snow earlier that afternoon, once her night dress was warm Iain handed it to Anne, she quickly pulled it over Lucy's head, Lucy hugged herself, 'mmm that's warm' she chuckled.

'Daddy can yoo tell ma more of tha story?' Iain sat back in his chair, 'not much else ta tell lass' he pondered for a moment, Lucy could see he was trying to think of something to say, 'aye a noo come here lassie,' Lucy pulled from Anne's arms and jumped back onto Iain's lap, 'noo lassie get off a'm trying ta get ma wallet,' Iain arched his back as he tried to remove his wallet from the back pocket of his trousers, much to Anne's amusement, 'tight as a Scotsman, yoo are,' she joked.

Having finally managing to release his wallet from his tight pocket, Iain patted his lap for Lucy to jump back up, she didn't need asking twice, up she jumped, she was fascinated as Iain fumbled through bits of paper stuffed in the back of his wallet 'ahh here it is' Iain held up a tatty piece of paper, it was an old photo, 'can yoo see it's a picture of tha Fairy Flag?' Lucy looked closely, it was hard to make out, it looked like a grey thing with dark grey spots on it, never the less Lucy was going to hold it, 'ba careful lass, all tha MacLeod's a know carry a picture of the Fairy flag, fa luck.' Lucy carried on looking at the picture as if expecting it to suddenly do something magical, 'can a hold it fa a while daddy?' Iain looked at Lucy as if he had some difficulty making up his mind, 'aye yoo can lassie, make sure yoo give it back afor the morning mind,' a wide smile rose on Lucy's face, 'aye daddy a will.'

After a few more precious minutes sitting on Iain's lap Lucy's eyes slowly began to close, she had got warm, that with all the running about she had done earlier outside began to catch up on her, very soon she was fast asleep.

Anne put her finger to her mouth telling Iain not to speak in case he woke Lucy, he nodded in agreement, slowly Iain moved to the front of his chair, he gently cradled Lucy in his arms and carried her to bed.

Anne went up before them to remove the hot water bottle she had placed in Lucy's bed earlier, her bed was nice and warm, Iain placed Lucy on the bed while Anne covered her up, Iain lent over, 'nite, nite lassie, sweet dreams,' a soft voice came back, 'nite, nite daddy,' Iain held Anne's hand as they left the room.

CHAPTER TWENTY-SIX
Iain's farewell

A bright ray of sunshine shone it's fingers through the bedroom curtains onto Anne's face, Iain was already awake, he lay looking at her face, so beautiful and peaceful he thought to himself, he lay thinking for a while, why did he have to leave, why did this stupid war have to be now, it was going to be hard to leave, he would have to be strong for Anne and Lucy, why should little Lucy even begin to understand why he had to go.

He decided to lie next to Anne for a while, he would miss her warmth, her smell and above all her love, Anne had remained constant ever since they were at school, there was something about her he could not resist, a kind of magic pulling him to her, he tenderly touched her hair brushing it further from her face, she stirred without opening her eyes, her hand moved across his thigh, then down toward his already stiffing manhood, Iain responded by caressing her breasts until her nipples stood erect, kissing the nape of her neck his lips slowly moved down to her breasts, he began to gently suck her nipples, Anne started to breath deeper and deeper, by the time Iain's hand reached between Anne's open thighs she was already wet with anticipation, she groaned with delight as his fingers entered her body and slowly gyrated within her, Iain withdrew his fingers and replaced them with his erect manhood.

Anne let out a deep sigh, he began to move inside her, he held the weight of his body above her on his strong outstretched arms.

Iain could feel Anne's body tightening around him, her breast moving up and down as her breathing became heavier, her body withering under the force of Iain's penetration, she reached the height of her climax arching her body into his, he could not contain the rush of pleasure welling inside his loins any longer, one last thrust left them both exhausted in each others arms.

They lay silently together words would only spoil the moment, Anne's hand found Iain's he turned to her and smiled, she touched his face, 'what a we going ta do ma wee man?' Iain let out a deep long sigh, 'a don't nor ma bonnie lass,' it was as if neither of them wanted to be the first to get up and break this special moment, they knew as soon as they got up the rest of the day would be about Iain leaving.

They lay in silence both thinking about the last few precious days, occasionally one of them would smile as a special memory came to mind, this was going to be their last minutes together as lovers for a long time, both of them continued to hold each other, neither prepared to sacrifice their time to it's place in history.

Anne started to talk about the first night Iain arrived and how pleased she had been to see him, he responded telling her how nervous he was before he opened the door

Am Bratach Sith of Dunvegan

that night, in case she was still mad at him for leaving in the first place, he told her how lucky he felt to have her as his wife and he would always be beside her even if they were miles apart, she would be able to feel his presence with her, his body may be elsewhere but his spirit remains with her.

Lucy knocked the bedroom door, she would normally just barge in, for some reason this morning she didn't, Iain looked at Anne she shrugged her slim shoulders as if to say don't ask me, 'come in lass,' Iain said in an enquiring voice, slowly the door creaked open, Lucy was holding the door knob hanging off it as if it was a one handed swing, 'what's that noise?' Iain looked at Anne they both burst into laughter, 'nothing lass, just mummy an daddy playing, come here an give us a cuddle,' Iain held out his arms, Lucy was still not sure, but a cuddle is a cuddle she bounced onto the bed between Iain and Anne.

Time passed quickly, Iain had a lot to do before he left, he had left packing his things because he hadn't wanted to spoil yesterday, Anne had given it some thought, she had stacked Iain's underwear in a separate draw to make it easier, her thinking was the quicker Iain was packed and ready the longer they would have together before he left.

Lucy would normally make a game out of something like this but this was different some how, she didn't want her daddy to leave, when he went before, he said he would be back before she knew it, it seemed forever to her, now he was going again, no matter what Iain did Lucy remained quiet, after he had packed his things Iain decided to have a talk to Lucy, he sat her down and tried to explain why he had to leave and how he wanted her to look after mummy for him until he gets back, Lucy did manage a couple of smiles especially after Iain told her he wanted to remember her with a happy face not a sad one.

Anne had prepared breakfast while Iain had been talking to Lucy, she had saved some ham and eggs for this occasion, Iain loved scrambled eggs and ham, he often said all good days should start with ham and eggs.

Anne didn't want this one to be any different, not many words were spoken during breakfast, it was as if this special breakfast said all there was to say, Lucy didn't want to say the wrong thing so she kept quiet anyway, with breakfast over it was time for Iain to leave, he had a long drive to Edinburgh, then an even longer train journey to the airfield, at least the weather was good, Iain hoped the roads to Edinburgh would be clear, he would have enough trouble getting to the main road let alone getting to Edinburgh.

Lucy helped Iain carry his kit to the car, Anne sat in the car, she knew how to start it while Iain cranked it up from the front, Iain always joked with Lucy telling her he had to wind up a spring under the bonnet to make the car go.

Iain gave the starting handle a couple of turns, nothing happened, he tried again and again, just as he was beginning to lose patience the engine turned over and spluttered, then started, Anne kept the revs going.

After a few minutes Iain thought it was safe for Anne to let her foot off the accelerator peddle, she got out of the car, Iain held her tight in his arms, he could just feel her through his heavy coat, he didn't want a long goodbye, they both felt they had said and done all there was while they were in bed that morning.

Am Bratach Sith of Dunvegan

Lucy gripped hold of Iain so tight her little hands started to turn white, Iain tried to reassure her, Anne had to prise Lucy's fingers away from Iain's coat, tears were streaming down Lucy's face, 'am sorry daddy a canny smile, a don't want yoo ta go,' Lucy was in Anne's arm's sobbing uncontrollably.

Iain gave them both one last hug and got into the car pausing for a moment to look back at Anne, Lucy and the cottage, he gave a couple of heavy revs to the engine released the hand break, slowly the car moved onto the track and went off sliding it's way southeast to Edinburgh.

Anne stood with Lucy in the crisp morning air watching until Iain was gone, Anne whispered, 'safe journey ma love come back soon,' Lucy moved her head as if to look for who Anne was talking to 'come on lassie lets go in' Anne carried Lucy into the cottage and closed the door behind them.

Iain was having a worse journey than he had expected, the roads weren't very good at the best of times, in places the snow hadn't been moved off the roads at all, when he reached Sean's house he was at least an hour behind, if he was going to make the train they would have to leave at once, as luck would have it Sean knew of a short cut to Edinburgh train station.

They set out, even the roads on the outskirts of Edinburgh were covered in snow, after about an hour they arrived at Edinburgh train station with a couple of minutes to spare, Iain rushed into the station at the kiosk he was told the train had been delayed so he had plenty of time.

Back out at the car Sean had taken Iain's kit from the boot, Sean carried Iain's kit bag into the station, the train had been delayed an hour in Carlisle, at least it gave Iain time to catch up with Sean, they exchanged stories, Sean told Iain he was joining the army in a couple of weeks, his wife didn't know yet but he had been to sign up last week, he didn't know how to tell her, he felt he had to do something, all the other chaps in is street had already signed up and were on their way, people were starting to believe he was a coward or something.

Iain knew Sean was no coward and it would take a brave man who called him a coward to his face, the train pulled into the station before they had expected, Iain shook hands with Sean, they wished each other well, Iain boarded the train it was not due to leave for a while but Sean didn't want to hang around because the weather was starting to close in again.

Iain stuck his head out of the carriage window and shouted after Sean, 'look after ma car,' Sean turned and stuck two fingers up to Iain much to the disgust of a number of other travellers.

Laughing Iain sat down in his seat, his kit bag occupying the seat next to him, until the train filled up with other passengers, Iain was surprised the train was full, some passengers were standing, the train seemed to stand in the station for ages before the sound of carriage doors could be heard slamming shut, that was always a sign the train was about to depart.

One long loud blow from the guards whistle signalled to the train driver it was time and safe to move off, the carriages clattered as the steam engine powered into action, it's wheels skidding round on the tracks trying to find enough grip, in a couple of seconds the engines great iron wheels started to bite into the track, one by one the engine pulled the weight of the carriages until all were moving, slowly at first then faster as the train cleared the station.

Other passengers were leaning out of the door windows waving goodbye to relatives and loved ones, Iain could smell the smoke from the engine as it bellowed through the open windows, the commotion soon came to a close, door windows were closed, passengers found their seats, with many like Iain preparing themselves for a long journey.

Iain looked round the carriage people sat reading newspapers or books, two woman were already busy knitting, he wondered, how do they do that, both woman had young children with them, not only were they knitting they were keeping the children amused, it seemed effortless.

Iain had often watched Anne knitting during the evenings, she looked so relaxed, he had tried to knit once, much to Anne's amusement, he was all fingers and thumbs, he pulled his kit bag over to release the tie on the top, he had packed his book on the top, he removed the book and started to lose himself as he became 'Jack Strand secret agent.'

The train seemed to stop at about every station from Edinburgh to London, the journey seemed as if it would never end, Iain was able to stretch his legs at Crewe station the stop there was twenty minutes.

As he walked along the cold draughty platform, his thoughts turned to home, Anne would be getting the tea, Lucy would be helping in her own way, outside the snow glistening under the frosty moonlight, he could feel himself becoming homesick already, how was he going to survive months away, soon after he was back sitting on the train as it once again powered it's way to London.

Finally he reached London Euston, now all he had to do was get to his squadron, there were numerous troop movements towards the south coast, Iain was going to try and cadge a lift, as he walked through London's streets he was horrified to the level of destruction that had been inflicted on the capital since he left a week earlier, whole streets lay in ruins, locals left to sift through the rubble trying to recover personal items or loved ones, still missing from the last air raid, Iain had heard Clydeside had suffered air raids but not on this scale, it was as if Hitler wanted to completely wipe London off the face of the earth, the evening air was heavy with smoke and dust, London was smoggy at the best of times, this was unbearable.

As if set by a clock the air raid sirens started up, Iain looked round him, people just made their way to the nearest air raid shelters, normally the underground stations, Iain was no exception, he followed the other's they appeared to know where they were going.

No sooner had he stood on the underground station, the first anti aircraft guns were heard firing at the oncoming German aircraft, it wasn't long before the nights helping of bombs started dropping, wave after wave it seemed relentless, 'their after the docks again,' one woman commented, most of the bombs dropped on the east side of London.

It was four in the morning when Iain decided to make a move, most of the others in the underground would stay there all night, Iain had other ideas, as he emerged from the underground, the sky over east London was red with fire, Hitler's bombers had certainly hit their targets tonight.

Iain walked as far as he could before being stopped by a air raid warden, 'sorry sir, unexploded bomb, you'll have go along the embankment west,' that's all Iain needed more delays.

Daylight finally came, Iain had been walking for nearly four hours, he was just about to give up and sit down for a rest when he heard a lorry coming behind him, he stood in the middle of the road waving his arms, the lorries breaks making a screeching noise as it came to a stand still, the drivers head appeared out of the side window, 'get out the way man,' Iain walked round the front of the lorry, 'are yoo going south?' the driver looked Iain up and down 'a need ta get ta ma squadron, a'm already late,' the driver looked at Iain again, 'a pilot are ya, hop in the back, I can give ya a lift ta Farnborough I'm going ta Aldershot,' Iain hurried to the back of the lorry, 'that'll do ma, thank-yoo,' he wasn't the only passenger at the back of the lorry a hand suddenly appeared from the darkness, 'give you a hand up old chap?' Iain grasped hold and scrambled up into the back of the lorry, 'thank-yoo,' there were two other pilot's in the lorry both late returning to their respective squadrons, 'don't worry old man, they're so short of pilots, they'll just be glad you came back at all,' Iain nodded in agreement.

All three got off at Farnborough to find their squadron's almost wiped out, the RAF had lost a lot of aircraft and pilots over the last week, Iain was given a Spitfire, it had so many patches on it and pieces from other planes to keep it in the air, he wondered if it would get off the ground at all, he would soon find out, within hours of returning to the airfield, Iain's squadron was scrambled to intercept in bound German bombers.

CHAPTER TWENTY-SEVEN
The lost picture

Iain didn't have time to properly introduce himself to his new squadron members before they were scrambled into action, his replacement Spitfire appeared to be held together by string and wire.

He had given it the once over, the amount of patches concerned him, it looked as if the Germans enjoyed shooting at this plane a little too much for Iain's liking.

He sat in the cockpit, the controls seemed loose enough, he wouldn't really be able to tell until he got into the air, the ground crew assured him his Spitfire was as good as any in the air, which didn't help to increase Iain's confidence in the rest of the aircraft in the squadron, he was however surprised when the Merlin engine started at the first time of asking, it roared like a lion as only Merlin engine's can.

The squadron swept into the clear winter sky, Iain carried out a couple of manoeuvres to get used to the plane and controls, everything appeared to work, he didn't have much time until he would find out how good his plane really was.

The formation of German bombers they were looking for were sighted below them and to their right, a shout came over the radio, 'tally-ho bandits at four o'clock,' they didn't appear to have a fighter escort, this was perfect, with the sun behind them the bombers wouldn't see them until it was too late.

Iain peeled off to carry out the first attack, the rest of the squadron followed close behind, it was like a turkey shoot, Iain brought down two bombers in his first attack, he saw two more plunge towards the ground and one more blew up in mid air, they kept on with the attack bringing down a further five planes without loosing a single Spitfire, they were joined by a squadron of Hurricanes, they were more than happy to carry on where the Spitfires had finished, almost out of ammunition Iain led his squadron home.

Iain's luck continued to hold, each of the squadrons were continually being scrambled to try and stem the relentless tide of German bombers, the only good thing was the bombers were attacking more and more without fighter escort, this made their job a lot easier, the Spitfire and Hurricane fighters were normally too quick for the bombers gun crews to hit them, that wasn't to say there wasn't any losses but not as many as there would have been if they had German fighters to contend with before attacking the bombers.

Christmas and the New Year came and went, Iain didn't feel there was much to celebrate while being miles away from Anne and Lucy, he spent a lot of his limited spare time writing to Anne, he received post from Anne but it was slow to arrive, each letter he received gave him mixed emotions, on one hand he was glad to hear from her and catch up on her news, on the other her letters were a constant reminder of how much he missed her and Lucy.

In general his spirits were raised following the arrival of a letter, he also received letters from his parents, not many but it was always nice to hear from them, the rest of the time was spent relaxing or down the local pub with the rest of the squadron, it sometimes got a bit crowded, there was no such thing as a quiet drink, the mentality of the pilots was sometimes unbelievable, they were as mad as march hares.

Iain put this down to the loss of other pilots and being expected to carry out sortie after sortie with little rest or sleep, each time they went up could be their last, all the pilots knew too many good men who had lost their lives over the last few months, friends were made easily and lost ever more easily, the general attitude among the pilots was enjoy today it may be your last.

Most pilots were like Iain, long distances from home and loved ones, in some ways it was not surprising given all leave had been cancelled for months, unless on compassionate grounds, many of Iain's mates had found some comfort by dating local girls, even though they had wives and girlfriends back home.

Iain found himself more and more distracted by thoughts of holding Anne as he did on the morning before he had to return to this wretched war, he made a vow to himself never to leave Anne on her own again, he wanted to spend as much time with her as he could.

God must have been on the British side for once, a few days of bad weather stopped the German bombers crossing the Channel, this gave the ground crew time to spoil the aircraft with some genuine maintenance instead of 'patch it up and get it back in the air' although leave was still cancelled it was nice to relax knowing the squadron wouldn't be scrambled.

Time was spent as ever sleeping, writing or drinking in the pub, with the occasional game of darts, if the pub was not too busy, as with all good things, they come to an end, at the first sign of a break in the weather Hitler sent his bombers to see if we were still there, not wanting to disappoint him, Iain's squadron was one of the first to pay there respects by bringing a record seven bombers down in one sortie without the loss of a single Spitfire.

Over the following weeks moral was surprisingly high, everyone felt Hitler was both running out of patience and bombers, day time bombing raids were increasing, the bombers that got through did cause more devastation but more bombers were brought down by the RAF and anti-aircraft guns, the only problem was the RAF was still stretched to breaking point both in resources and man power.

Iain sat on a deck chair outside the bunk house chatting to Michael O'Kay a new recruit to the squadron, he had replaced Iain's number two, who had been injured when he was shot down in a dog fight with a German fighter over the channel.

Michael was telling Iain how he came to join the RAF even though he was from southern Ireland which had remained a neutral country during the war, Michael turned out to be quite superstitious, not considered a good thing as a fighter pilot, even though nearly all pilots had

Am Bratach Sith of Dunvegan

some quirky ritual they always carried out before a sortie or an item they would carry for luck.

Michael always carried a four leafed clover with him, it was given to him by his grandmother who told him the fairies had given it to her mother, the clover was in a small round glass case, like two watch glasses stuck together, it couldn't be opened, Michael was proud to show off his lucky charm, 'keep it safe laddie, yoo'll need it,' Iain was half teasing him and half serious, Iain knew pilots needed all the luck they could get.

Michael's lucky charm made Iain think about the photo of the Fairy flag he carried with him, while Iain was searching through his wallet, he was trying to tell Michael of it's significance, Iain stopped talking, Michael could see Iain was becoming more nervous, by this time Iain had stood up and was leaning over the deck chair emptying the contents of his wallet into it, 'it was here, a'm sure it was,' he stood bolt upright clearly in deep thought, 'Lucy' he called out and shook his head, 'that young lassie, yoo wait till a see her,' Iain packed every piece of paper back into his wallet and sat back down as if nothing had happened, 'a canny show yoo tha Fairy flag, ma wee lassie has it,' Iain lit his pipe sitting silent, his only movements was him sucking on his pipe and a visible nervous twitch of his right knee as his leg bounced up and down.

Michael could see Iain was unnerved about not having the photo, he tried to ease Iain by saying he could get another or Iain's wife could post it to him, Iain made light of it saying it's only a photo, it didn't mean anything, he had been without it since he left home, nothing had happened to him, quite the reverse, his plane hadn't been hit once by a German bullet.

Michael waited until Iain was away from the bunk house, he found Iain's address from one of his letters and wrote to Anne explaining as best he could Iain's reaction when he hadn't got the photo, he posted the letter, hoping the reply would get back quickly, Michael thought it better not to tell Iain what he had done, in case he resented his involvement.

The next few days went off without any serious involvement with enemy aircraft, another piece of luck as far as Michael was concerned, Iain sprained his ankle, when his foot went down a rabbit hole during a game of cricket between the squadrons, Iain could hardly stand let alone climb into a plane, this meant Iain would not fly for at least a week.

Every day came the post was sorted, each letter Iain received Michael was expressing an unwelcome interest in, Iain was becoming suspicious of Michael, he decided to keep a close eye on him, two or three days later Iain caught Michael going through his letters, 'what do yoo think ya doing laddie, that's ma personal things, now put them back before I break ya thieving neck,' Michael was stunned at first, then he knew he had to explain, 'it's not what ya think Iain, I wasn't taking anything,' Michael was trying to find the words to explain, 'the photo, I wrote to your wife asking her to post it to you, you looked that shocked when it wasn't there.'

This made Iain stop and think, 'yoo telling ma yoo wrote ta ma Anne, when?' Michael thought for a second, 'the day after, may be the next, I don't remember,' Iain sat on the edge of the bed, 'yoo stupid wee mon, a thought aboot it an wrote ta her telling her ta keep it, it would protect her an Lucy, now she'll have posted it before she

Am Bratach Sith of Dunvegan

gets ma letter an neither of us has it,' Iain sat on the bed, his head in his hands, 'sorry Iain I was only trying to help,' Iain nodded to acknowledge Michael's words, 'ya never know it might turn up in ta morrow's post,' Michael slowly edged towards the door, still unsure if Iain would attack him, 'leave ma be, laddie,' Iain didn't take his hands from over his face.

Michael could not find any words to show Iain how sorry he was for deceiving him by going behind his back and getting involved in something that was not his problem, Michael edged towards the door closing it behind him.

Bright sunshine greeted the next day, ideal weather to engage the enemy, Iain was in a bright but physiological mood, saying things like, 'lets get at um, before they get us,' and, 'what yoo waiting for yoo only live once,' this was so unlike Iain normally he was focused on the job in hand, of anyone Iain would not take the enemy lightly.

Michael thought he should tell someone about what had happened, it was nine-thirty, the post had normally arrived by now, he kept looking over at the administration hut, then over at Iain, still nothing, suddenly the sound Michael didn't want to hear, the telephone, it was picked up, to everyone's relief it was put back down.

A couple of minutes later a motorcyclist pulled into the airfield, the post had arrived, Michael started to walk towards the administration hut when the telephone rang again, this time the squadron was placed on standby, Michael carried on towards the hut, as he got to the door it swung open, the administration officer stood there, handing out the post was a main and responsible duty as far as he was concerned, the Kings Mail had to be hand delivered by the authorised person, 'haa O'Kay one letter for you lad,' the letter was thrust at Michael, 'any post for Iain MacLeod?' a stern look came back, 'now, now laddie, you know better than that, any post for Squadron leader MacLeod will be handed to him by myself,' on that the administration officer proceeded to walk off towards the bunk houses, once again the telephone rang, 'scramble,' in an instant all the pilots were running towards their aircraft, ground crew were ready to remove the blocks from the wheels as soon as the engines were fired up.

One by one the Merlin engines roared into action, Iain was one of the first into the air, Michael one of the last, he was the furthest away from his aircraft when the shout went up, he watched Iain take off 'hold fast Iain, hold fast.'

As usual the enemy planes were already over the south coast, Iain's squadron was not the first to engage this time they were backing up another squadron, as they approached the enemy the sky was full of dog fights, the bombers were being escorted by a large number of fighters, this could only mean one thing, Hitler was after a major target, they wanted as many bombers to get through as possible.

The call came over from air control to engage, Iain peeled off taking two other aircraft with him, the idea was to take the German fighters from above out of the sun, again they had instant success four fighters were downed, this was by far the biggest dog fight Iain had ever been in, he rounded on another enemy fighter, a short burst of gun fire released smoke from the fighters engine, Iain tilted his Spitfire to confirm the fighter was down.

There was a lot of chatter over the radio, the dog fight was not going all their own way, three Spitfires and four

Am Bratach Sith of Dunvegan

Hurricanes had been shot down, Iain spotted an enemy fighter coming up behind Michael, Iain warned him over the radio, Michael could not shift the fighter, Iain swooped in behind the enemy plane, two short blasts of his cannons was enough to bring down the plane and save Michael's skin.

Iain was so preoccupied in saving Michael he didn't spot the enemy fighter behind him, a stream of bullets tore through his cockpit, he felt a burning sensation in his back, the engine caught fire, he had to get out, he pushed open the cockpit cover and pulled himself clear with the plane crashing towards the sea, he managed to throw himself clear.

After the battle, numerous planes from both sides had been shot down, the battle was judged to be a success for the RAF, as only eight of the thirty bombers had got through, their intended target was thought to have been Buckingham Palace which did not receive any major damage.

As the aircraft returned to the air field, some just limping back having sustained damage, many would be out of action for a number of days, the grim task of counting the human cost began. Michael O'Kay confirmed his kills, he also confirmed seeing Iain MacLeod parachuting into the sea just off the coast after he had shot down, by an enemy aircraft that was on his own tail, he could not confirm if he was alive, they would have to wait for the rescue boats to bring him ashore.

In Iain's room a letter had arrived that morning, the administration officer left it on the draws by Iain's bed.

CHAPTER TWENTY-EIGHT
Iain comes home

Anne was up bright and early, the spring sun felt warm through the bedroom window, Lucy stayed in bed later than usual, she had to go to school, she liked school but still liked to stay with Anne, she felt her mummy would get lonely without her, with daddy being away, because of the war, the school was closed more than it was open, it had been used to house people evacuated from Glasgow, until they could be found places to stay.

Anne thought it would be an idea to have a couple of evacuated children to stay with her and Lucy, they had a spare room and it would be nice for Lucy to make new friends, she hadn't mentioned it to Lucy, she knew Lucy would pester her until they arrived, what she would do, is ask Lucy what she thought about it first.

It was a long walk to the school, about thirty minutes, they had to set off early, Anne had a letter she wanted to post to Iain, one of his friends Michael, had wrote to her saying Iain had left the photo of the Fairy flag when he left, Iain was concerned about not having the photo,

Michael didn't think Iain would ask her to send it in case she thought he was being silly.

Anne had forgotten about the photo, when Michael's letter arrived she had to ask Lucy if she had seen it, Lucy had put it safe, the night after Iain had left, Lucy went to bed, she felt something in the bed, it was the photo, she remembered holding it in her hand when her daddy had carried her to bed, she must have gone to sleep still holding it, she put the photo in a box, where she kept all her secret things, she had meant to give it to Anne but forgot.

Anne was hoping someone in the village would be going to one of the towns or cities, she would ask them if they would post it from there, it would get there days earlier that way, she was in luck a couple of local men had signed up and were on there way to Edinburgh to join their regiment, they offered to take Anne's letter along with the other letters and parcels people had given them to take. Anne walked Lucy to the school, waved her off, Lucy went off playing with her friends, Anne would be back to pick Lucy up later, while she was in the village Anne took the opportunity to visit the village hall, she wanted to ask about having evacuees to stay with her, she was told by Margaret the person responsible for arranging homes for evacuated children, they were expecting a number of children in the next few weeks.

Clydebank had been coming under heavy bombing in the last few days, the Ministry of Defence were expecting the bombing to get worse, what Margaret was saying didn't come as a surprise to Anne, she had heard the bombs during the night, it sounded like thunder in the distance, sometimes late at night, out of her bedroom window which faced in a southerly direction, she could see a orange glow

Am Bratach Sith of Dunvegan

in the sky, she had guessed it was the dock yards being bombed.

Margaret was quite pleased, Anne was willing to give refuge for two children, normally she had to twist peoples arms or beg people to take in the poor little mites, Margaret had always been a mother hen, she never had children of her own, Anne thought it was a shame, she had a heart of gold where children were concerned, Anne thought two lassie's about the same age as Lucy would be a good idea, Margaret agreed to see what she could arrange, but they didn't always know what children would arrive.

Anne asked Margaret not to mention it to Lucy if she saw her, she wanted to discuss it with her first, before Anne walked back home she went to see her friend Jane, they had been friends for ever, Jane had two children William and Susan, they went to the same school as Lucy but were a little older, with the children out of the way they could sit and catch up on all the gossip.

Jane's husband had enlisted in the army, he was somewhere down south, last Jane heard he was camped somewhere on Salisbury Plain, Jock, her husband wasn't very good at sending letters, Jane thought he was having too much of a good time, what Jane didn't know, Jock was nearer than she knew, he was currently training with the Special Forces Commandoes north of Fort William, along with the others specially chosen for Special Forces training, he was not allowed to send letters or have contact with his family and friends.

Anne ended up staying with Jane all day until they went to collect Lucy, William and Susan from school, Anne gave Jane a big hug and thanked her for her company, it had really lifted her spirits, Lucy was still full of beans on the way home, she didn't stop talking, when they reached the cottage, the fire had nearly gone out, Anne tossed on a couple of logs, within minutes it was roaring away. Lucy took the opportunity to sit with Anne, she cuddled into Anne's soft breast, it was as if she couldn't get close enough, both seemed transfixed by the flames, 'Lucy, what do yoo think aboot a couple a lassies coming ta stay with us?' Lucy didn't move, 'fa good?' Anne wanted to choose her words carefully, 'noo until tha war ends, until daddy comes home,' Lucy didn't reply for a few seconds, 'can a play we them?' Anne smiled, 'that's tha idea,' this time Lucy looked round at Anne 'when will tha ba coming?' Anne squeezed Lucy, 'in a couple a days, a week, a doon't noo,' Lucy was deep in thought, 'aye a suppose so, as long as tha don't have ma room,' Anne smiled, 'noo lass they'll have tha spare room,' both sat taking in the warmth of the fire, after a while Lucy sat up, 'a'll have two sisters,' Anne stroked Lucy's golden hair, 'a hope so, ma bonnie lass, a hope so,' a tear gently rolled down the side of Anne's nose onto her flushed red lips, before disappearing into the corner of her delicate mouth, if only that could be true, she thought to herself.

There would be a full moon that night a 'bombers moon' not one cloud could be seen ghosting it's way across the clear sky, the stars shone bright like pin holes in a black-out curtain, it was a fine spring night, her thoughts turned to Iain, it was one of those nights they had used to walk for hours when they were teenagers, getting into trouble when they got back for being out so late.

Anne stood outside the cottage with only the familiar sounds of the night for company, Lucy was tucked up in bed, this was Anne's time and she would milk every minute of it, she felt warm with an inner glow, like a dram of fine malt whisky on a cold winters night, she could smell Iain

Am Bratach Sith of Dunvegan

around her, feel his strong arms holding her, shielding her from harm.

Anne was late going to bed, she had stood outside for over two hours, she looked in on Lucy, who was fast asleep, one arm round her favourite teddy, the other over the top of her head, Anne quickly dropped off into a deep sleep, she was tired and contented.

Suddenly a deafening bang, more like an explosion, pounded Anne's ears waking her in an instant, she sat upright in bed, the window, she pulled back the curtains, in the distance she could see a fire near the village, overhead the drone of aircraft engines, 'Lucy?' she shouted, she turned towards the bedroom door grabbing her dressing gown, a burst of bright light blinded her, followed by a rush of wind that knocked her to the floor.

'Lucy?' she shouted again, Anne couldn't see a thing, she squealed with pain, her eyes felt as if they had been pierced by hot needles, she smelt something burning, the heat of flames, she stepped forward towards the bedroom door, every step she was treading on stones or something, she had to get to Lucy.

Anne held her arms out in front of her, trying to feel for the door, a small hand touched hers, 'Lucy?' she knelt down, 'mummy,' Lucy threw her arms round Anne's neck, 'thank god your alright, what's happened, a canny see?' her question was followed by a short silence, 'Lucy what's happened?' Lucy pulled Anne's arm, 'come on mummy we have ta go with tha lady,' Lucy pulled at Anne's arm, 'what lady, Lucy what lady?' another hand touched her arm warm, gentle, delicate as silk, Anne could tell it wasn't Lucy's.

She could feel Lucy pulling her other arm, 'come on mummy we have ta go,' Lucy became insistent, Anne could feel a searing heat as she was led down the stairs, her feet felt as if they were burning, she kept wincing with pain, all Anne could smell was hot smoke that burned her lungs when she tried to breath, Lucy kept encouraging Anne to keep going, she had little choice, she knew something bad had happened.

At the bottom of the stairs Anne expected to hear the front door open, instead she felt a sudden coldness in front of her, 'come on mummy a few more steps,' a light breeze whispered round Anne's face, Lucy stopped, 'yoo can sit here mummy, tha lady's gone,' Anne sat down guiding herself with her arm feeling for what ever she was supposed to sit on, she felt a log or something, the only log she could remember was the one Iain used as a block to chop wood, that was at the side of the cottage by the lane.

After about half an hour Andrew Askew arrived 'my god Anne, are you alright?' his voice took Anne by surprise, she nodded at first, then broke down in tears, 'a canny see, Andrew, a canny see,' Andrew sat on another log the other side of Anne, 'a you alright Lucy?' Andrew looked at Lucy, 'not a scratch, a Lucy,' he answered to reassure Anne, 'what's happened Andrew?' he looked at the cottage, 'it looks like you had a direct hit, if you ask me your both lucky to be alive.'

Anne picked her head up 'a bomb, is there much damage?' her question wasn't answered, 'can you manage to walk Anne?' she stood up, Lucy had found their wellington boots, they had been by the back door and must have been blown out by the blast.

Andrew helped Anne to put on her wellington boots, Lucy was having difficulty as always, Andrew helped her out, 'right lets go to the house,' Andrew took off his coat and placed it round Anne's shoulders, he then put his arm round Anne, 'come on Lucy lead the way,' Lucy didn't leave Anne's side.

When they arrived at Andrew's house Anne was exhausted, Andrew took her and Lucy to the spare bedroom, 'lucky it's a double bed,' Anne removed Andrew's coat and felt for the bed, Lucy tried to guide her, once she was in bed Lucy climbed beside her Anne put her arms round Lucy as if she would never let her go.

Anne woke to a strange noise, it was Andrew's heavy footsteps on the wooden stair, 'good morning, how are we today?' Anne looked towards Andrew's voice, 'your just a blur,' Andrew had brought some breakfast for Anne and Lucy, boiled eggs and soldiers, 'the doctors on his way, he should be here in an hour or so,' Lucy tucked into her breakfast, 'thank yoo Andrew, a doon't noo what we have done if yoo hadn't been there,' Anne felt for Andrew's hand, he grasped her 'now don't be silly, I'm just glad your safe,' a loud rap at the door made Anne jolt, 'that's the doctor, earlier than I thought' Andrew went down to let him in.

At first Doctor MacLeish, looked a strange sort of person to be a doctor, Anne could picture him as Count Dracula, she had once read Bram Stokers book, scared her for ages after, Dr MacLeish would make a good vampire, tall, slim, black hair swept back and so slick he was almost oily, 'bit of a night eh Mrs MacLeod?' he gave Anne a thorough examination, then Lucy 'I think you had better go into hospital for a couple of days observation, we need to make sure your eye sight returns.' Anne was too tired to argue, 'Lucy can stay here, until you come home, I was going to have one of those evacuee's but Lucy can stay instead.'

Anne held out her hand towards Lucy, she caught hold and squeezed it tight, 'don't ba away long,' Lucy lent over and hugged Anne, 'not long, yoo ba good for Andrew,' Dr MacLeish had to drive Anne to Stirling Hospital, all the available ambulances were at the docks, the bombing had been heavy leaving a lot of injured requiring medical attention, Lucy waved as Anne drove off with Dr MacLeish.

Within a couple of days Anne's eyesight was back to normal, the hospital doctor wanted to examine them once more before she would be discharged, he shone a bright light into her eyes as he pulled her eye lids back, 'every thing seems alright, you had a lucky escape I hear, it's a blessing you didn't lose your baby,' Anne looked at the doctor, 'yes Lucy escaped without a scratch,' the doctor held her hand, 'you didn't know, you were pregnant, did you?' Anne could hardly take in what the doctor had said 'a canny ba pregnant, it's noo possible, there must ba some mistake,' the doctor shook his head, 'no mistake your as pregnant as any woman could be,' reality started to dawn on Anne, 'ma Iain's been away nearly four months, a canny ba four months pregnant,' she stared at the doctor 'just, but still pregnant,' this was more than Anne could cope with, she tried to explain to the doctor she hadn't had sex since her husband returned to his squadron last December, 'well lassie unless your going to call it the immaculate conception, you'll have to admit to something.'

Dr MacLeish agreed to take Anne home, she was still in a daze when he arrived, she told him how shocked she was to be told she was pregnant, again he told her you can't be pregnant without having intercourse, he went on to say that one day it might be possible but possibly not in their lifetime, his words went over her head, what would she tell

Am Bratach Sith of Dunvegan

Lucy, what would people think of her, some kind of loose woman, worst of all, what would Iain say, how could he believe her when no-one else would.

As they approached Andrew's house, Anne's heart sank, she should be happy after all she was told she would never be able to have any other children, as the car stopped Lucy ran out to greet her, 'mummy, mummy,' Lucy was full of happiness, it was as if Anne had been away for months, 'let your mummy get into the house Lucy,' Andrew was doing his best to control Lucy, he may as well have saved his breath, they went into the house, Anne almost fell back into the chair no sooner was she sitting than Lucy bounced on her lap, 'a'm glad your better, is ya baby better too?' Anne stared at Lucy.

'A'm sorry Anne,' Andrew shrugged his shoulders, 'she keeps saying she's having a baby brother, I think she's confused with the evacuees,' Lucy turned round, 'noo tha lady told ma, she did mummy, she did,' Anne caught hold of Lucy's arms, 'Lucy what did tha lady say, when did she say it?' Lucy started to cry, 'tha night, tha fire come, she said he would ba like me, she did mummy, she did,' Anne wrapped her arms round Lucy, 'a noo lass, a noo.'

Later on a car pulled up, Andrew answered the door, Anne could hear muffled talking, she assumed it was Andrew's business and didn't want to interfere, Andrew took his visitor into the drawing room, after a while Andrew came into the kitchen, 'Anne, eh, this is Wing Commander Jarvis, Iain's squadron,' Anne smiled, 'helloo pleased ta meet yoo,' she held out her hand, he shook hands with her. 'it's David' she nodded, something clicked in her head, 'is there something wrong, is Iain alright?' Andrew looked at David 'let's go and sit down shall we?' Andrew tried to coax Anne to the lounge, 'what's wrong, tell ma, it's Iain?' tears started to well up in her eyes, 'I'm sorry to have to inform you Iain was lost in action three days ago, despite efforts to find him, his body was only recovered last night,' David carried on talking, Anne was oblivious to anything else he said, 'when can a see him?' David looked again at Andrew, 'Iain's body will arrive in Edinburgh on Friday.' Anne was still stunned, she couldn't believe it, how will she tell Lucy, 'ma god, Lucy, a'v got ta find Lucy,' Anne stood up, ' she's out the back, I'll fetch her,' Andrew went to get up, 'noo I'v got ta do this ma own way,' she turned to David, 'a thank yoo for ya kind words, a would like yoo ta leave noo,' David nodded in agreement, he picked up his hat and coat from the coat stand, 'thank-you Andrew,' he shook Andrew's hand.

Andrew closed the door behind him, Anne was outside with Lucy, 'would yoo like ta walk with ma lass,' Lucy had been playing with Andrews dog a 'Westie terrier' they walked down the lane towards the cottage, Lucy was holding Anne's hand, Anne didn't know where to begin, 'mummy,' Lucy looked up at Anne, 'why didn't yoo wake ma when daddy was here before tha fire?' Anne stopped walking, 'he was nee here lass, he couldn't have been,' Lucy's head dropped, 'tha lady told ma mummy would ba alright, daddy add come ta her before he left.'

Anne held Lucy's shoulder's, 'a have something important ta tell yoo, daddy wont ba coming home, he's gone away ta heaven,' tear's filled Lucy's eyes, she grabbed Anne round the waist, she held tight sobbing uncontrollably, tear's flowed down Anne's pale cheeks, 'come on lass, lets go ta tha cottage,' the short walk seemed to take forever.

Anne looked at her beloved cottage, it lay in ruins, half was completely destroyed by the bomb, the other half gutted by the fire, Anne sat on the same log she had sat on after escaping the fire, 'tell ma aboot tha lady?' Lucy told her it was the lady from the Loch, she had woke her up before the bomb had gone off and she had helped them down the stairs, Lucy said she was frightened because the stairs were covered in flames but the Lady told her the flames would not hurt them, she told her about daddy visiting Anne earlier that night and about the baby.

Anne decided to move back to her parents house after Iain's funeral, there was enough room there for her and Lucy, Iain's parents also offered them the option to stay with them, Anne needed time to sort things out.

Iain had always joked about being buried on Skye at Dunvegan, Anne didn't know if that's what he really wanted but that's what she would do for him, it took a little while to gain permission, she wrote to Chief MacLeod of MacLeod, asking for help in granting Iain's wishes, within two weeks Iain MacLeod was buried within the shadow of his beloved Dunvegan Castle, Anne stood over his grave, in the twilight of a fine spring evening looking towards the proud silhouette of Dunvegan castle, against the setting sun, 'hear me, fairies of Dunvegan, look after Iain MacLeod, a true son of Scotland, his body is no longer mine, I'm returning his spirit to you for safe keeping, one day destiny will give him back to me.'

CHAPTER TWENTY-NINE
Home to Skye

Iain's death changed Anne in ways she could never explain, life carried on, Lucy went with Anne to stay with her parents, Anne tried to explain how she became pregnant, her mother made some effort to understand, her father never did.

When Iain John MacLeod was born he had the reddest hair and emerald green eyes, Anne was convinced he was Iain's child, but how? She only had the memories of how close she felt to Iain the night before the cottage was bombed along with Lucy's account of the Lady she said she had seen.

The one thing that always played on Anne's mind was Iain must have already been dead that night.

Anne's father could never accept Iain John as his true grandson, it wasn't too bad during the first couple of years but then her father started more and more to spoil Lucy while ignoring Iain John, Anne soon found she could not stand by and see her own father treat Iain's son this way.

She had been in regular contact with Iain's parents since the funeral, in a letter she asked them if she could go and stay with them for a while, they willingly agreed, within a couple of weeks Anne moved to Portree on Skye, her father never spoke to her again.

Life became a lot clearer for Anne, Iain's parents took to Iain John without any questions, Iain's mother had a picture of Iain as a boy, a close friend of hers was an artist he had drew the picture for her on Iain's fifth birthday, Iain John's likeness to the picture became stronger and stronger, Iain's parents were in no doubt who Iain John MacLeod's father was.

Anne would often take the children to Dunvegan to visit Iain's grave, she would try and retell the stories Iain had told Lucy years before, Lucy would correct her on bits she got wrong, Lucy thought Skye was a magical isle, her favourite place had to be the Fairy bridge, the first time she went to the Fairy bridge, she sat dangling her legs over the side.

Anne sat with Iain John on the banks of the burn, about twenty yards away, Lucy was nine years old, as she sat eating an oatcake, she heard a voice, it seemed to be coming from under the bridge, she looked down in the rippling water she could see the Lady, the same Lady she had seen at Loch Lomond and again at the cottage.

Anne watched Lucy staring into the stream, 'careful Lucy, don't fall in,' there was no depth to the water, Anne just didn't want her to hurt herself or get wet, 'a'm alright, a'm just looking.'

Anne became curious to what Lucy was looking at, she picked Iain John up and walked towards Lucy, 'what yoo looking at Lucy?' Lucy hadn't noticed Anne walking

Am Bratach Sith of Dunvegan

up to her, the closeness of Anne's voice startled Lucy, she thought for a second, 'err, nothing, just tha water,' Anne smiled 'come on lass it's time we were away home.'

Anne noticed Lucy was quiet on the way home, normally she was full of chatter, she asked if anything was wrong, Lucy just shrugged her shoulders and said nothing.

Lucy knew what the Lady under the fairy bridge told her had some meaning but she couldn't figure what, she kept saying the words over and over in her head, 'my strength is your strength, use it well, stay true to who you are,' Lucy never forgot these words she often repeated them to herself , thinking she would someday understand the meaning, with the knowledge of when the Lady had talked to her before she hadn't known the reason of her words, yet the night the cottage was bombed she understood completely, Lucy decided to wait and see what happened, hoping it wouldn't be anything bad.

The war finally ended, people celebrated all over Skye, within a few months families began to be reunited with loved ones returning home, it was a time of reflection for many woman including Anne.

Lucy shared a number of quiet cuddles with Anne, it was one of those periods in time, when nothing said everything.

As the years passed Lucy grew into a pretty young woman, Iain John was everything a boy should be, he was always getting into mischief, Anne worked for a local bakery in the square in Portree, Lucy had gained a place at Edinburgh University, studying History, as for Iain John, he was still at school, he wanted to travel the world, his grandfather said, he was just like his father at that age, never still always wanting to know what's round the next corner, before he got there.

In general life was slow and relaxed, not that the pace of life was ever quick on Skye no-one could have predicted their lives would again descend into turmoil.

Anne collapsed after feeling faint at the bakery, her doctor admitted her to hospital in Fort William, she was diagnosed to have an inoperable tumour in her brain, Lucy arrived at the hospital from Edinburgh just hours before Anne fell into a coma, Anne died three days later, twelve years to the day after the bomb hit the cottage.

Iain John was inconsolable, he always had difficulty with not knowing who his father really was, for some reason, he had started to blame himself for Iain's death, Lucy had tried to reassure him especially over the last few years, she would tell him how their father had always wanted a son, he never seemed to believe her.

Lucy was beginning to understand the words the woman had said to her at the Fairy bridge a few years previous, she would need to find the strength for both Iain John and herself.

Anne was buried with Iain at Dunvegan, at last they would be together again, the fairies would return Iain to his beloved Anne, Lucy had contacted Anne's parents while Anne was in hospital, they didn't go to the hospital or the funeral.

Lucy tried to carry on with her studies at University, she found herself returning home more and more, to be with Iain John, he couldn't get over Anne's death, he missed school more than he attended, getting into trouble all the time, he was becoming too much for his grandparents to cope with, until finally he ran off.

Am Bratach Sith of Dunvegan

Iain John was picked up by the Police in Glasgow after trying to steal food from a shop, he wasn't charged and he returned to Portree, over the coming years he ran off more and more, the last time he was found by Lucy in Newcastle.

Shortly after his sixteenth birthday following a long talk with Lucy and his grandfather Iain John signed up to join the Royal Navy, it was the making of him, within ten years he had risen up the ranks, his life for once had a meaning.

When Iain John left the Navy after fifteen years, he had become an officer and very much a gentleman, Lucy somehow completed her studies and gained a degree in History, she stayed in Edinburgh for some years working with the Edinburgh Museum, her favourite subject was the History of the Scottish Highlands and Islands, she also became one of Scotland's leading authorities on Scottish Myths and Legends.

Iain John had met and married a lass called Janet from Fife, it was a love at first sight, married within a few months sort of romance, Lucy didn't know anything about Iain John getting married until they turned up together in Portree.

When Iain John was discharged from the Royal Navy, he couldn't settle back in Scotland, they eventually immigrated to Australia, leaving Lucy on her own, Iain's parents had both died the previous year within three months of each other.

Lucy was now in no doubt behind the meaning of the words spoken at the Fairy bridge, she didn't know how she had coped with everything, where had she gained her strength from?

Lucy kept in touch with her brother and Janet, she visited them on one occasion but found Australia too hot and she didn't like the travelling, she soon started to become home sick, Iain John had become more Australian over the years, he hardly asked about Scotland in his letters, more about the football, that was mainly the English teams, Anne could never understand why he supported Portsmouth, of all teams, he said it was the first team he had ever seen play, he went with one of his mates from the Navy while he was on leave, Portsmouth won three-nil, he had supported them ever since.

One of his letters caught Lucy off guard, she was stunned to read Janet had died, she was bitten by a snake when they were camping in the outback, by the time the letter reached Lucy, Janet had been buried, Iain John didn't want Lucy to go out there, he knew how much she hated to travel, he impressed on her he would be alright.

Time marched past the months rolled into years, Lucy was busy investigating the myth of a Witch from Wester Ross who was reputed to have been burnt at the stake in Ullerpool, she was disturbed by a knock at the door, to her surprise there stood Iain John with his new wife Catherine, it was a complete shock.

It was time to catch up, where had the years gone? Lucy couldn't help but notice, Catherine was some years younger than Iain John, he said he had married a young woman to stay young, her brother was happy, that's all that mattered to Lucy.

Iain John and Catherine had come to Britain on their honeymoon, he wanted to show Catherine all the sight's before they went back to Oz, speaking to Iain John Lucy could see there was nothing left of Scotland in Iain John,

Am Bratach Sith of Dunvegan

he was all Australian, even his passport had him as an Australian national. Iain John had become an Australian citizen, return they did, Lucy was left once again to hide away in the past.

The next letter she received from her brother contained even better news, Catherine was pregnant, Lucy wrote time after time, until she received the letter she was waiting for, Catherine had given birth to a baby boy Iain jnr, both doing well, the letter also contained a photo, on the back her brother had wrote, 'do you think he's a MacLeod?' Lucy looked at the photo and laughed to herself and nodded in agreement.

Iain jnr had red hair and green eyes, how could there be any doubt, Lucy sent present after present for Iain jnr, she thought even if she can't see him, he will know who she is, they didn't have any other children, 'not for the want of trying,' Iain John would always say much to Catherine's embarrassment. Their contact was made easier when Iain John had a telephone installed, Lucy telephoned them all the while no matter what the cost; she thought it was worth it to hear her Nephew's voice.

Lucy reached across to take hold of Iain jnr's hand, 'that's where your family come from, if yoo don't noo where ya from, how can yoo noo were your going?' Iain jnr stood looking at the graves, Lucy had a headstone put on the graves after Anne had died, Iain jnr read out the inscription, 'here lies Iain MacLeod with his beloved wife Anne, true to Scotland, forever in the arms of the past, held in the minds of the future,' he placed a single thistle wrapped in heather on the grave, 'come on away laddie a want ta show yoo something,' Lucy grabbed his arm.

As they walked Lucy tried to explain why she had sent him the ticket to fly to Scotland, she hoped he would understand, they soon reached the main gate to Dunvegan castle, Lucy paid the entrance fee, 'a don't noo why a still pay, a could tell am more than they know aboot this place,' they walked round the gardens past the waterfalls, through the walled garden all the while Lucy reeled off detail after detail about the Clan MacLeod and Dunvegan Castle.

She pointed out every part of the castle, the Fairy Tower, the Keep, the original sea gate, inside the castle her knowledge of the items on display and many that weren't proved boundless, only now Iain jnr started to understand some of the things she had been telling him about, Lucy could see he was more than interested, 'am a boring yoo laddie?'

Iain jnr was looking at the Jacobite relics, 'struth no, aunt Lucy, I didn't expect all this, I thought you were havin a laugh, you know, makin it up, tellin a story,' Lucy stopped, she looked sternly at Iain jnr, 'a can assure yoo it's all true, every last word,' they slowly walked round the rooms Iain jnr found it difficult to take in all these people in the portraits were part of his families past, all he knew before today was his grandfather and father were from Scotland, but that hadn't meant much just another place in the world, he was Australian and proud of it.

Lucy stopped at the Fairy flag, she stood looking, other people pushed by, to most of them it must have looked like a bit of rag put in a frame for the benefit of the tourists, Lucy never stopped looking at the Fairy flag, 'what do yoo see laddie?' Iain jnr looked a bit surprised at Lucy's question 'eh, the Fairy flag?' Lucy let out one of those sighs that could only mean wrong answer, 'what dose tha

Am Bratach Sith of Dunvegan

Fairy flag mean ta yoo?' Iain jnr really wanted to give Lucy the right answer, 'to be honest, if the MacLeod Clan have believed in this flag for so many years and all that you have said is true, I guess I must believe in fairies, if I don't I can't believe any of it, which means I wouldn't believe in myself and who I am,' Lucy nodded her approval of his answer, 'a start laddie, a start.'

Lucy unclipped her handbag and started to rummage though looking for something, 'aye, here yoo are,' she held up a large square locket on a gold chain, it was the biggest locket Iain jnr had ever seen, it must have been over an inch square, it gently spun round as Lucy held it up by the gold chain, she handed it to Iain jnr, 'open it, go on laddie,' he found it difficult to open, once he could force his finger nails into the join, he managed to prise the locket open, inside one half was the picture of the Fairy flag, Iain had left with her when he returned to the war, on the other side was a photo of Iain, Lucy's father, taken from the drawing her grandfather had, she had the photo taken and shrunk down to be able to fit in the locket, the locket she had made specially to fit the photo of the Fairy flag, 'a want yoo ta have this, if ya believe in tha fairies they will protect yoo, a know yoo going ta join tha Royal Australian Air Force, ya grandfather Iain MacLeod would have wanted yoo ta have tha flag.'

Iain jnr couldn't take his eyes off the locket, 'I'll treasure it aunt Lucy, promise,' they left Dunvegan castle, 'now laddie there's one thing yoo can do for ya old aunt,' Iain looked at Lucy, 'anythin aunt Lucy, anythin,' she carried on walking, 'a would ask yoo ta take ma one last time orr the sea from Skye, a want ta hear tha fairies call ma back, one last time.'

They left Armadale on the ferry to Mallaig as the sun began to set over Skye, a lone piper stood on the harbour wall sounding out rebel tunes as a mist began to form between the trees, a gentle stiffing breeze blew across the ferry, Lucy could hear voices from the past, she could see ghost riders, the white foam on the crest of the waves giving them away as they rode by, Skye would call Lucy back one last time, she had found her peace.

Iain jnr joined the Royal Australian Air Force as planned, Lucy died of Cancer a month after Iain jnr left Scotland, she knew of her condition, as always she had "Held fast" Lucy was cremated at her request, no mourners were to be present, and a simple message was read out,

'I Lucy MacLeod return to whence I came, happy in heart, clear in sight, proud of those held dear and true, this daughter of the Loch returns to you.'

The next morning following Lucy's cremation, the urn containing her ashes was found on the Fairy bridge on the Isle of Skye by a young girl out walking with her mother, the girl had skipped off some distance in front, as she knelt down to pick up the urn, she heard a voice from beneath the bridge, she gently lay down and peered into the twilight under the bridge, she reached for the urn and removed the top, holding the urn downwards the contents flowed into the water.

The girls mother had by now caught up with her, 'what a yoo doing Sandra, get up,' the girl slowly got to her feet, she never took her eyes from the water, 'what's that in ya hand?' the girl looked at her mother, 'it was on tha bridge, tha lady told ma ta empty it inta tha water,' the girl was grabbed by the arm, 'put it doon, ya don't noo where it's been, what have a told yoo aboot making things up?' Sandra started to cry, 'but mummy there was a lady under tha bridge, she told ma not ta be afraid of tha fire,' her mother stopped walking, 'Sandra MacLeod tha only fire a can see is tha red of ya hair, noo come on or we'll be late.'

THE END (for now)

Printed in the United Kingdom
by Lightning Source UK Ltd.
129619UK00001B/46-63/P